Diana Wynne Jones

HOUSE OF MANY WAYS

Illustrated by Tim Stevens

HarperCollins *Children's Books*

The official Diana Wynne Jones fansite is at
www.leemac.freeserve.co.uk

First published in paperback in Great Britain by HarperCollins *Children's Books* 2009
First published in hardback in Great Britain by HarperCollins *Children's Books* 2008
Harper Collins *Children's Books* is a division of HarperCollins *Publishers* Ltd
77-85 Fulham Palace Road, Hammersmith, London, W6 8JB

www.harpercollins.co.uk

4

Text copyright © Diana Wynne Jones 2008
Illustrations copyright © Tim Stevens 2008

ISBN 13: 978 0 00 727568 7

The author and the illustrator assert the moral right to be
identified as the author and illustrator of the work.

**Mixed Sources**
Product group from well-managed
forests and other controlled sources
www.fsc.org   Cert no. SW-COC-1806
© 1996 Forest Stewardship Council

FSC is a non-profit international organisation established to promote the
responsible management of the world's forests. Products carrying the FSC
label are independently certified to assure consumers that they come
from forests that are managed to meet the social, economic and
ecological needs of present and future generations.

Find out more about HarperCollins and the environment at
**www.harpercollins.co.uk/green**

*To my granddaughter, Ruth, together with*

*Sharyn's laundry and also to Lilly B.*

Dear Reader,

Here is my new book, *House of Many Ways*, which I hope you will enjoy. It is a sequel to *Howl's Moving Castle* and *Castle in the Air*, set in the world where such things as seven-league boots and flying carpets are not only possible but real. For this one we move to the mountainous kingdom of High Norland, where the elderly King and his almost equally elderly daughter are busy cataloguing their huge library, but not too busy to notice that they are getting poorer and poorer. Their Royal Wizard falls ill and is unable to help them, which is how we come to meet Charmain, a cross-grained teenager who has been brought up so respectably that she knows almost nothing about anything except books. Charmain is volunteered to look after the Royal Wizard's house while he is ill. But of course a wizard's house is bound to be peculiar, and this one is, very.

While Charmain struggles with its peculiarities and with a very small and very greedy dog called Waif, she runs into the fearsome lubbock, a cocksure boy called Peter, a tribe of kobolds, and the inhabitants of the moving castle – Sophie, her son Morgan, Calcifer the fire demon and Wizard Howl in a very irritating disguise. Oh, and there are elves too, not to speak of Jamal the cook and his surly dog.

I had fun writing this. I hope you will have equal fun reading it.

*Diana Wynne Jones*

# CONTENTS

# CHAPTER ONE

### In which Charmain is volunteered to look after a wizard's house

"Charmain must do it," said Aunt Sempronia. "We can't leave Great Uncle William to face this on his own."

"Your Great Uncle William?" said Mrs Baker. "Isn't he—" She coughed and lowered her voice because this, to her mind, was not quite nice. "Isn't he a *wizard*?"

"Of course," said Aunt Sempronia. "But he has—" Here she too lowered her voice. "He has a *growth*, you know, on his insides, and only the elves can help him. They have to carry him off in order to cure him, you see, and *someone* has to look after his house. Spells, you know, *escape* if there's no one there to watch them. And *I* am far too busy to do it. My stray dogs' charity alone — "

"Me too. We're up to our ears in wedding cake orders this month," Mrs Baker said hastily. "Sam was saying only this morning — "

"Then it has to be Charmain," Aunt Sempronia decreed. "Surely she's old enough now."

"Er — " said Mrs Baker.

They both looked across the parlour to where Mrs Baker's daughter sat, deep in a book, as usual, with her long, thin body bent into what sunlight came in past Mrs Baker's geraniums, her red hair pinned up in a sort of birds' nest and her glasses perched on the end of her nose. She held one of her father's huge juicy pasties in one hand and munched it as she read. Crumbs kept falling on her book and she brushed them off with the pasty when they fell on the page she was reading.

"Er… did you hear us, dear?" Mrs Baker said anxiously.

"No," Charmain said with her mouth full. "What?"

"That's settled, then," Aunt Sempronia said. "I'll leave it to you to explain to her, Berenice, dear." She stood up, majestically shaking out the folds of her stiff silk dress and then of her silk parasol. "I'll be back to fetch her tomorrow morning," she said. "Now I'd better go and tell poor Great Uncle William that Charmain will be taking care of things for him."

She swept out of the parlour, leaving Mrs Baker to wish that her husband's aunt was not so rich or so bossy, and to wonder how she was going to explain to Charmain, let alone to Sam. Sam never allowed Charmain to do anything that was not utterly respectable. Nor did Mrs Baker either, except when Aunt Sempronia took a hand.

Aunt Sempronia, meanwhile, mounted into her smart little pony trap and had her groom drive her out of the other side of town where Great Uncle William lived.

"I've fixed it all up," she announced, sailing through the magic ways to where Great Uncle William sat glumly writing in his study. "My great niece Charmain is coming here tomorrow. She will see you on your way and look after you when you come back. In between, she will take care of the house for you."

"How very kind of her," said Great Uncle William. "I take it she is well versed in magic, then?"

"I have no idea," said Aunt Sempronia. "What I *do* know is that she never has her nose out of a book, never does a hand's turn in the house and is treated like a sacred object by both her parents. It will do her *good* to do something normal for a change."

"Oh dear," said Great Uncle William. "Thank you for warning me. I shall take precautions then."

"Do that," said Aunt Sempronia. "And you had better make sure there is plenty of food in the place. I've never *known* a girl who eats so much. And remains thin as a witch's besom with it. I've *never* understood it. I'll bring her here tomorrow before the elves come, then."

She turned and left. "Thank you," Great Uncle William said weakly to her stiff, rustling back. "Dear, dear," he added, as the front door slammed. "Ah, well. One has to be grateful to one's relatives, I suppose."

Charmain, oddly enough, was quite grateful to Aunt Sempronia too. Not that she was in the least grateful for being volunteered to look after an old, sick wizard whom she had never met. "She might have asked *me*!" she said, rather often, to her mother.

"I think she knew you would say no, dear," Mrs Baker suggested eventually.

"I might have," Charmain said. "Or," she added, with a secretive smile, "I might not have."

"Dear, I'm not expecting you to *enjoy* it," Mrs Baker said tremulously. "It's not at all *nice*. It's just that it would be so very kind—"

"You know I'm not kind," Charmain said, and she went away upstairs to her white frilly bedroom, where she sat at her nice desk, staring out of her window at the

*12*

roofs, towers and chimneys of High Norland City, and then up at the blue mountains beyond. The truth was, this was the chance she had been longing for. She was tired of her respectable school and *very* tired of living at home, with her mother treating her as if Charmain were a tigress no one was sure was tame, and her father forbidding her to do things because they were not nice, or not safe, or not usual. This was a chance to leave home and do something – the *one* thing – Charmain had always wanted to do. It was worth putting up with a wizard's house just for that. She wondered if she had the courage to write the letter that went with it.

For a long time she had no courage at all. She sat and stared at the clouds piling along the peaks of the mountains, white and purple, making shapes like fat animals and thin swooping dragons. She stared until the clouds had wisped away into nothing but faint mist against a blue sky. Then she said, "Now or nothing." After that she sighed, fetched her glasses up on the chain that hung round her neck, and got out her good pen and her best writing paper. She wrote, in her best writing:

> Your Majesty,
>     Ever since I was a small child and first heard of your great collection of books and manuscripts, I have longed to work in your

library. Although I know that you yourself, with the aid of your daughter, Her Royal Highness Princess Hilda, are personally engaged in the long and difficult task of sorting and listing the contents of the Royal Library, I nevertheless hope that you might appreciate my help. Since I am of age, I wish to apply for the post of librarian assistant in the Royal Library. I hope Your Majesty will not find my application too presumptuous.

 Yours truly,
  Charmain Baker
  12 Corn Street
  High Norland City


Charmain sat back and reread her letter. There was no way, she thought, that writing like this to the old King could be anything other than sheer cheek, but it seemed to her that the letter was quite a good one. The one thing in it that was dubious was the "I am of age." She knew that was supposed to mean that a person was twenty-one – or at least eighteen – but she felt it was not *exactly* a lie. She had not said what age she was *of*, after all. And she hadn't, either, said that she was hugely learned or highly qualified, because she knew she was not. She hadn't even said that she loved books more than anything else in the world, although this was perfectly true. She would just have to trust her love of books shone through.

I'm quite sure the King will just scrumple the letter up and throw it on the fire, she thought. But at least I tried.

She went out and posted the letter, feeling very brave and defiant.

The next morning, Aunt Sempronia arrived in her pony trap and loaded Charmain into it, along with a neat carpet bag that Mrs Baker had packed full of Charmain's clothes, and a much larger bag that Mr Baker had packed, bulging with pasties and tasties, buns, flans and tarts. So large was this second bag, and smelling so strongly of savoury herbs, gravy, cheese, fruit, jam and spices, that the groom driving the trap turned round and sniffed in astonishment, and even Aunt Sempronia's stately nostrils flared.

"Well, you'll not starve, child," she said. "Drive on."

But the groom had to wait until Mrs Baker had embraced Charmain and said, "I know I can trust you, dear, to be good and tidy and considerate."

That's a lie, Charmain thought. She doesn't trust me an inch.

Then Charmain's father hurried up to peck a kiss on Charmain's cheek. "We know you'll not let us down, Charmain," he said.

That's another lie, Charmain thought. You know I will.

"And we'll miss you, my love," her mother said, nearly in tears.

That may not be a lie! Charmain thought, in some surprise. Though it beats me why they even like me.

"*Drive on!*" Aunt Sempronia said sternly, and the groom did. When the pony was sedately ambling through the streets, she said, "Now, Charmain, I know your parents have given you the best of everything and you've never had to do a thing for yourself in your life. Are you prepared to look after yourself for a change?"

"Oh, yes," Charmain said devoutly.

"*And* the house *and* the poor old man?" Aunt Sempronia persisted.

"I'll do my best," Charmain said. She was afraid Aunt Sempronia would turn round and drive her straight back home if she didn't say this.

"You've had a good education, haven't you?" Aunt Sempronia said.

"Even music," Charmain admitted, rather sulkily. She added hastily, "But I wasn't any good at it. So don't expect me to play soothing tunes to Great Uncle William."

"I don't," Aunt Sempronia retorted. "As he's a wizard, he can probably make his own soothing tunes. I was simply trying to find out whether you've had a proper grounding in magic. You have, haven't you?"

Charmain's insides seemed to drop away downwards somewhere and she felt as if they were taking the blood from her face with them. She did not dare confess that she knew not the first thing about magic. Her parents – particularly Mrs Baker – did not think magic was nice. And theirs was such a respectable part of town that Charmain's school never taught anyone magic. If anyone wanted to learn anything so vulgar, they had to go to a private tutor instead. And Charmain knew her parents would never have paid for any such lessons. "Er…" she began.

Luckily, Aunt Sempronia simply continued. "Living in a house full of magic is no joke, you know."

"Oh, I won't ever think of it as a joke," Charmain said earnestly.

"Good," said Aunt Sempronia, and sat back.

The pony clopped on and on. They clopped through Royal Square, past the Royal Mansion looming at one end of it with its golden roof flashing in the sun, and on through Market Square, where Charmain was seldom allowed to go. She looked wistfully at the stalls and at all the people buying things and chattering, and stared backwards at the place as they came into the older part of town. Here the houses were so tall and colourful and so different from one another – each one seemed to have steeper gables and more oddly placed windows than the one before it – that Charmain began to have hopes that living in Great Uncle William's house might prove to be very interesting after all. But the pony clopped onward, through the dingier, poorer parts, and then past mere cottages, and then out among fields and hedges, where a great cliff leaned over the road and only the occasional small house stood backed into the hedgerows, and the mountains towered closer and closer above.

Charmain began to think they were going out of High Norland and into another country altogether. What would it be? Strangia? Montalbino? She wished she had paid more attention to geography lessons.

Just as she was wishing this, the groom drew up at a small mouse-coloured house crouching at the back of a long front garden. Charmain looked at it across its small iron gate and felt utterly disappointed. It was the most boring house she had ever seen. It had a window on either side of its brown front door and the mouse-coloured roof came down above them like a scowl. There did not seem to be an upstairs at all.

"Here we are," Aunt Sempronia said cheerfully. She got down, clattered open the little iron gate, and led the way up the path to the front door. Charmain prowled gloomily after her while the groom followed them with Charmain's two bags. The garden on either side of the path appeared to consist entirely of hydrangea bushes, blue, green-blue and mauve.

"I don't suppose you'll have to look after the garden," Aunt Sempronia said airily. I should hope not! Charmain thought. "I'm fairly sure William employs a gardener," Aunt Sempronia said.

"I hope he does," Charmain said. The most she knew about gardens was the Bakers' own back yard, which contained one large mulberry tree and a rosebush, plus the window boxes where her mother grew runner beans. She knew there was earth under the plants and that the earth contained worms. She shuddered.

Aunt Sempronia clattered briskly at the knocker on the brown front door and then pushed her way into the house, calling out, "Coo-ee! I've brought Charmain for you!"

"Thank you kindly," said Great Uncle William.

The front door led straight into a musty living room, where Great Uncle William was sitting in a musty, mouse-coloured armchair. There was a large leather suitcase beside him, as if he were all ready to depart. "Pleased to meet you, my dear," he said to Charmain.

"How do you do, sir," Charmain replied politely.

Before either of them could say anything else, Aunt Sempronia said, "Well, then, I'll love you and leave you. Put her bags down there," she said to her groom. The groom obediently dumped the bags down just inside the front door and went away again. Aunt Sempronia followed him in a sizzle of expensive silks, calling, "Goodbye, both of you!" as she went.

The front door banged shut, leaving Charmain and Great Uncle William staring at each other. Great Uncle William was a small man and mostly bald except for some locks of fine, silvery hair streaked across his rather domed head. He sat in a stiff, bent, crumpled way that showed Charmain he was in quite a lot of pain. She was surprised to find that she felt sorry for him, but she did wish he wouldn't stare at her so steadily. It made her feel guilty. And his lower eyelids drooped from his tired blue eyes, showing the insides all red, like blood. Charmain disliked blood almost as much as she disliked earthworms.

"Well, you seem a very tall, competent-looking young lady," Great Uncle William said. His voice was tired and gentle. "The red hair is a good sign, to my mind. Very good. Do you think you can manage here while I'm gone? The place is a little disordered, I'm afraid."

"I expect so," Charmain said. The musty room seemed quite tidy to her. "Can you tell me some of the things I ought to do?" Though I hope I shan't be here long, she thought. Once the King replies to my letter...

"As to that," said Great Uncle William, "the usual household things, of course, but magical. Naturally, most of it's magical. As I wasn't sure what grade of magic you'll have reached, I took some steps—"

Horrors! Charmain thought. He thinks I know magic!

She tried to interrupt Great Uncle William to explain, but at that moment they were both interrupted. The front door clattered open and a procession of tall, tall elves walked quietly in. They were all most medically dressed in white, and there was no expression on their beautiful faces at all. Charmain stared at them, utterly unnerved by their beauty, their height, their neutrality and, above all, by their complete silence. One of them moved her gently aside and she stood where she was put, feeling clumsy and disorderly, while the rest clustered around Great Uncle William with their dazzling fair heads bent over him. Charmain was not sure what they did, but in next to no time Great Uncle William was dressed in a white robe and they were lifting him out of his chair. There were what seemed to be three red apples stuck to his head. Charmain could see he was asleep.

"Er… haven't you forgotten his suitcase?" she said, as they carried him away towards the door.

"No need for it," one of the elves said, holding the door open for the others to ease Great Uncle William out through it.

After that, they were all going away down the garden path. Charmain dashed to the open front door and called after them, "How long is he going to be away?" It suddenly seemed urgent to know how long she was going to be left in charge here.

"As long as it takes," another of the elves replied.

Then they were all gone before they reached the garden gate.

# Chapter Two

### In which Charmain
### explores the house

Charmain stared at the empty path for a while and then shut the front door with a bang. "*Now* what do I do?" she said to the deserted, musty room.

"You will have to tidy the kitchen, I'm afraid, my dear," said Great Uncle William's tired, kindly voice out of thin air. "I apologise for leaving so much laundry. Please open my suitcase for more complicated instructions."

Charmain shot the suitcase a look. So Great Uncle William had meant to leave it, then. "In a minute," she said to it. "I haven't unpacked for myself yet." She picked up her two bags and marched with them to the only other door. It was at the back of the room and, when Charmain had tried to open it with the hand that held the food bag, then with that hand and with both bags in the other hand, and finally with both hands and with both bags on the floor, she found it led to the kitchen.

She stared for a moment. Then she dragged her two bags round the door just as it was shutting and stared some more.

"What a *mess*!" she said.

It ought to have been a comfortable, spacious kitchen. It had a big window looking out on to the mountains, where sunlight came warmly pouring through. Unfortunately, the sunlight only served to highlight the enormous stacks of plates and cups piled into the sink and on the draining board and down on the floor beside the sink. The sunlight then went on – and Charmain's dismayed eyes went with it – to cast a golden glow over the two big canvas laundry bags leaning beside the sink. They were stuffed so full with dirty washing that Great Uncle William had been using them as a shelf for a pile of dirty saucepans and a frying pan or so.

Charmain's eyes travelled from there to the table in the middle of the room. Here was where Great Uncle William appeared to keep his supply of thirty or so teapots and the same number of milk jugs – not to speak of several that had once held gravy. It was all quite neat in its way, Charmain thought, just crowded and not clean.

"I suppose you *have* been ill," Charmain said grudgingly to the thin air.

There was no reply this time. Cautiously, she went over to the sink, where, she had a feeling, something was missing. It took her a moment or so to realise that there were no taps. Probably this house was so far outside town that no water pipes had been laid. When she looked through the window, she could see a small yard outside and a pump in the middle of it.

"So I'm supposed to go and pump water and then bring it in, and *then* what?" Charmain demanded. She looked over at the dark, empty fireplace. It was summer, after all, so naturally there was no fire, nor anything to burn that she could see. "I heat the water?" she said. "In a dirty saucepan, I suppose, and— Come to think of it, how do *I* wash? Can't I ever have a bath? Doesn't he have any bedroom, or a bathroom at all?"

She rushed to the small door beyond the fireplace and dragged it open. All Great Uncle William's doors seemed to need the strength of ten men to open, she thought angrily. She could almost feel the weight of magic holding them shut. She found herself looking into a small pantry. It had nothing on its shelves apart from a small crock of butter, a stale-looking loaf and a large bag mysteriously labelled CIBIS CANINICUS that seemed to be full of soapflakes. And piled into the back part of it were two more large laundry bags as full as the ones in the kitchen.

"I shall scream," Charmain said. "How *could* Aunt Sempronia do this to me? How could Mother let her do it?"

In this moment of despair, Charmain could only think of doing what she always did in a crisis: bury herself in a book. She dragged her two bags over to the crowded table and sat herself down in one of the two chairs there. There she unbuckled the carpet bag, fetched her glasses up on to her nose and dug eagerly among the clothes for the books she had put out for Mother to pack for her.

Her hands met nothing but softness. The only hard thing proved to be the big bar of soap among her washing things. Charmain threw it across the room into the empty hearth and dug further. "I don't *believe* this!" she said. "She must have put them in first, right at the bottom." She turned the bag upside down and shook everything out on to the floor. Out fell wads of beautifully folded skirts, dresses, stockings, blouses, two knitted jackets, lace petticoats and enough other underclothes for a year. On top of those flopped her new slippers. After that, the bag was flat and empty.

Charmain nevertheless felt all the way round the inside of the bag before she threw it aside, let her glasses drop to the end of their chain and wondered whether to cry. Mrs Baker had actually *forgotten* to pack the books.

"Well," Charmain said, after an interval of blinking and swallowing, "I suppose I've never really been away from home before. Next time I go anywhere, I'll pack the bag *myself* and fill it with books. I shall make the best of it for now."

Making the best of it, she heaved the other bag on to the crowded table and shoved to make room for it. This shunted four milk jugs and a teapot off on to the floor. "And I *don't care*!" Charmain said as they fell. Somewhat to her relief, the milk jugs were empty and simply bounced, and the teapot did not break either. It just lay on its side leaking tea on to the floor. "That's probably the good side to magic," Charmain said, glumly digging out the topmost meat pasty. She flung her skirts into a bundle between her knees, put her elbows on the table and took a huge, comforting, savoury bite from the pasty.

Something cold and quivery touched the bare part of her right leg.

Charmain froze, not daring even to chew. This kitchen is full of big magical slugs! she thought.

The cold thing touched another part of her leg. With the touch came a very small whispery whine.

Very slowly, Charmain pulled aside skirt and tablecloth and looked down. Under the table sat an extremely small and ragged white dog, gazing up at her piteously and shaking all over. When it saw Charmain looking down at it, it cocked uneven, frayed-looking white ears and flailed at the floor with its short, wispy tail. Then it whispered out a whine again.

"Who are *you*?" Charmain said. "Nobody told me about a dog."

Great Uncle William's voice spoke out of the air once more. "This is Waif. Be very kind to him. He came to me as a stray and he seems to be frightened of everything."

Charmain had never been sure about dogs. Her mother said they were dirty and they bit you and would never have one in the house, so Charmain had always been extremely nervous of any dog she met. But this dog was so small. It seemed extremely white and clean. And it looked to be far more frightened of Charmain than Charmain was of it. It was still shaking all over.

"Oh, do stop trembling," Charmain said. "I'm not going to hurt you."

Waif went on trembling and looking at her piteously.

Charmain sighed. She broke off a large lump of her pasty and held it down towards Waif. "Here," she said. "Here's for not being a slug after all."

Waif's shiny black nose quivered towards the lump.

He looked up at her, to make sure she really meant this, and then, very gently and politely, he took the lump into his mouth and ate it. Then he looked up at Charmain for more. Charmain was fascinated by his politeness. She broke off another lump. And then another. In the end, they shared the pasty half and half.

"That's all," Charmain said, shaking crumbs off her skirt. "We'll have to make this bagful last, as there seems to be no other food in this house. Now show me what to do next, Waif."

Waif promptly trotted over to what seemed to be the back door, where he stood wagging his wisp of a tail and whispering out a tiny whine. Charmain opened the door – which was just as difficult to open as the other two – and followed Waif out into the backyard, thinking that this meant she was supposed to pump water for the sink. But Waif trotted past the pump and over to the rather mangy-looking apple tree in the corner, where he raised a very short leg and peed against the tree.

"I see," Charmain said. "That's what you're supposed to do, not me. And it doesn't look as if you're doing the tree much good, Waif."

Waif gave her a look and went trotting to and fro around the yard, sniffing at things and raising a leg against clumps of grass. Charmain could see he felt quite safe in this yard. Come to think of it, so did she. There was a warm, secure feeling, as if Great Uncle William had put wizardly protections around the place. She stood by the pump and stared up beyond the fence to the steeply rising mountains. There was a faint breeze blowing down from the heights, bringing a smell of snow and new flowers, which somehow reminded Charmain of the elves. She wondered if they had taken Great Uncle William up there.

And they'd better bring him back soon, she thought. I shall go mad after more than a day here!

There was a small hut in the corner by the house. Charmain went over to investigate it, muttering, "Spades, I suppose, and flowerpots and things." But when she had hauled its stiff door open, she found a vast copper tank inside and a mangle and a place to light a fire under the tank. She stared at it all, the way you stare at a strange exhibit in a museum, for a while, until she remembered that there was a similar shed in her own yard at home. It was a place just as mysterious to her as this one, since she had always been forbidden to go into it, but she did know that, once a week, a red-handed, purple-faced washerwoman came and made a lot of steam in this shed, out of which came clean clothes somehow.

Ah. A wash house, she thought. I think you have to put those laundry bags in the tank and boil them up. But how? I'm beginning to think I've led a much too sheltered life.

"And a good thing too," she said aloud, thinking of the washerwoman's red hands and mauve face.

But that doesn't help me wash dishes, she thought. Or about a bath. Am I supposed to boil myself in that tank? And where shall I sleep, for goodness' sake?

Leaving the door open for Waif, she went back indoors, where she marched past the sink, the bags of laundry, the crowded table and the heap of her own things on the floor, and dragged open the door in the far wall. Beyond it was the musty living room again.

"This is hopeless!" she said. "Where are bedrooms? Where is a *bathroom*?"

Great Uncle William's tired voice spoke out of the air. "For bedrooms and bathroom, turn left as soon as you open the kitchen door, my dear. Please forgive any disorder you find."

Charmain looked back through the open kitchen door to the kitchen beyond it. "Oh, yes?" she said.

"Well, let's see." She walked carefully backwards into the kitchen and shut the door in front of her. Then she hauled it open again, with what she was beginning to think of as the usual struggle, and turned briskly left into the door frame before she had time to think of it as impossible.

She found herself in a passageway with an open window at the far end. The breeze coming in through the window was strongly full of the mountain smell of snow and flowers. Charmain had a startled glimpse of a sloping green meadow and faraway blue distances, while she was busy turning the handle and shoving her knee against the nearest door.

This door came open quite easily, as if it were used rather a lot. Charmain stumbled forward into a smell that caused her instantly to forget the scents from the window. She stood with her nose up, sniffing delightedly. It was the delicious mildewy fragrance of old books. Hundreds of them, she saw, looking round the room. Books were lined up on shelves on all four walls, stacked on the floor and piled on the desk, old books in leather covers mostly, although some of the ones on the floor had newer looking coloured jackets. This was obviously Great Uncle William's study.

"Oooh!" Charmain said.

Ignoring the way the view from the window was of the hydrangeas in the front garden, she dived to look at the books on the desk. Big, fat, redolent books, they were, and some of them had metal clasps to keep them shut as if they were dangerous open. Charmain had the nearest one already in her hands when she noticed the stiff piece of paper spread out on the desk, covered with shaky handwriting.

"My dear Charmain," she read, and sat herself down in the padded chair in front of the desk to read the rest.

My dear Charmain,

Thank you for so kindly agreeing to look after this house in my absence. The elves tell me I should be gone for about two weeks. (*Thank goodness for that! Charmain thought.*) Or possibly a month if there are complications. (*Oh.*) You really must forgive any disorder you find here. I have been afflicted for quite some time now. But I am sure you are a resourceful young lady and will find your feet here quite readily. In case of any difficulty, I have left spoken directions for you wherever these seemed necessary. All you need do is speak your question aloud and it should be answered. More complex matters you will find explained in the suitcase. Please be kind to Waif, who has not been with me for long enough to feel secure, and please feel free to help yourself to any books in this study, apart from those actually on this desk, which are for the most part too powerful and advanced for you. (*Pooh. As if I cared for that! Charmain thought.*) Meanwhile I wish you a happy sojourn here and hope to be able to thank you in person before very long.

Your affectionate Great-Great Uncle-by-marriage,
William Norland

"I suppose he *is* by-marriage," Charmain said aloud. "He must be Aunt Sempronia's Great Uncle really, and she married Uncle Ned, who is Dad's uncle, except that he's dead now. What a pity. I was starting to hope I'd inherited some of his magic." And she said politely to the air, "Thank you very much, Great Uncle William."

There was no reply. Charmain thought, Well, there wouldn't be. That wasn't a question. And she set about exploring the books on the desk.

The fat book she had in her hand was called *The Book of Void and Nothingness*. Not surprisingly, when she opened it, the pages were blank. But she could feel under her fingers each empty page sort of purring and writhing with hidden magics. She put it down rather quickly and picked up one called *Wall's Guide to Astromancy* instead. This was slightly disappointing, because it was mostly diagrams of black dotted lines with numbers of square red dots spreading out from the black lines in various patterns, but almost nothing to read. All the same, Charmain spent longer looking at it than she expected. The diagrams must have been hypnotic in some way. But eventually, with a bit of a wrench, she put it down and turned to one called *Advanced Seminal Sorcery*, which was not her kind of thing at all. It was closely printed in long paragraphs that mostly seemed to begin, "If we extrapolate from our findings in my earlier work, we find ourselves ready to approach an extension of the paratypical phenomenology…"

No, Charmain thought. I don't think we are ready.

She put that one down too and lifted up the heavy, square book on the corner of the desk. It was called *Das Zauberbuch* and it turned out to be in a foreign language. Probably what they speak in Ingary, Charmain decided. But, most interestingly, this book had been acting as a paperweight to a pile of letters underneath it, from all over the world. Charmain spent a long time going nosily through the letters and becoming more and more impressed with Great Uncle William. Nearly all of them were from other wizards who were wanting to consult Great Uncle William on the finer points of magic – clearly, they thought of him as the great expert – or to congratulate him on his latest magical discovery. One and all of them had the most terrible handwriting. Charmain frowned and scowled at them and held the worst one up to the light.

Dear Wizard Norland (*it said, as far as she could read it*),

Your book, *Crucual Cantrips*, has been a great help to me in my dimensional (*or is that demented? Charmain wondered*) work, but I would like to draw your attention to a small discovery of mine related to your section on Murdoch's Ear (*"Merlin's Arm? Murphy's Law?" I give up! Charmain thought*). When I next find myself in High Norland, perhaps we could talk?

Yours alluringly (*"allergically? admiringly? antiphony?" Lord! What writing! Charmain thought*),

Wizard Howl Pendragon

"Dear, dear! He must write with a poker!" Charmain said aloud, picking up the next letter.

This one was from the King himself and the writing, though wavery and old-fashioned, was much easier to read.

Dear Wm (*Charmain read, with growing awe and surprise*),

We are now more than halfway through Our Great Task and as yet none the wiser. We rely on you. It is Our devout Hope that the Elves We sent you will succeed in restoring you to Health and that We will again shortly have the Inestimable Benefit of your Advice and Encouragement. Our Best Wishes go with you.

Yours, in Sincere Hope,

Adolphus Rex High Norland

So the King sent those elves! "Well, well," Charmain murmured, leafing through the final stack of letters. Every single one of these was written in different sorts of someone's best handwriting. They all seemed to say the same thing in different ways: "Please, Wizard Norland, I would like to become your apprentice. Will you take me on?" Some of them went on to offer Great Uncle William money. One of them said he could give Great Uncle William a magical diamond ring, and another, who seemed to be a girl, said rather pathetically, "I am not very pretty myself, but my sister is, and she says she will marry you if you agree to teach me."

Charmain winced and only flipped hastily through the rest of the stack. They reminded her so very much of her own letter to the King. And quite as useless, she thought. It was obvious to her that these were the kind of letters that a famous wizard would instantly write and say "No" to. She bundled them all back under *Das Zauberbuch* and looked at the other books on the desk. There was a whole row of tall, fat books at the back of the desk, all labelled *Res Magica*, which she thought she would look at later. She picked up two more books at random. One was called *Mrs Pentstemmon's Path: Signposts to the Truth* and it struck her as a trifle moralising. The other, when she had thumbed open its metal clasp and spread it out at its first page, was called

*The Boke of Palimpsest*. When Charmain turned over the next pages, she found that each page contained a new spell – a clear spell too, with a title saying what it did and, below that, a list of ingredients, followed by numbered stages telling you what you had to do.

"This is more like it!" Charmain said, and settled down to read.

A long time later, while she was trying to decide which was more useful, "A Spell to tell Friend from Foe" or "A Spell to Enlarge the Mind," or perhaps even "A Spell for Flying," Charmain suddenly knew that she had crying need of a bathroom. This tended to happen to her when she had been absorbed in reading. She sprang up, squeezing her knees together, and then realised that a bathroom was a place she had still not found.

"Oh, how do I find the bathroom from here?" she cried out.

Reassuringly, Great Uncle William's kind, frail voice spoke out of the air at once. "Turn left in the passage, my dear, and the bathroom is the first door on the right."

"Thank you!" Charmain gasped, and ran.

# CHAPTER THREE

## In which Charmain works
## several spells at once

The bathroom was as reassuring as Great Uncle William's kindly voice. It had a worn greenstone floor and a little window, at which fluttered a green net curtain. And it had all the fitments Charmain knew from home. And home has nothing but the best, she thought. Better still, it had taps and the toilet flushed. True, the bath and the taps were strange, slightly bulbous shapes, as if the person who installed them had not been quite sure what he or she was aiming at; but the taps, when Charmain experimentally turned them on, ran cold and hot water, just as they were supposed to, and there were warm towels on a rail under the mirror.

Perhaps I can put one of those laundry bags in the bath, Charmain mused. How would I squeeze it dry?

Across the corridor from the bathroom was a row of doors, stretching away into dim distance. Charmain went to the nearest one and pushed it open, expecting it to lead to the living room. But there was a small bedroom beyond it instead, obviously Great Uncle William's, to judge by the mess. The white covers trailed off the unmade bed, almost on top of several stripey nightshirts scattered over the floor. Shirts dangled out of drawers, along with socks and what looked like long underclothes, and the open cupboard held a musty-smelling uniform of some kind. Under the window were two more sacks stuffed full of laundry.

Charmain groaned aloud. "I suppose he's been ill for quite a time," she said, trying to be charitable. "But, mother-of-pearl, why do *I* have to deal with it all?"

The bed started twitching.

Charmain jumped round to face it. The twitching was Waif, curled up comfortably in the mound of bedclothes, scratching for a flea. When he saw Charmain looking at him, he wagged his flimsy tail and grovelled, lowered his frayed ears and whispered a pleading whine at her.

"You're not supposed to be there, are you?" she said

to him. "All right. I can see you're comfortable – and I'm blowed if I'm sleeping in that bed anyway."

She marched out of the room and opened the next door along. To her relief, there was another bedroom there almost identical to Great Uncle William's, except that this one was tidy. The bed was clean and neatly made, the cupboard was shut, and when she looked, she found the drawers were empty. Charmain nodded approval at the room and opened the next door along the corridor. There was another neat bedroom there, and beyond that another, each one exactly the same.

I'd better throw my things around the one that's mine or I'll never find it again, she thought.

She turned back into the corridor to find that Waif had come off the bed and was now scratching at the bathroom door with both front paws. "You won't want to go in there," Charmain told him. "None of it's any use to you."

But the door came open somehow before Charmain got to it. Beyond it was the kitchen. Waif trotted jauntily in there and Charmain groaned again. The mess had not gone away. There were the dirty crockery and the laundry bags, with the addition now of a teapot lying in a pool of tea, Charmain's clothes in a heap near the table and a large green bar of soap in the fireplace.

"I'd forgotten all this," Charmain said.

Waif put both tiny front paws on the bottom rung of the chair and raised himself to his full small length, pleadingly.

"You're hungry again," Charmain diagnosed. "So am I."

She sat in the chair and Waif sat on her left foot, and they shared another pasty. Then they shared a fruit tart, two doughnuts, six chocolate biscuits and a custard flan. After this Waif plodded rather heavily away to the inner door, which opened for him as soon as he scratched at it. Charmain gathered up her pile of clothes and followed him, meaning to put her things in the first empty bedroom.

But here things went a trifle wrong. Charmain pushed the door open with one elbow and, fairly naturally, turned right to go into the corridor with the bedrooms in it. She found herself in complete darkness. Almost at once she walked into another door, where she hit her elbow on its doorknob with a clang.

"Ouch!" she said, fumbled for the doorknob and opened this door.

It swung inward majestically. Charmain walked into a large room lit by arched windows all around it and found herself breathing a damp, stuffy, leathery, neglected smell. The smell seemed to come from the elderly leather seats of carved chairs arranged around the big carved table that took up most of the room. Each seat had a leather mat on the table in front of it, and an old, withered sheet of blotting paper on the mat, except for the large seat at the other end that had the arms of High Norland carved into the back of it. This one had a fat little stick on the table instead of a mat. All of it, chairs, table, and mats, was covered in dust and there were cobwebs in the corners of the many windows.

Charmain stared. "Is this the dining room or what?" she said. "How do I get to the bedrooms from here?"

Great Uncle William's voice spoke, sounding quite faint and far off. "You have reached the Conference Room," it said. "If you are there, you are rather lost, my dear, so listen carefully. Turn round once, clockwise. Then, still turning clockwise, open the door with your left hand only. Go through and let the door shut behind you. Then take two long steps sideways to your left. This will bring you back beside the bathroom."

And let's hope it does! Charmain thought, doing her best to follow these directions.

All went well, except for the moment of darkness after the door had swung shut behind her, when Charmain found herself staring into a totally strange stone corridor. An old, bent man was pushing a trolley along it, loaded with steaming silver teapot, jugs and chafing dishes and what looked like a pile of crumpets. She blinked a little, decided that she would not do any good, either to herself or the old man, by calling out to him, and took two long steps to the left instead. And then, to her relief, she was standing beside the bathroom, from where she could see Waif turning round and round on Great Uncle William's bed in order to get comfortable.

"Phew!" Charmain said, and went and dumped the pile of clothes on top of the chest of drawers in the next bedroom along.

After that she went along the corridor to the open window at the end, where she spent some minutes staring out at that sloping sunlit meadow and breathing the fresh, chilly air that blew in from it. A person could easily climb out of this, she thought. Or in. But she was not really seeing the meadow, or thinking of fresh air. Her real thoughts were with that enticing book of spells that she had left open on Great Uncle William's desk. She had never in her life been let loose among magic like this. It was hard to resist. I shall just open it at random and do the first spell I see, she thought. Just one spell.

In the study, *The Boke of Palimpsest* was, for some reason, now open at "A Spell to Find Yourself a Handsome Prince". Charmain shook her head and closed the book. "Who needs a prince?" she said. She opened the book again, carefully at a different place. This page was headed "A Spell for Flying".

"Oh yes!" Charmain said. "That's much more like it!"

She put her glasses on and studied the list of ingredients.

"A sheet of paper, a quill pen (*easy, there's both on this desk*), one egg (*kitchen?*), two flower petals – one pink and the other blue – six drops of water (*bathroom*), one red hair, one white hair and two pearl buttons."

"No problem at all," Charmain said. She took her glasses off and bustled about assembling ingredients. She hurried to the kitchen – she got to that by opening the bathroom door and turning left and was almost too excited to find that she had got this right – and asked the air, "Where do I find eggs?"

Great Uncle William's gentle voice replied, "Eggs are in a crock in the pantry, my dear. I think it's behind the laundry bags. I do apologise for leaving you with such disorder."

Charmain went into the pantry and leaned across the laundry bags, where sure enough she found an old pie dish with half a dozen brown eggs in it. She took one of them carefully back to the study. Since her glasses were dangling on their chain, she failed to notice that *The Boke of Palimpsest* was now open at "A Spell to Find Hidden Treasure". She bustled over to the study window, where the flower petals were ready to hand on a hydrangea bush that was one half pink and the other blue. She laid those beside the egg and rushed to the bathroom, where she collected the six drops of water in a tooth mug. On the way back, she went across the passage to where Waif was now curled up like a meringue on Great Uncle William's blankets. "Excuse me," Charmain said to him, and raked her fingers along his ragged white back. She came away with quite a number of white hairs, one of which she put beside the flower petals and added to that a red hair from her own head. As for the pearl buttons, she simply ripped two of them off the front of her blouse.

"Right," she said, and put her glasses eagerly on again to look at the instructions. *The Boke of Palimpsest* was now open at "A Spell for Personal Protection", but Charmain was too excited to notice. She looked only at the instructions, which were in five stages. Stage One said, "Place all ingredients except quill and paper in a suitable bowl."

Charmain, after taking her glasses off to stare searchingly around the room, and finding no bowl, suitable or not, was forced to go off to the kitchen again. While she was gone, lazily and slyly, *The Boke of Palimpsest* turned over another couple of pages. When Charmain came back with a slightly sugary bowl, having tipped all the sugar out on to a not-too-dirty plate, the

*Boke* was open at "A Spell to Increase Magical Power".

Charmain did not notice. She put the bowl down on the desk and piled into it the egg, the two petals, the two hairs and her two buttons, and dripped the water carefully in on top. Then she put her glasses on and leaned over the book to discover what she did next. By this time, *The Boke of Palimpsest* was displaying "A Spell to Become Invisible", but Charmain only looked at the instructions and did not see this.

Stage Two told her to "Mash all ingredients together, using only the pen."

It is not easy to mash up an egg with a feather, but Charmain managed it, stabbing with the sharpened end over and over until the shell fell to pieces, then stirring so hard that her hair fell down over her face in red strands, and finally, when nothing seemed to mix properly, whisking with the feather end. When she finally stood up, panting, and pushed her hair away with sticky fingers, the *Boke* had turned over yet another page. It now displayed "A Spell to Start a Fire", but Charmain was too busy trying not to get egg on her glasses to see. She put them on and studied Stage Three.

Stage Three of this spell said, "Recite three times 'Hegemony Gauda'."

"Hegemony gauda," Charmain intoned obediently over the bowl. She was not sure, but on the third

47

repetition she thought the bits of eggshell seethed around the pearl buttons a little. I think it's working! she thought. She pushed her glasses back on her nose and looked at Stage Four. By this time, she was looking at Stage Four in "A Spell to Bend Objects to the Will".

"Take up the quill," this said, "and, using the prepared mixture, write upon the paper the word *Ylf* surrounded by a five-sided figure. Care must be taken not to touch the paper while doing this."

Charmain took up the drippy, sticky feather pen, adorned with bits of eggshell and a piece of pink petal, and did her best. The mixture was not easy to write with and there seemed no way to hold the paper steady. It slipped and it slid, while Charmain dipped and scratched, and the word that was supposed to be *Ylf* came out gluey and semi-visible and crooked, and looked more like *Hoof* because the red hair in the bowl came out on the pen halfway through and did strange loopy things across the word. As for the five-sided figure, the paper slipped sideways while Charmain was trying to draw it and the most that could be said for it was that it had five sides. It finished as a sinister egg-yolk yellow shape with a dog hair sticking off one corner.

Charmain heaved up a breath, plastered her hair back with a now extremely sticky hand and looked at the final stage, Stage Five. It was now Stage Five of "A Spell to

Make a Wish Come True", but she was far too flustered to notice. It said, "Placing the feather back in the bowl, clap hands three times and say 'Tacs'."

"Tacs!" Charmain said, clapping hard and stickily.

Something evidently worked. The paper, the bowl and the quill pen all vanished, quietly and completely. So did most of the sticky trickles on Great Uncle William's desk. *The Boke of Palimpsest* shut itself with a *snap*. Charmain stood back, dusting crumby bits from her hands, feeling quite exhausted and rather let down.

"But I should be able to fly," she told herself. "I wonder where the best place is to test it out."

The answer was obvious. Charmain went out of the study and along to the end of the passage, to where the window stood invitingly open to the sloping green meadow. The window had a broad, low sill, perfect for climbing over. In a matter of seconds, Charmain was out in the meadow in the evening sunlight, breathing the cold, clean air of the mountains.

She was right up in the mountains here, with most of High Norland spread out beneath her, already blue with evening. Opposite her, lit up orange by the low sun and deceivingly near, were the snowy peaks that separated her country from Strangia, Montalbino and other foreign places. Behind her were more peaks where large dark grey and crimson clouds were crowding up ominously. It was going to rain up here soon, as it often did in High Norland, but for the moment it was warm and peaceful. There were sheep grazing in another meadow just beyond some rocks, and Charmain could hear mooing and bells tonkling from a herd of cows somewhere quite near. When she looked that way, she was a trifle startled to find that the cows were in a meadow above her and that there was no sign of Great Uncle William's house or the window she had climbed out of.

Charmain did not let this worry her. She had never been this high in the mountains before and she was astonished at how beautiful it was. The grass she was standing on was greener than any she had seen in the town. Fresh scents blew off it. These came, when she looked closely, from hundreds and hundreds of tiny, exquisite flowers growing low in the grass.

"Oh, Great Uncle William, you are lucky!" she cried out. "Fancy having this next door to your study!"

For a while, she wandered blissfully about, avoiding the bees that were busy among the flowers and picking herself a bunch that was supposed to be one of each kind. She picked a tiny scarlet tulip, a white one, a starry golden flower, a pale pigmy primrose, a mauve harebell, a blue cup, an orange orchid and one each from crowded clumps of pink and white and yellow. But the flowers that took her fancy most were tiny blue trumpets, more piercingly blue than any blue she could have imagined. Charmain thought they might be gentians and she picked more than one. They were so small, so perfect, and so blue. All the time, she was wandering farther down the meadow, to where there seemed to be a drop-off of some kind. She thought she might jump off there and see if the spell had made her really able to fly.

She reached the drop-off at the time when she found she had more flowers than she could hold. There were six new kinds at the rocky edge that she had to leave where they were. But then she forgot flowers and just stared.

The meadow ended in a cliff half the mountain high. Way, way below her, beside the little thread of the road, she could see Great Uncle William's house like a tiny grey box in a smudge of garden. She could see other houses, equally far off, scattered up and down the road, and lights coming on in them in tiny orange twinkles. They were so far below that Charmain gulped and her knees shook slightly.

"I think I'll give up flying practice for the moment," she said. But how do I get down? asked a subdued inner thought.

Don't let's think about that now, another inner thought replied firmly. Let's just enjoy the view.

She could see most of High Norland from up here, after all. Beyond Great Uncle William's house, the valley narrowed into a green saddle glinting with white waterfalls, where the pass led up into Montalbino. The other way, past the bulge of mountain where the meadow was, the thread of road joined the more winding thread of the river and both plunged in among the roofs, towers, and turrets of High Norland City. Lights were coming on there too, but Charmain could still see the soft shining of the famous golden roof on the Royal Mansion, with the flicker of the flag above it, and she thought she could even pick out her parents' house beyond it. None of it was very far away. Charmain was quite surprised to see that Great Uncle William really lived only just outside the town.

Behind the town, the valley opened out. It was lighter there, out of the shadow of the mountains, melting into twilight distance with orange pricks of lights in it. Charmain could see the long, important shape of Castel Joie, where the Crown Prince lived, and another castle she did not know about. This one was tall and dark, with smoke drifting from one of its turrets. Behind it, the land faded into bluer distance full of farms, villages and industries that formed the heart of the country. Charmain could actually see the sea, misty and faint, beyond that.

We're not a very big country, are we? she thought.

But this thought was interrupted by a sharp buzzing from the bunch of flowers she held. She held the bunch up to see what was making the noise. Up here in the meadow, the sun was still quite dazzlingly bright, bright enough for Charmain to see that one of her blue trumpet-shaped probably-gentians was shaking and vibrating as it buzzed. She must have picked one with a bee in it by mistake. Charmain held the flowers downward and shook them. Something purple and whirring fell out into the grass by her feet. It was not exactly bee-shaped, and instead of flying away as a bee would, it sat in the grass and buzzed. As it buzzed, it grew. Charmain took a nervous sideways step from it, along the edge of the cliff. It was bigger than Waif already and still growing.

I don't like this, she thought. What is it?

Before she could move – or even think – again, the creature shot up to twice the height of a person. It was dark purple and man-shaped, but it was not a man. It had small see-through purple wings on its back that were blurred and whirring with motion, and its face was— Charmain had to look away. Its face was the face of an insect, with groping bits and feeler bits, antennae and bulging eyes that had at least sixteen smaller eyes inside them.

"Oh, heavens!" Charmain whispered. "I think the thing's a lubbock!"

"I am *the* lubbock," the creature announced. Its voice was a mixture of buzz and snarl. "I am the lubbock and I own this land."

Charmain had heard of lubbocks. People at school had whispered of lubbocks and none of it was pleasant. The only thing to do, so they said, was to be very polite and hope to get away without being stung and then eaten. "I'm very sorry," Charmain said. "I didn't realise I was trespassing in your meadow."

"You are trespassing wherever you tread," the lubbock snarled. "All the land you can see is mine."

"What? All of High Norland?" Charmain said. "Don't talk nonsense!"

"I never talk nonsense." the creature said. "All is mine. You are mine." Wings whirring, it began to stalk towards her on most unnatural-looking wiry blobs of feet. "I shall come to claim my own very soon now. I claim you first." It took a whirring stride towards Charmain. Its arms came out. So did a pronged sting on the lower part of its face.

Charmain screamed, dodged and fell off the edge, scattering flowers as she fell.

# Chapter Four

### Introduces Rollo, Peter and mysterious changes in Waif

Charmain heard the lubbock give a whirring shout of rage, though not clearly for the rushing wind of her fall. She saw the huge cliff streaking past her face. She went on screaming. "Ylf, YLF!" she bellowed. "Oh, for goodness' sake! *Ylf!* I just did a flying spell. Why doesn't it work?"

It *was* working. Charmain realised it must be when the upwards rush of the rocks in front of her slowed to a crawl, then to a glide and then to a dawdle. For a moment, she hung in space, bobbing just above some gigantic spikes of rock in the crags below the cliff.

Perhaps I'm dead now, she thought.

Then she said, "This is ridiculous!" and managed, by means of a lot of ungainly kicking and arm waving, to turn herself over. And there was Great Uncle William's house, still a long way below her in the gloaming and about a quarter of a mile off. "And it's all very well floating," Charmain said, "but how do I move?" At this point, she remembered that the lubbock had wings and was probably at that moment whirring down from the heights towards her. After that, there was no need to ask how to move. Charmain found herself kicking her legs mightily and positively surging towards Great Uncle William's house. She shot in over its roof and across the front garden, where the spell seemed to leave her. She just had time to jerk herself sideways so that she was above the path, before she came down with a thump and sat on the neat crazy-paving, shaking all over.

Safe! she thought. Somehow there seemed to be no doubt that inside Great Uncle William's boundaries it was safe. She could feel it was.

After a bit, she said, "Oh, goodness! What a day! When I think that all I ever asked for was a good book and a bit of peace to read it in…! Bother Aunt Sempronia!"

The bushes beside her rustled. Charmain flinched away and nearly screamed again when the hydrangeas bent aside to let a small blue man hop out on to the path. "Are you in charge here now?" this small blue person demanded in a small hoarse voice.

Even in the twilight the little man was definitely blue, not purple, and he had no wings. His face was crumpled with bad-tempered wrinkles and almost filled with a mighty nose, but it was not an insect's face. Charmain's panic vanished. "What are you?" she said.

"Kobold, of course," said the little man. "High Norland is all kobold country. I do the garden here."

"At *night*?" Charmain said.

"Us kobolds mostly come out at night," said the small blue man. "What I said – *are* you in charge?"

"Well," Charmain said. "Sort of."

"Thought so," the kobold said, satisfied. "Saw the wizard carried off by the Tall Ones. So you'll be wanting all these hydrangeas chopped down, then?"

"Whatever for?" Charmain said.

"I like to chop things down," the kobold explained. "Chief pleasure of gardening."

Charmain, who had never thought about gardening in her life, considered this. "No," she said. "Great Uncle William wouldn't have them if he didn't like them. He's coming back before long, and I think he might be upset to find them all chopped down. Why don't you just do your usual night's work and see what he says when he's back?"

"Oh, he'll say no, of course," the kobold said gloomily. "He's a spoilsport, the wizard is. Usual fee, then?"

"What is your usual fee?" Charmain asked.

The kobold said promptly, "I'll take a crock of gold and a dozen new eggs."

Fortunately, Great Uncle William's voice spoke out of the air at the same time. "I pay Rollo a pint of milk nightly, my dear, magically delivered. No need to concern yourself."

The kobold spat disgustedly on the path. "What did I say? Didn't I say spoilsport? And a fat lot of work I can do, if you're going to sit in this path all night."

Charmain said, with dignity, "I was just resting. I'm going now." She got to her feet, feeling surprisingly heavy, not to speak of weak about the knees, and plodded up the path to the front door. It'll be locked, she thought. I shall look awfully silly if I can't get in.

The door burst open before she reached it, letting out a surprising blaze of light and with the light Waif's small scampering shape, squeaking and wagging and wriggling with delight at seeing Charmain again. Charmain was so glad to be home and welcomed that she scooped Waif up and carried him indoors, while Waif writhed and wriggled and reached up to lick Charmain's chin.

Indoors, the light seemed to follow you about magically. "Good," Charmain said aloud. "Then I don't need to hunt for candles." But her inner thoughts were saying frantically, I left that window open! The lubbock can get in! She dumped Waif on the kitchen floor and then rushed left through the door. Light blazed in the corridor as she raced along to the end and slammed the window shut. Unfortunately, the light made it seem so dark in the meadow that, no matter how hard she peered through the glass, she could not tell if the lubbock was out there or not. She consoled herself with the thought that she had not been able to see the window once she was in the meadow, but she still found she was shivering.

After that, she could not seem to stop shivering. She shivered her way back to the kitchen and shivered while she shared a pork pie with Waif, and shivered more because the pool of tea had spread out under the table, making the underside of Waif wet and brown. Whenever Waif came near her, parts of Charmain became clammy with tea too. In the end, Charmain took off her blouse, which was flapping open because of the missing buttons anyway, and wiped up the tea with it. This of course made her shiver more. She went and fetched herself the thick woollen sweater Mrs Baker had packed for her and huddled into it, but she still shivered. The threatened rain started. It beat on the window and pattered down the kitchen chimney, and Charmain shivered even more. She supposed it was shock really, but she still felt cold.

"Oh!" she cried out. "How do I light a fire, Great Uncle William?"

"I believe I left the spell in place," the kindly voice said out of the air. "Simply throw into the grate one thing that will burn and say aloud, 'Fire, light,' and you should have your fire."

Charmain looked round for one thing that would burn. There was the bag beside her on the table, but it still had another pork pie and an apple tart in it, and besides, it was a nice bag, with flowers that Mrs Baker had embroidered on it. There was paper in Great Uncle William's study, of course, but that meant getting up and fetching it. There was the laundry in the bags by the sink, but Charmain was fairly sure that Great Uncle William would not appreciate having his dirty clothes burned. On the other hand, there was her own blouse, dirty and teasoaked and missing two buttons, in a heap on the floor by her feet.

"It's ruined anyway," she said. She picked up the brown, soggy bundle and threw it into the fireplace. "Fire, light," she said.

The grate thundered into life. For a minute or so, there was the most cheerfully blazing fire that anyone could have wished for. Charmain sighed with pleasure. She was just moving her chair nearer to the warmth, when the flames turned to hissing clouds of steam. Then, piling up and up among the steam, crowding up the chimney and blasting out into the room, came bubbles. Big bubbles, small bubbles, bubbles glimmering with rainbow colours, they came thronging out of the fireplace into the kitchen. They filled the air, landed on things, flew into Charmain's face, where they burst with a soft sigh, and kept coming. In seconds, the kitchen was a hot, steamy storm of froth, enough to make Charmain gasp.

"I forgot the bar of soap!" she said, panting in the sudden wet heat.

Waif decided that the bubbles were personal enemies and retreated under Charmain's chair, yapping madly and snarling at the bubbles that burst. It was surprisingly noisy.

"Do shut up!" Charmain said. Sweat ran down her face, and her hair, which had come down over her shoulders, was dripping in the steam. She batted a cloud of bubbles away and said, "I think I'll take all my clothes off."

Someone hammered on the back door.

"Perhaps not," Charmain said.

The person outside hammered on the door again. Charmain sat where she was, hoping it was not the lubbock. But when the hammering came a third time, she got up reluctantly and picked her way among the storming bubbles to see who it was. It could be Rollo, she supposed, wanting to come in out of the rain.

"Who are you?" she shouted through the door. "What do you want?"

"I need to come in!" the person outside shouted back. "It's pouring with rain!"

Whoever it was sounded young, and the voice did not rasp like Rollo's or buzz like the lubbock's. And Charmain could hear the rain thrashing down, even through the hissing of steam and the continuous, gentle popping of the bubbles. But it could be a trick.

"*Let me in!*" the person outside screamed. "The wizard's *expecting* me!"

"That's not true!" Charmain shouted back.

"I wrote him a *letter*!" the person shouted. "My mother arranged for me to come. You've no right to keep me out!"

The latch on the door waggled. Before Charmain could do more than put both hands out to hold it shut, the door crashed open and a soaking wet boy surged inside. He was about as wet as a person could be. His hair, which was probably curly, hung round his young face in dripping brown spikes. His sensible-looking jacket and trousers were black and shiny with wet, and so was the big knapsack on his back. His boots squelched as he moved. He began to steam the moment he was indoors. He stood staring at the crowding, floating bubbles, at Waif yapping and yapping under the chair, at Charmain clutching her sweater and gazing at him between the red strands of her hair, at the stacks of dirty dishes and at the table loaded with teapots. His eyes turned to the laundry bags, and these things were obviously all too much for him. His mouth came open and he just stood there, staring around at all these things all over again and steaming quietly.

After a moment, Charmain reached over and took hold of his chin, where a few harsh hairs grew, showing he was older than he looked. She pushed upwards and his mouth shut with a clop. "Do you mind closing the door?" she said.

The boy looked behind him at the rain pelting into the kitchen. "Oh," he said. "Yes." He heaved at the door until it shut. "What's going on?" he said. "Are you the wizard's apprentice too?"

"No," said Charmain. "I'm only looking after the house while the wizard's not here. He was ill, you see, and the elves took him away to cure him."

The boy looked very dismayed. "Didn't he tell you I was coming?"

"He didn't really have time to tell me anything," Charmain said. Her mind went to the pile of letters under *Das Zauberbuch*. One of those hopeless requests for the wizard to teach people must have been from this boy, but Waif's yapping was making it difficult to think. "*Do* shut up, Waif. What's your name, boy?"

"Peter Regis," he said. "My mother's the Witch of Montalbino. She's a great friend of William Norland's and she arranged with him for me to come here. Do be quiet, little dog. I'm meant to be here." He heaved himself out of the wet knapsack and dumped it on the floor. Waif stopped barking in order to venture out from under the chair and sniff at the knapsack in case it might be dangerous. Peter took the chair and hung his wet jacket on it. His shirt underneath was almost as wet. "And who are you?" he asked, peering at Charmain among the bubbles.

"Charmain Baker," she told him and explained, "We always call the wizard Great Uncle William, but he's Aunt Sempronia's relation really. I live in High Norland. Where have you come from? Why did you come to the back door?"

"I came down from Montalbino," Peter said. "And I got lost, if you must know, trying to take the short cut from the pass. I did come here once before, when my mother was arranging for me to be Wizard Norland's apprentice, but I don't seem to have remembered the way properly. How long have you been here?"

"Only since this morning," Charmain said, rather surprised to realise she had not been here a whole day yet. It had felt like weeks.

"Oh." Peter looked at the teapots through the floating bubbles, as if he were calculating how many cups of tea Charmain had drunk. "It looks as if you'd been here for weeks."

"It was like this when I came," Charmain said coldly.

"What? Bubbles and all?" Peter said.

Charmain thought, I don't think I like this boy. "No," she said. "That was me. I forgot I'd thrown my soap into the grate."

"Ah," Peter said. "I thought it looked like a spell that's gone wrong. That's why I assumed you were an apprentice too. We'll just have to wait for the soap to be used up, then. Have you any food? I'm starving."

Charmain's eyes went grudgingly to her bag on the table. She turned them away quickly. "No," she said. "Not really."

"What are you going to feed your dog on, then?" Peter said.

Charmain looked at Waif, who had gone under the chair again in order to bark at Peter's knapsack. "Nothing. He's just had half a pork pie," she said. "And he's not my dog. He's a stray that Great Uncle William took in. He's called Waif."

Waif was still yapping. Peter said, "Do be quiet, Waif," and reached among the storming bubbles and past his wet jacket to where Waif crouched under the chair.

Somehow he dragged Waif out and stood up with Waif upside down in his arms. Waif uttered a squeak of protest, waved all four paws, and curled his frayed tail up between his back legs. Peter uncurled the tail.

"You've damaged his dignity," Charmain said. "Put him down."

"He isn't a he," Peter said. "He's a she. And she hasn't got any dignity, have you, Waif?"

Waif clearly disagreed and managed to scramble out of Peter's arms on to the table. Another teapot fell down and Charmain's bag tipped over. To Charmain's great dismay, the pork pie and the apple tart rolled out of it.

"Oh, good!" said Peter, and snatched up the pork pie just before Waif got to it. "Is this all the food you've got?" he said, biting deeply into the pie.

"Yes," Charmain said. "That was breakfast." She picked the fallen teapot up. The tea that had spilled out of it rapidly turned into brown bubbles, which whirled upwards to make a brown streak among the other bubbles. "Now look what you've done."

"A bit more won't make any difference to this mess," Peter said. "Don't you ever tidy up? This is a really good pie. What's this other one?"

Charmain looked at Waif, who was sitting soulfully beside the apple tart. "Apple," she said. "And if you eat it, you have to give some to Waif too."

"Is that a rule?" Peter said, swallowing the last of the pork pie.

"Yes," said Charmain. "Waif made it and he – I mean she – is very firm about it."

"She's magical then?" Peter suggested, picking up the apple tart. Waif at once made small soulful noises and trotted about among the teapots.

"I don't know," Charmain began. Then she thought of the way Waif seemed to be able to go anywhere in the house and how the front door had burst open for her earlier on. "Yes," she said. "I'm sure she is. *Very* magical."

Slowly and grudgingly, Peter broke a lump off the apple tart. Waif's frayed tail wagged and Waif's eyes soulfully followed his every movement. She seemed to know exactly what Peter was doing, no matter how many bubbles got in the way. "I see what you mean," Peter said, and he passed the lump to Waif. Waif gently took it in her jaws, jumped from the table to the chair and then to the floor, and went pattering away to eat it somewhere behind the laundry bags. "How about a hot drink?" Peter said.

A hot drink was something Charmain had been yearning for ever since she fell off the mountainside.

She shivered and hugged her sweater round herself. "What a good idea," she said. "Do make one if you can find out how."

Peter waved bubbles aside to look at the teapots on

the table. "*Someone* must have made all these pots of tea," he said.

"Great Uncle William must have made them," Charmain said. "It wasn't me."

"But it shows it can be done," Peter said. "Stop standing there looking feeble and find a saucepan or something."

"*You* find one," Charmain said.

Peter shot her a scornful look and strode across the room, waving bubbles aside as he went, until he reached the crowded sink. There he naturally made the discoveries that Charmain had made earlier. "There are no taps!" he said incredulously. "And all these saucepans are dirty. Where does he get water from?"

"There's a pump out in the yard," Charmain said unkindly.

Peter looked among the bubbles at the window, where rain was still streaming across the panes. "Isn't there a bathroom?" he said. And before Charmain could explain how you got to it, he waved and stumbled his way across the kitchen to the other door and arrived in the living room. Bubbles stormed in there around him as he dived angrily back into the kitchen. "Is this a joke?" he said incredulously. "He *can't* have only these two rooms!"

Charmain sighed, huddled her sweater further around herself, and went to show him. "You open the door again and turn left," she explained, and then had to grab Peter as he turned right. "No. That way goes to somewhere very strange. *This* is left. Can't you tell?"

"No," Peter said. "I never can. I usually have to tie a piece of string round my thumb."

Charmain rolled her eyes towards the ceiling and pushed him left. They both arrived in the corridor, which was loud with the rain pelting across the window at the end. Light slowly flooded the place as Peter stood looking around.

"*Now* you can turn right," Charmain said, pushing him that way. "The bathroom's this door here. That row of doors leads to bedrooms."

"Ah!" Peter said admiringly. "He's been bending space. That's something I can't wait to learn how to do. Thanks," he added, and plunged into the bathroom. His voice floated back to Charmain as she tiptoed towards the study. "Oh, good! Taps! Water!"

Charmain whisked herself into Great Uncle William's study and closed the door, while the funny twisted lamp on the desk lit up and grew brighter. By the time she reached the desk, it was almost bright as daylight in there. Charmain shoved aside *Das Zauberbuch* and picked up the bundle of letters underneath. She had to check. If Peter was telling the truth, one of the letters asking to be Great Uncle William's apprentice had to be from him. Because she had only skimmed through them before, she had no memory of seeing one, and if there wasn't one, she was dealing with an imposter, possibly another lubbock. She had to know.

Ah! Here it was, halfway down the pile. She put her glasses on and read:

> Esteemed Wizard Norland,
>
> With regard to my becoming your apprentice, will it be convenient for me to arrive with you in a week's time, instead of in the autumn as arranged? My mother has to journey into Ingary and prefers to have me settled before she leaves. Unless I hear from you to the contrary, I shall present myself at your house on the thirteenth of this month.
>
> Hoping this is convenient,
> Yours faithfully,
> Peter Regis

So *that* seems to be all right! Charmain thought, half relieved and half annoyed. When she had skimmed the letters earlier, her eye must have caught the word *apprentice* near the top and the word *hoping* near the bottom, and those words were in all the letters. So she had assumed it was just another begging letter. And it looked as if Great Uncle William had done the same. Or perhaps he had been too ill to reply. Whatever had happened, she seemed to be stuck with Peter. Bother! At least he's not sinister, she thought.

Here she was interrupted by dismayed yelling from Peter in the distance. Charmain hastily stuffed the letters back under *Das Zauberbuch*, snatched off her glasses, and dived out into the corridor.

Steam was blasting out of the bathroom, mixing with the bubbles that had strayed in there. It almost concealed something vast and white that was looming towards Charmain.

"What have you d—," she began.

This was all she had time to say before the vast white something put out a gigantic pink tongue and licked her face. It also gave out a huge trumpeting sound. Charmain reeled backwards. It was like being licked by a wet bath towel and whined at by an elephant. She leaned against the wall and stared up into the creature's enormous, pleading eyes.

"I know those eyes," Charmain said. "What has he *done* to you, Waif?"

Peter surged out of the bathroom, gasping. "I don't know what went wrong," he gasped. "The water didn't come out hot enough to make tea, so I thought I'd make it hotter with a Spell of Enlargement."

"Well, do it backwards at once," Charmain said. "Waif's the size of an elephant."

Peter shot the huge Waif a distracted look. "Only the size of a carthorse. But the pipes in here are red hot," he said. "What do you think I should do?"

"Oh, honestly!" Charmain said. She pushed the enormous Waif gently aside and went to the bathroom. As far as she could see through the steam, boiling water was gushing out of all four taps and flushing into the toilet, and the pipes along the walls were indeed glowing red. "Great Uncle William!" she shouted. "How do I make the bathroom water *cold*?"

Great Uncle William's kindly voice spoke among the hissing and gushing. "You will find further instructions somewhere in the suitcase, my dear."

"*That's* no good!" Charmain said. She knew there was no time to go searching through suitcases. Something was going to explode soon. "Go *cold*!" she shouted into the steam. "Freeze! All you pipes, go cold at once!" she screamed, waving both arms. "I *order* you to cool down!"

It worked, to her astonishment. The steam died away to mere puffs and then vanished altogether. The toilet stopped flushing. Three of the taps gurgled and stopped running. Frost almost instantly formed on the tap that *was* running – the cold tap over the washbasin – and an icicle grew from the end of it. Another icicle appeared on the pipes that ran across the wall and slid, hissing, down into the bath.

"That's better," Charmain said, and turned round to look at Waif. Waif looked sadly back. She was as big as ever. "Waif," Charmain said, "go small. Now. I order you."

Waif sadly wagged the tip of her monstrous tail and stayed the same size.

"If she's magic," Peter said, "she can probably turn herself back if she wants to."

"Oh, shut up!" Charmain snapped at him. "What did you think you were trying to do anyway? No one can drink scalding water."

Peter glowered at her from under the twisted, dripping ends of his hair. "I wanted a cup of tea," he said. "You make tea with boiling water."

Charmain had never made tea in her life. She shrugged. "Do you really?" She raised her face to the ceiling. "Great Uncle William," she said, "how do we get a hot drink in this place?"

The kindly voice spoke again. "In the kitchen, you tap the table and say 'Tea', my dear. In the living room, tap the trolley in the corner and say 'Afternoon tea'. In your bedroom—"

Neither Peter nor Charmain waited to hear about the bedroom. They dived forward and slammed the bathroom door, opened it again – Charmain giving Peter a stern push to the left – and jammed themselves through it into the kitchen, turned round, shut the door, opened it again and finally arrived in the living room, where they looked eagerly around for the trolley. Peter spotted it over in the corner and reached it ahead of Charmain. "Afternoon tea!" he shouted, hammering mightily upon its empty, glass covered surface. "Afternoon tea! Afternoon tea! Aftern—"

By the time Charmain got to him and seized his flailing arm, the trolley was crowded with pots of tea, milk jugs, sugar bowls, cups, scones, dishes of cream, dishes of jam, plates of hot buttered toast, piles of muffins and a chocolate cake. A drawer slid out of the end of it, full of knives, spoons and forks. Charmain and Peter, with one accord, dragged the trolley over to the musty sofa and settled down to eat and drink. After a minute, Waif put her huge head round the door, sniffing. Seeing the trolley, she shoved a bit and arrived in the living room too, where she crawled wistfully and mountainously over to the sofa and put her enormous hairy chin on the back of it behind Charmain. Peter gave her a distracted look and passed her several muffins, which she ate in one mouthful, with huge politeness.

A good half hour later, Peter lay back and stretched. "That was great," he said. "At least we won't starve. Wizard Norland," he added experimentally, "how do we get lunch in this house?"

There was no reply.

"He only answers me," Charmain said, a trifle smugly. "And I'm not going to ask now. I had to deal with a lubbock before you came and I'm exhausted. I'm going to bed."

"What are lubbocks?" Peter asked. "I think one killed my father."

Charmain did not feel up to answering him. She got up and went to the door.

"Wait," Peter said. "How do we get rid of the stuff on this trolley?"

"No idea," said Charmain. She opened the door.

"Wait, wait, wait!" Peter said, hurrying after her. "Show me my bedroom first."

I suppose I'll have to, Charmain thought. He can't tell left from right. She sighed. Unwillingly, she shoved Peter in among the bubbles that were still storming into the kitchen, thicker than ever, so that he could collect his knapsack, and then steered him left, back through the door to where the bedrooms were. "Take the third one along," she said. "That one's mine and the first one's Great Uncle William's. But there's miles of them, if you want a different one. Good night," she added and went into the bathroom.

Everything in there was frozen.

"Oh, well," Charmain said.

By the time she got to her bedroom and into her

somewhat tea-stained nightdress, Peter was out in the corridor, shouting, "Hey! This toilet's frozen over!" Bad luck! Charmain thought. She got into bed and was asleep almost at once.

About an hour later, she dreamed that she was being sat on by a woolly mammoth. "Get off, Waif," she said. "You're too big." After this she dreamed that the mammoth slowly got off her, grumbling under its breath, before she went off into other, deeper dreams.

# Chapter Five

### Wherein Charmain receives
### her anxious parent

When Charmain woke, she discovered that Waif had planted her vast head on the bed, across Charmain's legs. The rest of Waif was piled on the floor in a hairy white heap that filled most of the rest of the room.

"So you can't go smaller on your own," Charmain said. "I'll have to think of something."

Waif's answer was a series of giant wheezings, after which she appeared to go to sleep again. Charmain, with difficulty, dragged her legs out from under Waif's head and edged round Waif's vast body finding clean clothes and getting into them. When she came to do her hair, Charmain discovered that all the hairpins she usually put it up with seemed to have vanished, probably during her dive off the cliff. All she had left was a ribbon. Mother always insisted that respectable girls needed to have their hair in a neat knot on the top of their head. Charmain had never worn her hair any other way.

"Oh, well," she said to her reflection in the neat little mirror, "Mother's not here, is she?" And she did her hair in a fat plait over one shoulder and fastened it with the ribbon. Like that, she thought her reflection looked nicer than usual, fuller in the face and less thin and grumpy. She nodded at her reflection and picked her way around Waif to get to the bathroom.

To her relief, the bathroom had thawed overnight. The room was full of soft dripping sounds from water dewing all the pipes, but nothing else seemed to be wrong until Charmain tried the taps. All four of them ran ice cold water, no matter how long they ran for.

"I didn't want a bath anyway," Charmain said, as she went out into the corridor.

There was no sound from Peter. Charmain remembered Mother telling her that boys always were hard to wake in the morning. She did not let this worry her. She opened the door and turned left into the kitchen, into solid foam. Clots of foam and large single bubbles sailed past her into the corridor.

"Damnation!" Charmain said. She put her head down and her arms across her head and ploughed into the room. It was as hot in there as her father's bakehouse when he was baking for a big order. "Phew!" she said. "I suppose it takes days to use up a cake of soap." After that she said nothing else, because her mouth filled with soapy froth when she opened it. Bubbles worked up her nose until she sneezed, causing a small foamy whirlwind. She collided with the table and heard another teapot fall down, but she ploughed on until she ran into the laundry bags and heard the saucepans rattle on top of them. Then she knew where she was. She spared one hand from her face in order to fumble for the sink and then along the sink until she felt the back door under her fingers. She groped for the latch – for a moment she thought that had vanished in the night, until she realised it was on the other edge of the door – and finally flung the door open. Then she stood gulping in deep, soapy breaths and blinking her running, smarting, soap-filled eyes into a beautiful mild morning.

Bubbles sailed out past her in crowds. As her eyes cleared, Charmain stood admiring the way big shiny bubbles caught the sunlight as they soared against the green slopes of the mountains. Most of them, she noticed, seemed to pop when they got to the end of the yard, as if there was an invisible barrier there, but some sailed on and up and up as if they would go on for ever. Charmain followed them up with her eyes, past brown cliffs and green slopes. One of those green slopes must be that meadow where she had met the lubbock, but she was unable to tell which. She let her eyes go on to the pale blue sky above the peaks. It was a truly lovely day.

By this time there was a steady, shimmering stream of bubbles pouring out of the kitchen. When Charmain turned to look, the room was no longer solid foam, but there were still bubbles everywhere and more piling out of the fireplace. Charmain sighed and edged back indoors, until she could lean over the sink and throw the window open too. This helped enormously. Two lines of bubbles now sailed out of the house, faster than before, and made rainbows in the yard. The kitchen emptied rapidly. It was soon clear enough for Charmain to see that there were now four bags of laundry leaning beside the sink, in place of last night's two.

"Bother that!" Charmain said. "Great Uncle William, how do I get breakfast?"

It was good to hear Great Uncle William's voice among the bubbles. "Just tap the side of the fireplace and say 'Breakfast, please,' my dear."

Charmain rushed hungrily over there at once. She

gave the soapy paintwork there an impatient tap. "Breakfast, please." Then found she was having to back away from a floating tray, nudging at the glasses dangling on her chest. In the centre of this tray was a sizzling plate of bacon and eggs, and crammed in around it were a coffee pot, a cup, a rack of toast, jam, butter, milk, a bowl of stewed plums and cutlery in a starched napkin.

"Oh, *lovely*!" she said, and before it could all get too soapy, she seized the tray and carried it away into the living room. To her surprise, there was no sign of the afternoon tea feast that she and Peter had had last night, and the trolley was neatly back in its corner; but the room was very musty and there were quite a few escaped bubbles coasting around in it. Charmain went on and out through the front door. She remembered that, while she was picking the pink and blue petals for the spell from *The Boke of Palimpsest*, she had noticed a garden table and bench outside the study window. She carried the tray round the corner of the house to look for it.

She found it, in the place where the morning sun was strongest, and above it, over the pink and blue bush, the study window, even though there was no space in the house for the study to be. Magic is interesting, she thought as she set the tray on the table. Though the bushes around her were still dripping from overnight rain, the bench and the table were dry.

Charmain sat down and consumed the most enjoyable breakfast she had ever had, warm in the sun and feeling lazy, luxurious, and extremely grown up. The only thing missing is a chocolate croissant, like Dad makes, she thought, sitting back to sip her coffee. I must tell Great Uncle William when he comes back.

She had an idea that Great Uncle William must have sat here often, enjoying his breakfast. The blooms on the hydrangeas around her were the finest in the garden, as if for his special pleasure. Each bush had more than one colour of flowers. The one in front of her had white flowers and pale pink and mauve. The next one over started blue on the left side and shaded over into a deep sea green on the right. Charmain was feeling rather pleased that she had not allowed the kobold to cut these bushes down, when Peter stuck his head out through the study window. This rather destroyed Charmain's pleasure.

"Hey, where did you get that breakfast?" Peter demanded.

Charmain explained, and he put his head inside and went away. Charmain stayed where she was, expecting Peter to arrive any moment and hoping that he wouldn't. But nothing happened. After basking in the sun a while longer, Charmain thought she would find a book to read. She carried the tray indoors and through to the kitchen first, congratulating herself on being so tidy and efficient. Peter had obviously been there, because he had shut the back door, leaving only the window open, so that the room was once more filled with bubbles, floating gently towards the window and then streaming swiftly out of it. Among these bubbles loomed the great white shape of Waif. As Charmain arrived, Waif stretched out her huge frayed tail and wagged it sharply against the mantelpiece. A very small dog dish, piled with the amount of food suitable for a very small dog, landed among the bubbles by her enormous front paws. Waif surveyed it sadly, lowered her vast head, and slurped up the dog food in one mouthful.

"Oh, poor Waif!" Charmain said.

Waif looked up and saw her. Her huge tail began to wag, thrumming against the fireplace. A new tiny dog dish appeared with each wag. In seconds, Waif was surrounded in little dog dishes, spread all over the floor.

"Don't overdo it, Waif," Charmain said, edging among the dishes. She put the tray down on one of the two new laundry bags and said to Waif, "I'll be in the study looking for a book, if you want me," and edged her way back there. Waif ate busily and took no notice.

Peter was in the study. His finished breakfast tray was on the floor beside the desk and Peter himself was in the chair, busily leafing through one of the large leather books from the row at the back of the desk. He looked far more respectable today. Now that his hair was dry, it was in neat tawny curls and he was wearing what was obviously his second suit, which was of good green tweed. It was crumpled from his knapsack and had one or two round wet patches on it where bubbles had burst, but Charmain found that she quite approved of it. As Charmain came in, he slammed the book shut with a sigh and pushed it back in its place. Charmain noticed that he had a piece of green string tied round his left thumb. So that's how he managed to get in here, she thought.

"I can't make head or tail of these," he said to her. "It *must* be in here somewhere, but I can't find it."

"What are you trying to find?" Charmain asked.

"You said something last night about a lubbock," Peter said, "and I realised that I didn't really know what they are. I'm trying to look them up. Or do you know all about them?"

"Not really – except that they're very frightening," Charmain confessed. "I'd like to find out about them too. How do we?"

Peter pointed his thumb with the green string round it at the row of books. "These. I know these are a wizards' encyclopedia, but you have to know the sort of thing you're looking for before you can even find the right volume to look in."

Charmain pulled her glasses up and bent to look at the books. Each one was called *Res Magica* in gold, with a number under that and then a title. *Volume 3*, she read, *Giroloptica*; *Volume 5, Panacticon*; then down at the other end, *Volume 19, Advanced Seminal*; *Volume 27, Terrestrial Oneiromancy*; *Volume 28, Cosmic Oneiromancy*. "I see your problem," she said.

"I'm going through them in order now," Peter said. "I've just done Five. It's all spells I can't make head or tail of." He pulled out Volume 6, which was labelled simply *Hex*, and opened it. "You do the next one," he said.

Charmain shrugged and pulled forward Volume 7. It was called, not very helpfully, *Potentes*. She took it over to the windowsill, where there was space and light, and opened it not far from the beginning. As soon as she did, she knew it was the one. "Demon: powerful and sometimes dangerous being," she read, "often confused with an Elemental *qv*," and leafing on a few pages, "Devil: a creature of hell...." After that she was at "Elfgift: contains powers gifted by Elves *qv* for the safety of a realm... ," and then, a wad of pages later, "Incubus: specialised Devil *qv*, inimical mostly to women...." She turned the pages over very slowly and carefully after that, and twenty pages on, she found it. "Lubbock. Got it!" she said.

"Great!" Peter slammed *Hex* shut. "This one's

nearly all diagrams. What does it say?" He came and leaned on the windowsill beside Charmain and they both read the entry.

"LUBBOCK: a creature fortunately rare. A lubbock is a purple-hued insectile being of any size from grasshopper to larger than human. It is very dangerous, though nowadays luckily only to be encountered in wild or uninhabited areas. A lubbock will attack any human it sees, either with its pincer-like appendages or its formidable proboscis. For ten months of the year, it will merely tear the human to pieces for food, but in the months of July and August it comes into its breeding season and is then especially dangerous; for in those months it will lie in wait for human travellers and, having caught one, it will lay its eggs in that human's body. The eggs hatch after twelve months, whereupon the first hatched will eat the rest, and this single new lubbock will then carve its way out of its human host. A male human will die. A female human will give birth in the normal fashion, and the offspring so born will be a lubbockin (see below). The human female then usually dies."

My goodness, I had a narrow escape! Charmain thought and her eyes, and Peter's, scudded on to the next entry.

"LUBBOCKIN: the offspring of a LUBBOCK *qv* and a human female. These creatures normally have the appearance of a human child except that they invariably have purple eyes. Some will have purple skin, and a few may even be born with vestigial wings. A midwife will destroy an obvious lubbockin on sight, but in many cases lubbockins have been mistakenly reared as if they were human children. They are almost invariably evil, and since lubbockins can breed with humans, the evil nature does not disappear until several generations have passed. It is rumoured that many of the inhabitants of remote areas such as High Norland and Montalbino owe their origins to a lubbockin ancestor."

It was hard to describe the effect of reading this on both Charmain and Peter. They both wished they had not read it. Great Uncle William's sunny study suddenly felt entirely unsafe, with queer shadows in the corners. In fact, Charmain thought, the whole house did. She and Peter both found themselves staring around uneasily and then looking urgently out of the window for danger in the garden. Both jumped when Waif gave an outsize yawn somewhere in the corridor. Charmain wanted to dash out there and make sure that window at the end was quite, quite shut. But first she had to look at Peter very, very carefully for any signs of purple in him. He said he came from Montalbino after all.

Peter had gone very white. This showed up quite a few freckles across his nose, but they were pale orange freckles, and the meagre new hairs that grew on his chin were a sort of orange too. His eyes were a rusty sort of brown, nothing like the greenish yellow of Charmain's own eyes, but not purple either.

She could see all this easily because Peter was staring at her quite as carefully. Her face felt cold. She could tell it had gone as white as Peter's. Finally, they both spoke at once.

Charmain said, "You're from Montalbino. Is your family purple?"

Peter said, "You met a lubbock. Did it lay any eggs in you?"

Charmain said, "No."

Peter said, "My mother's *called* the Witch of Montalbino, but she's from High Norland really. And she is not purple. Tell me about this lubbock you met."

Charmain explained how she had climbed out of the window and arrived in the mountain pasture where the lubbock lurked inside the blue flower and—

"But did it touch you?" Peter interrupted.

"No, because I fell off the cliff before it could," Charmain said.

"Fell off the— Then why aren't you dead?" Peter demanded. He backed away from her slightly, as if he thought she might be some kind of zombie.

"I worked a spell," Charmain told him, rather airily

because she was so proud of having worked real magic. "A flying spell."

"Really?" said Peter, half eager, half suspicious. "What flying spell? Where?"

"Out of a book in here," Charmain said. "And when I fell, I started to float and came down quite safely in the garden path. There's no need to look so disbelieving. There was a kobold called Rollo in the garden when I came down. Ask him, if you don't believe me."

"I will," Peter said. "What was this book? Show me."

Charmain tossed her plait haughtily across her shoulder and went over to the desk. *The Boke of Palimpsest* seemed to be trying to hide. It was certainly not where she had left it. Perhaps Peter had moved it. She found it in the end, squeezed in among the row of *Res Magica*, pretending to be another volume of the encyclopedia. "There," she said, banging it down on top of *Hex*, "and how dare you doubt my word! Now I'm going to find a book to read."

She marched to one of the bookshelves and began picking out likely titles. None of the books seemed to have stories in them, which Charmain would have preferred, but some of the titles were quite interesting. What about *The Thaumaturge as Artist*, for instance, or *Memoirs of an Exorcist*? On the other hand, *The Theory and Practice of Choral Invocation* looked decidedly dry, but Charmain rather fancied the one next to it, called *The Twelve-Branched Wand*.

Peter meanwhile sat himself down at the desk and leafed eagerly through *The Boke of Palimpsest*. Charmain was just discovering that *The Thaumaturge as Artist* was full of off-putting sayings like "thus our happy little magician can bring a sweet, fairylike music to our ears," when Peter said irritably, "There's no spell for flying in here. I've looked right through."

"Perhaps I used it up," Charmain suggested vaguely. She took a look inside *The Twelve-Branched Wand* and found it a very promising read.

"Spells don't work like that," Peter said. "Where did you find it, really?"

"In there. I told you," Charmain said. "And if you can't believe a word I say, why do you keep asking me?" She dropped her glasses off her nose, snapped the book shut, and carried a whole pile of likely volumes out into the corridor, where she slammed the study door on Peter and marched off backwards and forwards through the bathroom door until she reached the living room. There, in spite of the mustiness, she decided to stay. After that entry in *Res Magica*, outside in the sun did not seem safe anymore. She thought of the lubbock looming above the hydrangeas and sat herself firmly down on the sofa instead.

She was deep in *The Twelve-Branched Wand*, and even beginning to understand what it was about, when there was a sharp rapping at the front door. Charmain thought, just as she usually did, Someone else can answer that, and read on.

The door opened with an impatient rattle. Aunt Sempronia's voice said, "Of *course* she's all right, Berenice. She just has her nose in a book, as usual."

Charmain tore herself out of the book and snatched off her glasses in time to see her mother following Aunt Sempronia into the house. Aunt Sempronia, as usual, was most impressively clothed in stiff silk. Mrs Baker was at her most respectable in grey, with shining white collar and cuffs, and wore her most respectable grey hat.

How lucky I put on clean clothes this – , Charmain was beginning to think, when it dawned on her that the rest of the house was simply not fit for either of these two ladies to see. Not only was the kitchen full of dirty human dishes and dirty dog dishes, bubbles, laundry and a vast white dog, but Peter was sitting in the study. Mother would probably only find the kitchen, and that was bad enough. But Aunt Sempronia was (pretty certainly) a witch, and she would find the study and come across Peter. Then Mother would want to know what an unknown boy was doing here. And when Peter was explained, Mother would say that in that case Peter could look after Great Uncle William's house for him, and Charmain must do the respectable thing and come home at once. Aunt Sempronia would agree, and off home Charmain would be forced to go. And there would be an end to peace and freedom.

Charmain jumped to her feet and smiled terrifically, so broadly and welcomingly that she thought she might have sprained her face. "Oh, *hallo*!" she said. "I didn't hear the door."

"You never do," said Aunt Sempronia.

Mrs Baker peered at Charmain, full of anxiety. "Are you all right, my love? *Quite* all right? Why haven't you put your hair up properly?"

"I like it like this," Charmain said, shuffling across so that she was between the two ladies and the kitchen door. "Don't you think it suits me, Aunt Sempronia?"

Aunt Sempronia leaned on her parasol and looked at her judiciously. "Yes," she said. "It does. It makes you look younger and plumper. Is that how you want to look?"

"Yes, it is," Charmain said defiantly.

Mrs Baker sighed. "Darling, I wish you wouldn't talk in that bold way. People don't like it, you know. But I'm very glad to see you looking so well. I lay awake half the night listening to the rain and hoping that the roof on this house didn't leak."

"It doesn't leak," Charmain said.

"Or fearing that you might have left a window open," added her mother.

Charmain shuddered. "No, I shut the window," she said, and immediately felt sure that Peter was at that moment opening the window on to the lubbock's meadow. "You really have nothing to worry about, Mother," she lied.

"Well, to tell the truth, I was a little worried," Mrs Baker said. "Your first time away from the nest, you know. I spoke to your father about it. He said you might not be managing to feed yourself properly." She held up the bulging embroidered bag she was carrying. "He packed you some more food in this. I'll just go and put it in the kitchen for you, shall I?" she asked, and pushed past Charmain towards the inner door.

*No!* Help! Charmain thought. She took hold of the embroidered bag in what she hoped was a most gentle, civilised way, rather than the grab for it that she would have liked to make, and said, "You needn't bother, Mother. I'll take it in a moment and fetch the other one for you—"

"Oh why? It's no trouble, my love," her mother protested, hanging on to the bag.

"—because I've got a surprise for you first," Charmain said hurriedly. "You go and sit down. That sofa's very comfortable, Mother." And it has its back to this door. "*Do* take a seat, Aunt Sempronia—"

"But it won't take me a moment," Mrs Baker said. "If I leave it on the kitchen table where you can find it—"

Charmain waved her free hand. Her other hand was hanging on to the bag for dear life. "Great Uncle William!" she cried out. "Morning coffee! Please!"

To her enormous relief, Great Uncle William's kind voice replied, "Tap the trolley in the corner, my dear, and say 'Morning coffee'."

Mrs Baker gasped with amazement and looked round to see where the voice was coming from. Aunt Sempronia looked interested, looked quizzical, and went over to give the trolley a smart rap with her parasol. "Morning coffee?" she said.

Instantly the room filled with a warm smell of coffee. A tall silver coffee pot stood on the trolley, steaming, together with tiny gilded cups, a gilded cream jug, a silver sugar boat and a plate of little sugary cakes. Mrs Baker was so astonished that she let go of the embroidered bag. Charmain put it quickly behind the nearest armchair.

"Very elegant magic," Aunt Sempronia said. "Berenice, come and sit down here and let Charmain wheel the trolley over beside this sofa."

Mrs Baker obeyed, looking dazed, and to Charmain's acute relief, the visit started to turn into an elegant, respectable coffee morning. Aunt Sempronia poured coffee, while Charmain handed round the sugary cakes. Charmain was standing facing the kitchen door, holding the plate out to Aunt Sempronia, when the door swung open and Waif's huge face appeared round the edge of it, obviously fetched by the smell of little sugary cakes.

"Go *away*, Waif!" Charmain said. "Shoo! I mean it! You can't come in here unless you're... you're... you're *respectable*. Go!"

Waif stared wistfully, sighed hugely and backed away. By the time Mrs Baker and Aunt Sempronia, each carefully holding a brimming little coffee cup, had managed to turn round to see who Charmain was talking to, Waif was gone and the door was shut again.

"What was that?" Mrs Baker asked.

"Nothing," Charmain said soothingly. "Only Great Uncle William's guard dog, you know. She's terribly greedy—"

"You have a *dog* here!" Mrs Baker interrupted, in the greatest alarm. "I'm not sure I like that, Charmain. Dogs are so dirty. And you could get *bitten*! I hope you keep it chained up."

"No, no, no, she's terribly clean. And obedient," Charmain said, wondering if this was true. "It's just – it's just that she overeats. Great Uncle William tries to keep her on a diet, so of course she was after one of these cakes—"

The kitchen door opened again. This time it was Peter's face that came round the edge of it, with a look on it that suggested that Peter had something urgent to say. The look turned to horror as he took in Aunt Sempronia's finery and Mrs Baker's respectability.

"Here she is again," Charmain said, rather desperately. "Waif, go away!"

Peter took the hint and vanished, just before Aunt Sempronia could turn round again and see him. Mrs Baker looked more alarmed than ever.

"You worry too much, Berenice," Aunt Sempronia said. "I admit that dogs are smelly and dirty and noisy, but there's nothing to beat a good guard dog for keeping a house safe. You should be glad that Charmain has one."

"I suppose so," Mrs Baker agreed, sounding wholly unconvinced. "But – but didn't you tell me this house is protected by – your Great Uncle's... er... wizardly arts?"

"Yes, yes, it *is*!" Charmain said eagerly. "The place is *doubly* safe!"

"Of course it is," said Aunt Sempronia. "I believe that nothing can get in here that hasn't been invited over the threshold."

As if to prove Aunt Sempronia completely wrong there, a kobold suddenly appeared on the floor beside the trolley. "Now, look here!" he said, small and blue and aggressive.

Mrs Baker gave a shriek and clutched her coffee cup

to her bosom. Aunt Sempronia drew her skirts back from him in a stately way. The kobold stared at them, clearly puzzled, and then looked at Charmain. He was not the garden kobold. His nose was bigger, his blue clothing was of finer cloth and he looked as if he was used to giving orders.

"Are you an important kobold?" Charmain asked him.

"Well," the kobold said, rather taken aback, "you could say that. I'm chieftain in these parts, name of Timminz. I'm leading this deputation, and we're all pretty annoyed. And now we're told that the wizard isn't here, or won't see us, or—"

Charmain could see he was working himself into a rage. She said quickly, "That's true. He's not here. He's ill. The elves have taken him away to cure him, and I'm looking after his house while he's away."

The kobold hunched his eyes over his great blue nose and glowered at her. "Are you telling the truth?"

I seem to have spent all *day* being told I'm lying! Charmain thought angrily.

"It is the exact truth," Aunt Sempronia said. "William Norland is not here at present. So will you be so kind as to take yourself off, my good kobold. You are frightening poor Mrs Baker."

The kobold glowered at her and then at Mrs Baker. "Then," he said to Charmain, "I don't see any chance of this dispute being settled, ever!" And he was gone as suddenly as he had come.

"Oh, my goodness!" Mrs Baker gasped, holding her chest. "So little! So blue! How did it get in? Don't let it run up your skirt, Charmain!"

"It was only a kobold," Aunt Sempronia said. "Pull yourself together, Berenice. Kobolds as a rule do not get on with humans, so I have no idea what it was doing here. But I suppose Great Uncle William must have had some sort of dealings with the creatures. There's no accounting for wizards."

"*And* I've spilled coffee—" Mrs Baker wailed, mopping at her skirt.

Charmain took the little cup and soothingly filled it with coffee again. "Have another cake, Mother," she said, holding the plate out. "Great Uncle William has a kobold to do the gardening, and that one was angry too when I met him—"

"What was the gardener doing in the *living room*?" Mrs Baker demanded.

As often happened, Charmain began to despair of getting her mother to understand. She's not stupid, she just never lets her mind out, she thought. "That was a different kobold," she began.

The kitchen door opened and Waif trotted in. She was the right size again. That meant that she was, if anything, smaller than the kobold and very pleased with herself for shrinking. She trotted jauntily across to Charmain and raised her nose wistfully towards the cake plate.

"Honestly, Waif!" Charmain said. "When I think how much you ate for breakfast!"

"Is that the guard dog?" Mrs Baker quavered.

"If it is," Aunt Sempronia opined, "it would come off second best against a mouse. How much did you say it ate for breakfast?"

"About fifty dog dishes full," Charmain said without thinking.

"*Fifty*!" said her mother.

"I was exaggerating," Charmain said.

Waif, seeing them all looking at her, sat up into begging position with her paws under her chin. She contrived to look enchanting. It was the way she managed to make one ragged ear flop that did it, Charmain decided.

"Oh, what a sweet little doggie!" Mrs Baker cried out. "Is ooh hungwy, then?" She gave Waif the rest of the cake she was eating. Waif took it politely, ate it in one gulp and continued to beg. Mrs Baker gave her a whole cake from the plate. This caused Waif to beg more soulfully than ever.

"I'm disgusted," Charmain told Waif.

Aunt Sempronia graciously handed a cake over to Waif too. "I must say," she said to Charmain, "with this great hound to guard you, no one need fear for your safety, although you might go rather hungry yourself."

"She's good at barking," Charmain said. And there's no need to be sarcastic, Aunt Sempronia. I know she isn't a guard dog. But Charmain had no sooner thought this than she realised that Waif *was* guarding her. She had taken Mother's attention completely away from kobolds, or the kitchen, or any dangers to Charmain herself, and she had contrived to reduce herself to the right size to do it. Charmain found herself so grateful that she gave Waif a cake as well. Waif thanked her very charmingly, by nosing her hand, and then turned her expectant attention to Mrs Baker again.

"Oh, she is so *sweet!*" Mrs Baker sighed, and rewarded Waif with a fifth cake.

She'll burst, Charmain thought. Nevertheless, thanks to Waif, the rest of the visit went off most peacefully, until right at the end, when the ladies got up to go. Mrs Baker said, "Oh, I nearly forgot!" and felt in her pocket. "This letter came for you, darling." She held out to Charmain a long, stiff envelope with a red wax seal on the back of it. It was addressed to "Mistress Charmain Baker" in elegant quavery writing.

Charmain stared at the letter and found her heart

was banging away in her ears and her chest like a blacksmith at an anvil. Her eyes went fuzzy. Her hand shook as she took the letter. The King had replied to her. He had actually answered. She knew it was the King. The address was in the same quavery writing that she had found on the letter in Great Uncle William's study. "Oh. Thanks," she said, trying to sound casual.

"Open it, dear," her mother said. "It looks very grand. What do you think it is?"

"Oh, it's nothing," Charmain said. "It's only my Leavers' Certificate."

This was a mistake. Her mother exclaimed, "*What?* But your father is expecting you to stay on at school and learn a little *culture*, darling!"

"Yes, I know, but they always give everyone a certificate at the end of the tenth year," Charmain invented. "In case some of us do want to leave, you know. My whole class will have got one too. Don't worry."

In spite of this explanation, which Charmain considered quite brilliant, Mrs Baker did worry. She might have made a very great fuss, had not Waif suddenly sprung up on to her hind legs and walked at Mrs Baker, with her front paws most appealingly tucked under her chin again.

"Oh, you *sweetheart*!" Mrs Baker exclaimed. "Charmain, if your Great Uncle lets you bring this darling little dog home with you when he's better, I shan't mind a bit. I really shan't."

Charmain was able to stuff the King's letter into her waistband and kiss her mother and then Aunt Sempronia good-bye without either of them mentioning it again. She waved them happily off down the path between the hydrangeas and shut the front door behind them with a gasp of relief. "*Thank* you, Waif!" she said. "You clever dog!" She leaned against the front door and started to open the King's letter – though I know in advance he's bound to say no, she told herself, shivering with excitement. *I* would say no, if it was me!.

Before she had the envelope more than half open, the other door was flung open by Peter. "Have they gone?" he said. "At last? I need your help. I'm being mobbed by angry kobolds in here."

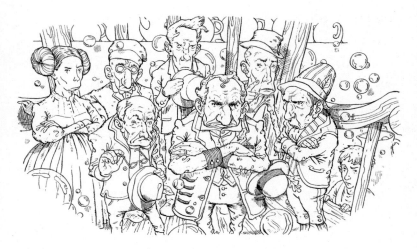

# CHAPTER SIX

### Which concerns the
### colour blue

Charmain sighed and stuffed the King's letter into her pocket. She did not feel like sharing whatever it said with Peter. "Why?" she said. "Why are they angry?"

"Come and see," Peter said. "It all sounds ridiculous to me. I told them that you were in charge and they had to wait until you had finished being polite to those witches."

"Witches!" said Charmain. "One of them was my mother!"

"Well, my mother's a witch," Peter said. "And you

only had to look at the proud one in silk to see that *she* was a witch. Do come on."

He held the door open for Charmain and she went through, thinking that Peter was probably right about Aunt Sempronia. No one in the Bakers' respectable house ever mentioned witchcraft, but Charmain had thought that Aunt Sempronia was a witch for years, without ever putting it to herself so baldly.

She forgot about Aunt Sempronia as soon as she entered the kitchen. There were kobolds everywhere. Little blue men with different shapes of large blue noses were standing anywhere there was a space on the floor that was not full of dog dishes or spilled tea. They were on the table between teapots and in the sink balanced on dirty dishes. There were little blue women too, mostly perched on the laundry bags. The women were distinguished by their smaller, gentler noses and their rather stylish flounced blue skirts. I'd like a skirt like that, Charmain thought. Only larger, of course. There were so many kobolds that it took Charmain a moment to notice that the bubbles from the fireplace were nearly gone.

All the kobolds raised a shrill shout as Charmain came in. "We seem to have got the whole tribe," Peter said.

Charmain thought he was probably right. "Very well," she said above the yelling. "I'm here. What's the problem?"

The answer was such a storm of yelling that Charmain put her hands over her ears.

"That'll do!" she shouted. "How can I understand a word you say when you all scream at once?" She recognised the kobold who had appeared in the living room, standing on a chair with at least six others. His nose was a very memorable shape. "*You* tell me. What was your name again?"

He gave her a curt little bow. "Timminz is my name. I understand you are Charming Baker and you speak for the wizard. Am I right?"

"More or less," Charmain said. There did not seem to be much point in arguing about her name. Besides, she rather liked being called Charming. "I told you the wizard's ill. He's gone away to get cured."

"So you say," Timminz answered. "Are you sure he hasn't *run* away?"

This produced such yells and jeers from all over the kitchen that Charmain had to shout again to get heard. "Be quiet! Of course he hasn't run away. I was here when he went. He was very unwell and the elves had to carry him. He would have died if the elves hadn't taken him."

In the near-silence that followed this, Timminz said sulkily, "If you say so, we believe you, of course. Our quarrel is with the wizard, but maybe you can settle it. And I tell you we don't like it. It's indecent."

"What is?" Charmain asked.

Timminz squeezed his eyes up and glowered over his nose. "You are not to laugh. The wizard laughed when I complained to him."

"I promise not to laugh," Charmain said. "So what is it?"

"We were very angry," Timminz said. "Our ladies refused to wash his dishes for him and we took away his taps so that he couldn't wash them himself, but all he did was smile, and say he hadn't the strength to argue—"

"Well, he was ill," Charmain said. "You know that now. So what is it *about*?"

"This garden of his," Timminz said. "The complaint came first from Rollo, but I came and took a look and Rollo was quite right. The wizard was growing bushes with blue flowers, which is the correct and reasonable colour for flowers to be, but by his magic he had made half the same bushes *pink*, and some of them were even green or white, which is disgusting and incorrect."

Here Peter was unable to contain himself. "But hydrangeas are *like* that!" he burst out. "I've *explained* it to you! Any gardener could tell you. If you don't put the bluing powder under the whole bush, some of the flowers are going to be pink. Rollo's a gardener. He must have known."

Charmain looked around the crowded kitchen but

could not see Rollo anywhere among the swarms of blue people. "He probably only told you," she said, "because he likes to chop things down. I bet he kept asking the wizard if he could chop the bushes down and the wizard said no. He asked me last night—"

At this, Rollo popped up from beside a dog dish, almost at Charmain's feet. She recognised him mostly by his grating little voice when he shouted, "And so I did ask her! And she sits there in the path, having just floated down from the sky, cool as you please, and tells me I only wants to enjoy myself. As bad as the wizard, *she* is!"

Charmain glared down at him. "You're just a destructive little beast," she said. "What you're doing is making trouble because you can't get your own way!"

Rollo flung out an arm. "Hear her? Hear that? Who's wrong here, her or me?"

A dreadful shrill clamour arose from all over the kitchen. Timminz shouted for silence, and when the clamour had died into muttering, he said to Charmain, "So will you now give permission for these disgraceful bushes to be lopped down?"

"No, I will not," Charmain told him. "They're Great Uncle William's bushes and I'm supposed to look *after* all his things for him. And Rollo is just making trouble."

Timminz said, squeezing his glower at her, "Is that your last word?"

"Yes," said Charmain. "It is."

"Then," Timminz said, "you're on your own. No kobold is going to do a hand's turn for you from now on."

And they were all gone. Just like that, the blue crowd vanished from among teapots and dog dishes and dirty crockery, leaving a little wind stirring the last few bubbles about and the fire now burning brightly in the grate.

"That was stupid of you," Peter said.

"What do you mean?" Charmain asked indignantly. "You're the one who said those bushes were supposed to be like that. And you could see Rollo had got them all stirred up on purpose. I couldn't let Great Uncle William come home to find his garden all chopped down, could I?"

"Yes, but you could have been more tactful," Peter insisted. "I was expecting you to say we'd put down a bluing spell to make all the flowers blue, or something."

"Yes, but Rollo would still have wanted to cut them all down," Charmain said. "He told me I was a spoilsport last night for not letting him."

"You could have made them see what he was like," Peter said, "instead of making them all even angrier."

"At least I didn't laugh at them like Great Uncle William did," Charmain retorted. "He made them angry, not me!"

"And look where that got him!" Peter said. "They took away his taps and left all his dishes dirty. So now we've got to wash them all without even any hot water in the bathroom."

Charmain flounced down into the chair and began, again, to open the King's letter. "Why have we got to?" she said. "I haven't the remotest idea how to wash dishes anyway."

Peter was scandalised. "You haven't? Why ever not?"

Charmain got the envelope open and pulled out a beautiful, large, stiff, folded paper. "My mother brought me up to be respectable," she said. "She never let me near the scullery, or the kitchen either."

"I don't believe this!" Peter said. "Why is it respectable not to know how to do things? Is it respectable to light a fire with a bar of soap?"

"That," Charmain said haughtily, "was an accident. Please be quiet and let me read my letter." She pulled her glasses up on to her nose and unfolded the stiff paper.

Dear Mistress Baker, she read.

"Well, I'm going to get on and try," Peter said. "I'm blowed if I'm going to be bullied by a crowd of little blue people. And I should think you had enough pride to help me do it."

"Shut up," said Charmain and concentrated on her letter.

Dear Mistress Baker,

How kind of you to offer Us your services. In the normal way, We would find the assistance of Our Daughter, the Princess Hilda, sufficient for Our need; but it so happens that the Princess is about to receive Important Visitors and is obliged to forgo her Work in the Library for the duration of the Visit. We therefore gratefully accept your Kind Offer, on a temporary basis. If you would be so Good as to present yourself at the Royal Mansion this coming Wednesday Morning, at around ten-thirty, We shall be happy to receive you in Our Library and instruct you in Our Work.

Your Obliged and Grateful
Adolphus Rex Norlandi Alti

Charmain's heart banged and bumped as she read the letter, and it was not until she reached the end of it that she realised that the amazing, unlikely, unbelievable thing had happened: the King had agreed to let her help him in the Royal Library! Tears came into her eyes, she was not sure why, and she had to whisk her glasses off. Her heart hammered with joy. Then with alarm. Was today Wednesday? Had she missed her chance?

She had been hearing, without attending, Peter crashing saucepans about and kicking dog dishes aside as he went to the inner door. Now she heard him come back again.

"What day is it today?" she asked him.

Peter set the large saucepan he was carrying down, hissing, on the fire. "I'll tell you if you tell me where he keeps his soap," he said.

"Bother you!" said Charmain. "It's in the pantry in a bag labelled something like Caninitis. Now, what day is it?"

"Cloths," said Peter. "Tell me where cloths are first. Did you know there are two new bags of laundry in this pantry now?"

"I don't know where cloths are," Charmain said. "What day is it?"

"Cloths first," said Peter. "He doesn't answer me when I ask."

"He didn't know you were coming," Charmain said. "Is it Wednesday yet?"

"I can't think why he didn't know," Peter said. "He got my letter. Ask for cloths."

Charmain sighed. "Great Uncle William," she said, "this stupid boy wants to know where cloths are, please."

The kindly voice replied, "Do you know, my dear, I nearly forgot cloths. They're in the table drawer."

"It's Tuesday," Peter said, pouncing on the drawer

and dragging it open almost into Charmain's stomach. He said as he fetched out wads of towelling and dishcloths, "I know it must be Tuesday, because I set off from home on Saturday and it took me three days to walk here. Satisfied?"

"Thank you," Charmain said. "Very kind of you. Then I'm afraid I'll have to go into town tomorrow. I may be gone all day."

"Then isn't it lucky that I'm here to look after the place for you?" Peter said. "Where are you skiving off to?"

"The King," Charmain said, with great dignity, "has asked me to go and help him. Read this, if you don't believe me."

Peter picked up the letter and looked it over. "I see," he said. "You've arranged to be in two places at once. Nice for you. So you can darned well help me wash these dishes *now*, when the water's hot."

"Why? I didn't get them dirty," Charmain said. She pocketed her letter and stood up. "I'm going into the garden."

"I didn't get them dirty either," Peter said. "And it was your uncle who annoyed the kobolds."

Charmain simply swept past him towards the living room.

"You've got nothing to *do* with being respectable!" Peter shouted after her. "You're just lazy."

Charmain took no notice and swept onward to the front door. Waif followed her, bustling appealingly around her ankles, but Charmain was too annoyed with Peter to bother with Waif. "Always criticising!" she said. "He's never stopped once since he got here. As if *he* was perfect!" she said as she flung open the front door.

She gasped. The kobolds had been busy. Very busy, very quickly. True, they had not cut down the bushes because she had told them not to, but they had cut off every single pink bloom and most of the mauve or white ones. The front path was strewn with pink and lilac umbrellas of hydrangea flowers and she could see more lying among the bushes. Charmain gave a cry of outrage and rushed forward to pick them up.

"Lazy, am I?" she muttered as she collected hydrangea heads into her skirt. "Oh, *poor* Great Uncle William! What a mess. He *liked* them all colours. Oh, those little blue *beasts*!"

She went to tip the flowers out of her skirt on to the table outside the study window and discovered a basket by the wall there. She took it with her among the bushes. While Waif scuttled and snorted and sniffed around her, Charmain scooped up snipped-off hydrangea heads by the basket load. She chuckled rather meanly when she discovered that the kobolds had not always been certain which were blue. They had left most of the ones that were greenish and some that were lavender-coloured, while there was one bush at which they must have had real trouble, because each flower on each of its umbrellas was pink in the middle and blue on the outside. To judge by the numbers of tiny footprints around this bush, they had held a meeting about it. In the end, they had cut the blooms off one half of the bush and left the rest.

"See? It's not that easy," Charmain said loudly, in case there were any kobolds around listening. "And what it really is is vandalism and I hope you're *ashamed*." She carried her last basketful back to the table, repeating, "Vandals. Bad behaviour. Little beasts," and hoping that Rollo at least was somewhere listening.

Some of the biggest heads had quite long stalks. Charmain collected those into a large pink, mauve and greenish white bunch, and spread the rest out on the table to dry in the sun. She remembered reading somewhere that you could dry hydrangeas and they would stay the same colour and make good decorations for winter. Great Uncle William would enjoy these, she thought.

"So you see it *is* useful to sit and read a lot!" she announced to the air. By this time, however, she knew she was trying to justify herself to the world – if not to Peter – because she had been rather too impressed with herself for getting a letter from the King. "Oh, well," she said. "Come on, Waif."

Waif followed Charmain into the house, but backed away from the kitchen door, trembling. Charmain saw why when she came into the kitchen and Peter looked up from his steaming saucepan. He had found an apron from somewhere and stacked all the crockery in neat heaps along the floor. He gave Charmain a look of righteous pain. "Very ladylike," he said. "I ask you to help me wash up and you pick flowers!"

"No, really," Charmain said. "Those beastly kobolds have cut off all the pink ones."

"They have?" Peter said. "That's too bad! Your uncle's going to be upset when he comes home, isn't he? You could put your flowers in that dish where the eggs are."

Charmain looked at the pie dish full of eggs crammed in beside the big bag of soapflakes among the teapots on the table. "Then where do we put the eggs? Just a moment." She went away to the bathroom and put the hydrangeas in the washbasin. It was rather ominously moist and trickly in there, but Charmain preferred not to think about that. She went back to the kitchen and said, "Now I'm going to nurture the hydrangea bushes by emptying these teapots on them."

"Nice try," Peter said. "That'll take you several hours. Do you think this water is hot yet?"

"Only steaming," Charmain said. "I think it ought to bubble. And it won't take me hours. Watch." She sorted out two largish saucepans and began emptying teapots into them. She was saying, "There are some advantages to being lazy, you know," when she realised that, as soon as she had emptied a teapot and put it back on the table, the teapot disappeared.

"Leave us one," Peter said anxiously. "I'd like a hot drink."

Charmain thought about this and carefully put the last teapot down on the chair. It disappeared too.

"Oh, well," Peter said.

Since he was obviously trying not to be so unfriendly, Charmain said, "We can get afternoon tea in the living room after I've emptied these. And my mother brought another bag of food when she came."

Peter cheered up remarkably. "Then we can have a decent meal when we've done the washing up," he said. "We're doing that first, whatever you say."

And he held Charmain to it, in spite of her protests. As soon as she came in from the garden, Peter came and took the book out of her hands and presented her with a cloth to tie round her waist instead. Then he led her to the kitchen, where the mysterious and horrible process began. Peter thrust another cloth into her hands. "You wipe and I'll wash," he said, lifting the steaming saucepan off the fire and pouring half the hot water on the soapflakes sprinkled in the sink. He heaved up a bucket of cold water from the pump and poured half of that in the sink too.

"Why are you doing that?" Charmain asked.

"So as not to get scalded," Peter replied, plunging knives and forks into his mixture and following those with a stack of plates. "Don't you know *anything*?"

"No," Charmain said. She thought irritably that not one of the many books she had read had so much as mentioned washing dishes, let alone explained how you did it. She watched as Peter briskly used a dishcloth to wipe old, old dinner off a patterned plate. The plate came out of the suds bright and clean. Charmain rather liked the pattern now and was almost inclined to believe that this was magic. She watched Peter dip the plate in another bucket to rinse it. Then he handed it to her. "What do I do with this?" she asked.

"Wipe it dry, of course," he said. "Then stack it on the table."

Charmain tried. The whole horrible business took ages. The wiping cloth hardly seemed to soak up water at all and the plate kept nearly slithering out of her hands. She was so much slower at wiping than Peter was at washing, that Peter soon had a heap of plates draining beside the sink and began to get impatient. Naturally, at that point, the prettiest patterned plate slid out of Charmain's hands completely and fell on the floor. Unlike the strange teapots, it broke.

"Oh," Charmain said, staring down at the pieces. "How do you put them together?"

Peter rolled his eyes up towards the ceiling. "You don't," he said. "You just take care not to drop another." He collected the pieces of plate and threw them into another bucket. "I'll wipe now. You try your hand at washing, or we'll be all day." He let the now brownish water out of the sink, collected the knives, forks and spoons out of it, and dropped them in the rinsing bucket. To Charmain's surprise, they all seemed to be clean and shiny now.

As she watched Peter fill the sink again with more soap and hot water, she decided, crossly but quite reasonably, that Peter had chosen the easy part of the work.

She found she was mistaken. She did not find it easy at all. It took her slow ages on each piece of crockery, and she got soaked down the front of her in the process. And Peter kept handing back to her plates and cups, saucers and mugs, and saying they were still dirty. Nor would he let her wash any of the many dog dishes until the human crockery was done. Charmain thought this was too bad of him. Waif had licked each one so clean that Charmain knew they would be easier to wash than anything else. Then, on top of this, she was horrified to find that her hands were coming out of the suds all red and covered with strange wrinkles.

"I must be ill!" she said. "I've got a horrible skin disease!"

She was annoyed and offended when Peter laughed at her.

But the dreadful business was done at last. Charmain, damp in front and wrinkly in the hands, went sulkily off to the living room to read *The Twelve-Branched Wand* by the slanting light of the setting sun, leaving Peter to stack the clean things in the pantry. By this time, she was feeling she might go mad if she didn't sit and read for a while. I've hardly read a word all day, she thought.

Peter interrupted her much too soon by coming in with a vase he had found and filled with the hydrangeas, which he dumped down on the table in front of her. "Where's that food you said your mother brought?" he said.

"What?" Charmain said, peering at him through the foliage.

"I said *Food*," Peter told her.

Waif seconded him by leaning against Charmain's legs and groaning.

"Oh," Charmain said. "Yes. Food. You can have some if you promise not to dirty a single dish eating it."

"That's all right," Peter said. "I'm so hungry I could lick it off the carpet."

So Charmain reluctantly stopped reading and dragged

the bag of food out from behind the armchair, and they all three ate large numbers of Mr Baker's beautiful pasties, followed by Afternoon Tea, twice, from the trolley. In the course of this huge meal, Charmain parked the vase of hydrangeas on the trolley to be out of the way. When she next looked, they had vanished.

"I wonder where they went," Peter said.

"You can sit on the trolley and find out," Charmain suggested.

But Peter did not feel like going that far, to Charmain's disappointment. While she ate, she tried to think of ways of persuading Peter to go away, back to Montalbino. It was not that she utterly disliked him exactly. It was just annoying to share the house with him. And she knew, as clearly as if Peter had told her, that the next thing he was going to make her do was to empty the things out of those laundry bags and wash them too. The idea of more washing made her shudder.

At least, she thought I'm not going to be here tomorrow, so he can't make me do it then.

All at once she was hideously nervous. She was going to see the King. She had been crazy to write to him, quite mad, and now she was going to have to go and see him. Her appetite went away. She looked up from her last creamy scone and found it was now dark outside. The magical lighting had come on indoors, filling the room with what seemed like golden sunshine, but the windows were black.

"I'm going to bed," she said. "I've got a long day tomorrow."

"If that King of yours has any sense," Peter said, "he'll kick you straight out as soon as he sees you. Then you can come back here and do the laundry."

Since both these things were exactly what Charmain was afraid of, she did not answer. She simply picked up *Memoirs of an Exorcist* for some light reading, marched to the door with it and turned left to where the bedrooms were.

# CHAPTER SEVEN

## In which a number of people arrive at the Royal Mansion

Charmain had rather a disturbed night. Some of this was certainly due to *Memoirs of an Exorcist*, whose author had clearly been very busy among a lot of haunts and weirdities, all of which he described in a matter-of-fact way that left Charmain in no doubt that ghosts were entirely real and mostly very unpleasant. She spent a lot of the night shivering and wishing she knew how to turn on the light.

Some of the disturbance was due to Waif, who was determined she had a right to sleep on Charmain's pillow.

But most of the disturbance was nerves, pure and simple, and the fact that Charmain had no way of telling what the time was. She kept waking up, thinking, Suppose I oversleep! She woke in grey dawn, hearing birds twittering somewhere, and almost decided to get up then. But somehow she fell asleep again, and when she woke next it was in broad daylight.

"Help!" she cried out and flung back the covers, accidentally flinging Waif on to the floor too, and stumbled across the room to find the good clothes she had put out specially. As she dragged on her best green skirt, the sensible thing to do came to her at last. "Great Uncle William," she called out, "how do I tell what *time* it is?"

"Merely tap your left wrist," the kindly voice replied, "and say 'Time', my dear." It struck Charmain that the voice was fainter and weaker than it had been. She hoped it was simply that the spell was wearing off, and not that Great Uncle William was getting weaker himself, wherever he was.

"Time?" she said, tapping.

She expected a voice, or more probably a clock to appear. People in High Norland were great on clocks. Her own house had seventeen, including one in the bathroom. She had been vaguely surprised that Great Uncle William did not seem to have even one cuckoo clock somewhere, but she realised the reason for this when what happened was that she simply knew the time. It was eight o'clock. "And it'll take me at least an hour to walk there!" she gasped, ramming her arms into her best silk blouse as she ran for the bathroom.

She was more nervous than ever as she did her hair in there. Her reflection – with water trickling across it for some reason – looked terribly young with its hair in one rusty pigtail over its shoulder. He'll *know* I'm only a schoolgirl, she thought. But there was no time to dwell on it. Charmain rushed out of the bathroom and back through the same door leftward and charged into the warm, tidy kitchen.

There were now five laundry bags leaning beside the sink, but Charmain had no time to bother about that. Waif scuttled towards her, whining piteously, and scuttled back to the fireplace, where the fire was still cheerfully burning. Charmain was just about to tap the mantelpiece and ask for breakfast, when she saw Waif's problem. Waif was now too small to get her tail anywhere near the fireplace. So Charmain tapped and said, "Dog food, please," before asking for breakfast for herself.

As she sat at the cleared table hurrying through her breakfast, while Waif briskly cleaned up the dog dish at her feet, Charmain could not help grudgingly thinking that it was much nicer having the kitchen clean and tidy. I suppose Peter has his uses, she thought, pouring herself a last cup of coffee. But then she felt she ought to tap her wrist again. And she *knew* it was now six minutes to nine and jumped up in a panic.

"How did I take so *long*?" she said out loud, and raced back to her bedroom for her smart jacket.

Perhaps because she was putting on the jacket as she ran, she somehow turned the wrong way through the door and found herself in a very peculiar place. It was a long thin room with pipes running everywhere around it and, in the middle, a large, trickling tank, mystifyingly covered in blue fur.

"Oh, *bother*!" Charmain said, and backed out through the door.

She found herself back in the kitchen.

"At least I know the way from here," she said, diving through into the living room and running for the front door. Outside, she nearly tripped over a crock of milk which must have been meant for Rollo. "And he doesn't deserve it!" she said, as she shut the front door with a slam.

Down the front path she raced, between beheaded hydrangeas, and out through the gate, which shut with a *clash* behind her. Then she managed to slow down, because it was silly to try to run however many miles it was to the Royal Mansion, but she went down the road at a very brisk walk indeed, and she had just got to the first bend when the garden gate went *clash* again behind her. Charmain whirled round. Waif was running after her, pattering as fast as her little legs would take her. Charmain sighed and marched back towards her. Seeing her coming, Waif gambolled delightedly and made tiny squeaks of pleasure.

"No, Waif," Charmain said. "You can't come. Go home." She pointed sternly towards Great Uncle William's house. "*Home!*"

Waif drooped both ears and sat up and begged.

"*No!*" Charmain commanded, pointing again. "*Go home!*"

Waif dropped to the ground and became a miserable white lump, with just the tip of her tail wagging.

"Oh, *honestly!*" Charmain said. And since Waif seemed determined not to budge from the middle of the road, Charmain was forced to pick her up and rush back to Great Uncle William's house with her. "I *can't* take you with me," she explained breathlessly as they went. "I've got to see the King, and people just don't take dogs to see the King." She opened Great Uncle William's front gate and dumped Waif on the garden path. "There. Now, *stay!*"

She shut the gate on Waif's reproachful face and strode off down the road again. As she went, she tapped her wrist anxiously and said, "Time?" But she was outside Great Uncle William's grounds then and the spell did not work. All Charmain knew was that it was getting later. She broke into a trot.

Behind her the gate clashed again. Charmain looked back to see Waif once more racing after her.

Charmain groaned, whirled round, raced to meet Waif, scooped her up and dumped her back inside the gate. "Now be a good dog and *stay*!" she panted, rushing off again.

The gate clashed behind her and Waif once more came pelting after her. "I shall scream!" Charmain said. She turned back and dumped Waif inside the gate for the third time. "*Stay* there, you silly little dog!" This time she set off towards town at a run.

Behind her, the gate clashed yet again. Tiny footsteps pattered in the road.

Charmain whirled round and ran back towards Waif, crying out, "Oh, *blast* you, Waif! I shall be so *late*!" This time she picked Waif up and carried her towards the town, panting out, "All right. You win. I shall have to take you because I'll be late if I don't, but I don't *want* you, Waif! Don't you understand?"

Waif was delighted. She squirmed upwards and licked Charmain's chin.

"No, stop that," Charmain said. "I'm not pleased. I hate you. You're a real nuisance. Keep still or I'll drop you."

Waif settled into Charmain's arms with a sigh of contentment.

"Grrr!" Charmain said as she hurried on.

As she rounded the huge bulge of cliff, Charmain had meant to check upwards in case the lubbock came plunging down at her from the meadow above, but by then she was in such a hurry that she clean forgot about the lubbock and simply jogtrotted onwards. And greatly to her surprise, the town was almost in front of her when she came round the bend. She had not remembered it was so near. There were the houses and towers, rosy and twinkling in the morning sun, only a stone's throw away. I think Aunt Sempronia's pony made a meal of this journey, Charmain thought, as she strode in among the first houses.

The road dived in across the river and became a dirty town street. Charmain thought she remembered that this end of town was rather rough and unpleasant and marched on fast and nervously. But although most of the people she passed seemed quite poor, none of them seemed to notice Charmain particularly – or if they did, they only noticed Waif, peeping out enthusiastically from Charmain's arms. "Pretty little dog," remarked a woman carrying strings of onions to market as Charmain strode by.

"Pretty little *monster*," Charmain said. The woman

looked very surprised. Waif squirmed protestingly. "Yes, you are," Charmain told her, as they began to come among wider streets and smarter houses. "You're a bully and a blackmailer, and if you've made me late I shall never forgive you."

As they reached the market place, the big clock on the town hall struck ten o'clock. And Charmain went suddenly from needing to hurry to wondering how she was going to stretch ten minutes' walk into half an hour. The Royal Mansion was practically just round the corner from here. At least she could slow down and get cool. By now the sun had burned through the mist from the mountains, and what with that and Waif's warm body, Charmain was decidedly hot. She took a detour along the esplanade that ran high above the river, rushing swift and brown on its way to the great valley beyond the town, and dropped to a saunter. Three of her favourite bookshops were on this road. She pushed her way among other sauntering people and looked eagerly into windows. "Nice little dog," several people said as she went.

"Huh!" Charmain said to Waif. "Fat lot *they* know!"

She arrived in Royal Square as the big clock there began to chime the half hour. Charmain was pleased. But, as she crossed the square to the booming of the clock, she was somehow not pleased, and not hot any more either. She was cold and small and insignificant. She knew she had been stupid to come. She was a fool. They would take one look at her and send her away. The flashing of the golden tiles on the roof of the Royal Mansion daunted her completely. She was glad of Waif's small warm tongue licking her chin again. By the time she was climbing the steps to the heavy front door of the Mansion, she was so nervous that she almost turned round and ran away.

But she told herself firmly that this was the one thing in the world she really wanted to do – even though I'm not sure I *do* want to now, she thought. And everyone *knows* that those tiles are only tin enchanted to *look* like gold! she added, and she lifted the great gold-painted knocker and bravely hammered on the door with it. Then her knees threatened to fold under her and she wondered if she *could* run away. She stood there quivering and clutching Waif hard.

The door was opened by an old, old serving man. Probably the butler, Charmain thought, wondering where she had seen the old man before. I must have passed him in town on my way to school, she thought. "Er…" she said. "I'm Charmain Baker. The King wrote me a letter—" She let go of Waif with one hand in order to fetch the letter out of her pocket, but before she could get at it, the old butler held the door wide open.

"Please to come in, Miss Charming," he said in a quavery old voice. "His Majesty is expecting you."

Charmain found herself entering the Royal Mansion on legs that wobbled almost as badly as the old butler's did. He was so stooped with age that his face was on a level with Waif as Charmain wobbled in past him.

He stopped her with a shaky old hand. "Please to keep tight hold on the little dog, miss. It wouldn't do to have it wandering about here."

Charmain discovered herself to be babbling. "I do hope it's all right to bring her, she would keep following me, you see, and in the end I had to pick her up and carry her or I'd have been—"

"Perfectly all right, miss," the butler said, heaving the great door shut. "His Majesty is very fond of dogs. Indeed he has been bitten several times trying to make friends with— Well, the fact of the matter is, miss, that our Rajpuhti cook owns a dog that is not at all a nice creature. It has been known to slay other dogs when they impinge upon its territory."

"Oh dear," Charmain said weakly.

"Precisely," said the old butler. "If you will follow me, miss."

Waif squirmed in Charmain's arms because Charmain was clutching her so tightly as she followed the butler along a broad stone corridor. It was cold inside the Mansion and rather dark. Charmain was surprised to find that there were no ornaments anywhere and almost no hint of royal grandeur, unless you counted one or two large brown pictures in dingy gold frames. There were big pale squares on the walls every so often, where pictures had been taken away, but Charmain was by now so nervous that she did not wonder about this. She just became colder and thinner and more and more unimportant, until she felt she must be about the size of Waif.

The butler stopped and creakily pushed open a mighty square oak door. "Your Majesty, Miss Charming Baker," he announced. "And dog." Then he doddered away.

Charmain managed to dodder into the room. The shakiness must be catching! she thought, and did not dare curtsy in case her knees collapsed.

The room was a vast library. Dim brown shelves of books stretched away in both directions. The smell of old book, which Charmain normally loved, was almost overpowering. Straight in front of her was a great oak table, piled high with more books and stacks of old, yellow papers, and some newer, whiter paper at the near end. There were three big carved chairs at that end, arranged around a very small charcoal fire in an iron basket. The basket sat on a kind of iron tray, which in turn sat on an almost worn-out carpet. Two old people sat in two of the carved chairs. One was a big old man with a nicely trimmed white beard and – when Charmain dared to look at him – kindly, crinkled old blue eyes. She knew he had to be the King.

"Come here, my dear," he said to her, "and take a seat. Put the little dog down near the fire."

Charmain managed to do as the King said. Waif, to her relief, seemed to realise that one must be on one's best behaviour here. She sat gravely down on the carpet and politely quivered her tail. Charmain sat on the edge of the carved chair and quivered all over.

"Let me make my daughter known to you," said the King. "Princess Hilda."

Princess Hilda was old too. If Charmain had not known she was the King's daughter, she might have thought the Princess and the King were the same age. The main difference between them was that the Princess looked twice as royal as the King. She was a big lady like her father, with very neat iron-grey hair and a tweed suit so plain and tweed-coloured that Charmain knew it was a highly aristocratic suit. Her only ornament was a big ring on one veiny old hand.

"That is a very sweet little dog," she said, in a firm and forthright voice. "What is her name?"

"Waif, Your Highness," Charmain faltered.

"And have you had her long?" the Princess asked.

Charmain could tell that the Princess was making conversation in order to set her at her ease, and that made her more nervous than ever. "No... er... that is," she said. "The fact is she was a stray. Or... er... Great Uncle William said she was. And he can't have had her long because he didn't know she was... er... a bi... er... I mean a girl. William Norland, you know. The wizard."

The King and the Princess both said, "Oh!" at this and the King said, "Are you related to Wizard Norland, then, my dear?"

"Our great friend," added the Princess.

"I – er— He's my aunt Sempronia's great uncle really," Charmain confessed.

Somehow the atmosphere became much more friendly. The King said, rather longingly, "I suppose you have had no news of how Wizard Norland is yet?"

Charmain shook her head. "I'm afraid not, Your Majesty, but he did look awfully ill when the elves took him away."

"Not to be wondered at," stated Princess Hilda. "Poor William. Now, Miss Baker—"

"Oh – oh – please call me Charmain," Charmain stammered.

"Very well," the Princess agreed. "But we must get down to business now, child, because I shall have to leave you soon to attend to my first guest."

"My daughter is sparing you an hour or so," the King said, "to explain to you what we do here in the library and how you may best assist us. This is because we gathered from your handwriting that you were not very old – which we see is the case – and so probably inexperienced." He gave Charmain the most enchanting smile. "We really are most grateful to you for your offer of help, my dear. No one has ever considered that we might need assistance before."

Charmain felt her face filling with heat. She knew she was blushing horribly. "My pleasure, Your—" she managed to mutter.

"Pull your chair over to the table," Princess Hilda interrupted, "and we'll get down to work."

As Charmain got up and dragged the heavy chair over, the King said courteously, "We hope you may not be too hot in here with the brazier beside you. It may be summer now, but we old people feel the cold these days."

Charmain was still frozen with nerves. "Not at all, Sire," she said.

"And Waif at least is happy," the King said, pointing a gnarly finger. Waif had rolled over on to her back with all four paws in the air and was basking in the heat from the brazier. She seemed far happier than Charmain was.

"To work, Father," the Princess said severely. She fetched up the glasses hanging from a chain round her neck and planted them on her aristocratic nose. The King fetched up a pair of pince-nez. Charmain fetched up her own glasses. If she had not been so nervous, she would have wanted to giggle at the way they all had to do this. "Now," said the Princess, "we have in this library books, papers, and parchment scrolls. After a lifetime of labour, Father and I have managed to list roughly half the books – by name and author's name – and assigned each a number, together with a brief account of what is in each book. Father will continue doing this, while you make yourself responsible for my main task, which is to catalogue papers and scrolls. I have barely made a start there, I'm afraid. Here is my list." She opened a large folder full of sheets of paper covered in elegant spidery writing, and spread a row of them in front of Charmain. "As you see, I have several main headings: Family Letters, Household Accounts, Historic Writings, and so on. Your task is to go through each pile of paper and decide exactly what every sheet contains. You then write a description of it under the appropriate heading, after which you put the paper carefully in one of these labelled boxes here. Is this clear so far?"

Charmain, leaning forward to look at the beautifully written lists, was afraid that she seemed awfully stupid. "What do I do," she asked, "if I find a paper that doesn't fit any of your headings, ma'am?"

"A very good question," Princess Hilda said. "We are hoping that you will find a great many things that do not fit. When you do find one, consult my father at once, in case the paper is important. If it isn't, put it in the box marked Miscellaneous. Now here is your first packet of papers. I'll watch as you go through them to see how you go on. There is paper for your lists. Pen and ink are here. Please start." She pushed a frayed brown packet of letters, tied together with pink tape, in front of Charmain and sat back to watch.

I've never known anything so off-putting! Charmain thought. She tremulously unpicked the pink knot and tried spreading the letters out a little.

"Pick each one up by its opposite corners," Princess Hilda said. "Don't push them."

Oh, dear! Charmain thought. She glanced sideways at the King, who had taken up a wilted-looking soft leather book and was leafing carefully through it. I'd hoped to be doing that, she thought. She sighed and carefully opened the first crumbly brown letter.

"My dearest, gorgeous, wonderful darling," she read. "I miss you so hideously…"

"Um," she said to Princess Hilda, "is there a special box for love letters?"

"Yes, indeed," said the Princess. "This one. Record the date and the name of the person who wrote it. Who was it, by the way?"

Charmain looked on to the end of the letter. "Um. It says 'Big Dolphie'."

Both the King and the Princess said, "*Well!*" and laughed, the King most heartily. "Then they are from my father to my mother," Princess Hilda said. "My mother died many years ago now. But never mind that. Write it on your list."

Charmain looked at the crumbly brown state of the paper and thought it must have been very many years ago. She was surprised that the King did not seem to mind her reading it, but neither he nor the Princess seemed in the least worried. Perhaps royal people are different, she thought, looking at the next letter. It began "Dearest chuffy puffy one." Oh, well. She got on with her task.

After a while, the Princess stood up and pushed her chair neatly up to the table. "This seems quite satisfactory," she stated. "I must go. My guest will be arriving soon. I still wish I had been able to ask that husband of hers too, Father."

"Out of the question, my dear," the King said, without looking up from the notes he was making.

"Poaching. He's someone else's Royal Wizard."

"Oh, I know," Princess Hilda said. "But I am also aware that Ingary has two Royal Wizards. And our poor William is ill and may be dying."

"Life is never fair, my dear," the King said, still scratching away with his quill pen. "Besides, William had no more success than we have had."

"I'm aware of that too, Father," Princess Hilda said as she left the library. The door shut with a heavy thud behind her.

Charmain bent over her next pile of papers, trying to look as if she had not been listening. It seemed private. This pile of paper had been tied into a bundle for so long that each sheet had stuck to the next one, all dry and brownish, like a wasps' nest Charmain had once found in the attic at home. She became very busy trying to separate the layers.

"Er-hem," said the King. Charmain looked up to see that he was smiling at her, with his quill in the air and a sideways twinkle at her from above his glasses. "I see you are a very discreet young lady," he said. "And you must have gathered from our talk just now that we – and your Great Uncle with us – are searching for some very important things. My daughter's headings will give you some clue what to look out for. Your key words will be "treasury", "revenues", "gold" and "elfgift". If you find a mention of any of these, my dear, please tell me at once."

The idea of looking for such important things made Charmain's fingers on the frail paper go all cold and clumsy. "Yes. Yes of course, Your Majesty," she said.

Rather to her relief, that packet of papers was nothing but lists of goods and their prices – all of which seemed surprisingly low. "To ten pounds of wax candles at 2 pennies a pound, twenty pence," she read. Well, it did seem to date from two hundred years ago. "To six ounces of finest saffron, thirty pence. To nine logs of fragrant applewood for the scenting of the chief chambers, one farthing." And so on. The next page was full of things like "To forty ells of linen drapes, forty-four shillings." Charmain made careful notes, put those pages in the box labelled Household Accounts and peeled up the next sheet.

"Oh!" she said. The next sheet said, "To Wizard Melicot, for the enchanting of one hundred square feet of tinne tilings to give the appearance of a golden roofe, 200 guineas."

"What is it, my dear?" the King asked, putting his finger on his place in his book.

Charmain read the ancient bill out to him. He chuckled and shook his head a little. "So it was definitely done by magic, was it?" he said. "I must confess I had always hoped it would turn out to be real gold, hadn't you?"

"Yes, but it *looks* like gold anyway," Charmain said consolingly.

"And a very good spell too, to last two hundred years," the King said, nodding. "Expensive as well. Two hundred guineas was a lot of money in those days. Ah, well. I never did hope to solve our financial problems that way. Besides, it would look shocking if we climbed up and stripped all the tiles off the roof. Keep looking, my dear."

Charmain kept looking but all she found was someone charging two guineas to plant a rose garden and someone else getting paid ten guineas to refurbish the treasury – no, not someone else, the same Wizard Melicot who did the roof!

"Melicot was a specialist, I fancy," the King said, when Charmain had read this out. "Looks to me like a fellow who went in for faking precious metals. The treasury was certainly empty by that date. I've known my crown was a fake for years. Must be this Melicot's work. Are you getting peckish at all, my dear? A bit cold and stiff? We don't bother with regular lunch – my daughter doesn't hold with it – but I generally ask the butler to bring in a snack around this time. Why not get up and stretch your legs while I ring the bell?"

Charmain stood up and walked about, causing Waif to roll to her feet and watch inquiringly, while the King limped over to the bell rope by the door. He was decidedly frail, Charmain thought, and very tall. It was as if his height was too much for him. While they waited for someone to answer the bell, Charmain seized the chance to look at the books in the shelves. They seemed to be books about everything, higgledy-piggledy, travel books next to books of algebra and poems rubbing shoulders with geography. Charmain had just opened one called *Secrets of the Universe Revealed*, when the library door opened and a man in a tall cook's hat came in carrying a tray.

To Charmain's surprise, the King nimbly skipped behind the table. "My dear, pick up your dog!" he called out urgently.

Another dog had come in, pressed close to the cook's legs as if it felt unsafe, a bitter-looking brown dog with gnarly ears and a ratty tail. It was growling as it came. Charmain had no doubt that this was the dog that slew other dogs and she dived to pick Waif up.

But Waif somehow slipped through her hands and went trotting towards the cook's dog. The other dog's growls increased to a snarl. Bristles rose along its haggard brown back. It looked so menacing that Charmain did not dare go any nearer to it. Waif, however, seemed to feel no fear. She went right up to the snarling dog in her jauntiest way, raised herself on her tiny hind legs and cheekily dabbed her nose on its nose. The other dog started back, so surprised that it stopped snarling. Then it pricked its lumpy ears and, very cautiously, nosed Waif in return. Waif gave an excited squeak and frisked. Next second, both dogs were gambolling delightedly all over the library.

"Well!" said the King. "I suppose that's all right, then. What is the meaning of this, Jamal? Why are you here instead of Sim?"

Jamal – who had only one eye, Charmain noticed – came and apologetically put his tray down on the table. "Our princess has taken Sim away to receive the guest, Sire," he explained, "leaving no one but me to bring food. And my dog *would* come. I think," he added, watching the two prancing dogs, "that my dog has never enjoyed life until now." He bowed to Charmain. "Please bring your small white dog here again often, Miss Charming."

He whistled to his dog. It pretended not to hear. He went to the door and whistled again. "Food," he said. "Come for squid." This time both dogs came. And to Charmain's surprise and dismay, Waif went trotting out of the door beside the cook's dog, and the door shut after them both.

"Not to worry," the King said. "They seem to be friends. Jamal will bring her back. Very reliable fellow,

Jamal. If it wasn't for that dog of his, he'd be the perfect cook. Let's see what he's brought us, shall we?"

Jamal had brought a jug of lemonade and a platter piled with crisp brown things under a white cloth. The King said, "Ah!" as he eagerly lifted the cloth. "Have one while they're hot, my dear." Charmain did so. One bite was enough to assure her that Jamal was an even better cook than her father – and Mr Baker was renowned for being the best cook in town. The brown things were crunchy, but soft at the same time, with a rather hot taste that Charmain had never met before. They made you need the lemonade. She and the King polished off the whole platterful between them and drank all the lemonade. Then they got back to work.

By this time they were on extremely friendly terms. Charmain now had no shyness about asking the King anything she wanted to know. "Why would they need two bushels of rose petals, Sire?" she asked him, and the King answered, "They liked them underfoot in the dining saloon in those days. Messy habit, to my mind. Listen to what this philosopher has to say about camels, my dear." And he read out a page from his book that made them both laugh. The philosopher had clearly not got on with camels.

Quite a long time later, the library door opened and Waif trotted in, looking very pleased with herself. She was followed by Jamal. "Message from our Princess, Sire," he said. "The lady has settled in, and Sim is taking tea to the front parlour."

"Ah," said the King. "Crumpets?"

"Muffins too," Jamal said and went away.

The King banged his book shut and stood up. "I had better go and greet our guest," he said.

"I'll go on with the bills, then," Charmain said. "I'll make a pile of the ones I want to ask about."

"No, no," said the King. "You come too, my dear. Bring the little dog. Helps break the ice, you know. This lady is my daughter's friend. Never met her myself."

Charmain at once felt highly nervous again. She had found Princess Hilda thoroughly intimidating and much too royal for comfort, and any friend of hers was likely to be just as bad. But she could hardly refuse, when the King was expectantly holding the door open for her. Waif was already trotting after him. Charmain felt forced to get up and follow.

The front parlour was a large room full of faded sofas with slightly frayed arms and rather ragged fringes. There were more pale squares on the walls, where pictures must once have hung. The biggest pale square was over the grand marble fireplace, where to Charmain's relief a cheerful fire was burning. The parlour, like the library, was a cold room, and Charmain had gone cold with nerves again.

Princess Hilda was sitting bolt upright on a sofa beside the fireplace, where Sim had just pushed a large tea trolley. As soon as she saw Sim pushing a trolley, Charmain knew where she had seen Sim before. It was when she had got lost beside the Conference Room and had that glimpse of the old man pushing a trolley along a strange corridor. That's odd! she thought. Sim was in the act of shakily placing a plate of buttered crumpets in the hearth. At the sight of those crumpets, Waif's nose quivered and she made a dash towards them. Charmain was only just in time to catch her. As she stood up holding the wriggling Waif firmly in both arms, the Princess said, "Ah, my father, the King." Everyone else in the parlour stood up. "Father," said the Princess, "may I introduce my great friend, Mrs Sophie Pendragon?"

The King strode limpingly forward, holding out his hand and making the large room look quite a little smaller. Charmain had not realised before quite how large he was. Quite as tall as those elves, she thought.

"Mrs Pendragon," he said. "Delighted to meet you. Any friend of our daughter's is a friend of ours."

Mrs Pendragon surprised Charmain. She was quite young, younger than the Princess by a long way, and modishly dressed in a peacock blue that set off her red gold hair and blue-green eyes to perfection. She's *lovely*! Charmain thought, rather enviously. Mrs Pendragon dropped the King a little curtsy as they shook hands, and said, "I'm here to do my best, Sire. More I can't say."

"Quite right, quite right," the King replied. "Please be seated again. Everyone. And let's have some tea."

Everyone sat down, and a polite, courteous hum of conversation began, while Sim doddered around giving out cups of tea. Charmain felt a complete outsider. Feeling sure that she should not be here, she sat herself in the corner of the most distant sofa and tried to work out who the other people were. Waif meanwhile sat sedately on the sofa beside Charmain, looking demure. Her eyes keenly followed the gentleman who was handing round the crumpets. This gentleman was so quiet and colourless that Charmain forgot what he looked like as soon as she took her eyes off him and had to look at him again to remind herself. The other gentleman, the one whose mouth looked closed even when he was talking, she gathered was the King's Chancellor. He seemed to have a lot of secretive things to say to Mrs Pendragon, who kept nodding – and then blinking a bit, as if what the Chancellor said surprised her. The other lady, who was elderly, seemed to be Princess Hilda's lady-in-waiting and very good at talking about the weather.

"And I shouldn't be surprised if it didn't rain again tonight," she was saying, as the colourless gentleman arrived beside Charmain and offered her a crumpet. Waif's nose swivelled yearningly to follow the plate.

"Oh, thanks," Charmain said, pleased that he had not forgotten her.

"Take two," suggested the colourless gentleman. "His Majesty will certainly eat any that are left over." The King at that moment was eating two muffins, one squashed on top of the other, and watching the crumpets as eagerly as Waif was.

Charmain thanked the gentleman again and took two. They were the most buttery crumpets she had ever encountered. Waif's nose swivelled to dab gently against Charmain's hand. "All right, all right," Charmain muttered, trying to break off a piece without dripping butter on the sofa. Butter ran down her fingers and threatened to trickle up her sleeves. She was trying to get rid of it on her handkerchief, when the lady-in-waiting finished saying all anyone could possibly say about the weather, and turned to Mrs Pendragon.

"Princess Hilda tells me you have a charming little boy," she said.

"Yes. Morgan," Mrs Pendragon said. She seemed to be having trouble with butter too and was mopping her fingers with her handkerchief and looking flustered.

"How old will Morgan be now, Sophie?" Princess Hilda asked. "When I saw him he was just a baby."

"Oh – nearly two," Mrs Pendragon replied, catching a big golden drip of butter before it fell on her skirt. "I left him with—"

The door of the parlour opened. Through it came a small, fat toddler in a grubby blue suit, with tears rolling down his face. "Mum-mum-mum!" he was wailing as he staggered into the room. But as soon as he saw Mrs Pendragon, his face spread into a blinding smile. He stretched out both arms and rushed to her, where he buried his face in her skirt. "*Mum!*" he shouted.

Following him through the door came floating an agitated-looking blue creature shaped like a long teardrop with a face on the front of it. It seemed to be made of flames. It brought a gust of warmth with it and a gasp from everyone in the room. An even more agitated housemaid hurried in after it.

After the housemaid came a small boy, quite the most angelic child Charmain had ever seen. He had a mass of blond curls that clustered around his angelic pink and white face. His eyes were big and blue and bashful. His exquisite little chin rested on a frill of white, white lace, and the rest of his graceful little body was clothed in a pale blue velvet suit with big silver buttons. His pink rosebud mouth spread into a shy smile as he came in, showing a charming dimple in his delicate little cheek. Charmain could not *think* why

Mrs Pendragon was staring at him in such horror. He was surely a truly enchanting child. And what long, curly eyelashes!

"—with my husband and his fire demon," Mrs Pendragon finished. Her face had gone fiery red, and she glared at the little boy across the toddler's head.

# CHAPTER EIGHT

### In which Peter has trouble
### with the plumbing

"**O**h, ma'am, Sire!" the housemaid gasped. "I had to let them in. The little one was so upset!"

She said this into a room full of confusion. Everyone stood up and someone dropped a teacup. Sim plunged to rescue the cup and the King dived past him to pick up the plate of crumpets. Mrs Pendragon stood up with Morgan in her arms, still looking daggers at the small boy, while the blue teardrop creature bobbed in front of her face. "It's not my fault, Sophie!" it kept saying, in an agitated crackling voice. "I swear it's not my fault! We couldn't stop Morgan crying for you."

Princess Hilda rose quellingly to her feet. "You may go," she said to the housemaid. "There is no need for anyone to be upset. Sophie, dear, I had no idea that you didn't employ a nursemaid."

"No, I don't. And I was hoping for a break," Mrs Pendragon said. "You would think," she added, glowering at the angelic little boy, "that a wizard and a fire demon could manage one small toddler between them."

"Men!" said the Princess. "I have no opinion of men's ability to manage anything. Of course Morgan and the other little boy must be our guests too, now that they're here. What sort of accommodation does a fire demon require?" she asked the colourless gentleman.

He looked completely blank.

"I'd appreciate a good log fire," the fire demon crackled. "I see you have a nice one in this room. That's all I need. I'm Calcifer, by the way, ma'am."

The Princess and the colourless gentleman both looked relieved. The Princess said, "Yes, of course. I believe we met briefly in Ingary, two years ago."

"And who is this other little fellow?" the King asked genially.

"Thophie'th my auntie," the small boy answered in a sweet lisping voice, raising his angelic face and big blue eyes to the King's.

Mrs Pendragon looked outraged.

"Pleased to meet you," the King said. "And what's your name, my little man?"

"Twinkle," the little boy whispered, coyly ducking his curly blond head.

"Have a crumpet, Twinkle," the King said heartily, holding the plate out.

"*Fank* you," Twinkle said devoutly, taking a crumpet.

At this, Morgan held out a fat, imperious hand and boomed, "Me, me, me!" until the King gave him a crumpet too. Mrs Pendragon sat Morgan on a sofa to eat it. Sim looked around and resourcefully fetched a cloth from the trolley. It became soaked in butter almost at once. Morgan beamed up at Sim, the Princess, the lady-in-waiting, and the Chancellor, with his face all shiny. "Dumpet," he said. "*Dood* dumpet."

While this was going on, Charmain became aware that Mrs Pendragon had somehow trapped little Twinkle behind the sofa she was sitting on. She could not help but overhear Mrs Pendragon demanding, "What *do* you think you're *doing*, Howl?" She sounded so fierce that Waif jumped into Charmain's lap and cowered there.

"They forgot to invite me," Twinkle's sweet little voice replied. "That'th thilly. You can't thort out thith meth on your own, Thophie. You need me."

"No I do *not*!" Sophie retorted. "And do you *have* to lisp like that?"

"Yeth," said Twinkle.

"Doh!" said Sophie. "It's not funny, Howl. And you've dragged Morgan here—"

"I tell you," Twinkle interrupted her, "Morgan did not thtop crying from the moment you left. Athk Calthifer if you don't believe me!"

"Calcifer's as bad as you are!" Sophie said passionately. "I don't believe either of you so much as *tried* to stop him. Did you? You were just looking for an excuse to launch this – this *masquerade* on poor Princess Hilda!"

"She needth uth, Thophie," Twinkle said earnestly.

Charmain was quite fascinated by this conversation, but unfortunately Morgan looked round for his mother just then and spotted Waif trembling on Charmain's knee. He gave a loud cry of "*Doggie!*", slid off his sofa, trampling the cloth as he went, and rushed at Waif with both buttery hands out. Waif jumped desperately on to the back of the sofa, where she stood and yapped. And yapped, like a shrill version of someone with a hacking cough. Charmain was forced to pick Waif up and back away, out of Morgan's reach, so that all she heard next of the strange conversation behind the sofa was Mrs Pendragon saying something about sending Twinkle (or was his name Howl?) to bed without supper and Twinkle daring her to "jutht *try* it."

As Waif quieted down, Twinkle said wistfully, "Don't you fink I'm pwetty at all?"

There was a strange hollow thump then, as if Mrs Pendragon had so far forgotten good behaviour as to stamp her foot. "Yes," Charmain heard her say. "*Disgustingly* pretty!"

"Well," said Princess Hilda, over near the fire, while Charmain was still backing away from Morgan, "things are certainly *lively* with children around. Sim, give Morgan a muffin, *quickly*."

Morgan at once reversed direction and ran towards Sim and the muffins. Charmain heard her own hair frizzle. She looked round and found the fire demon hovering beside her shoulder, looking at her with flaming orange eyes.

"Who are you?" the demon said.

Charmain's heart thumped a little, although Waif seemed perfectly calm. If I hadn't just met a lubbock, Charmain thought, I'd be quite frightened of this Calcifer. "I... er... I'm only the temporary help in the library," she said.

"Then we'll need to talk to you later," Calcifer crackled. "You reek of magic, did you know? You and your dog."

"She's not my dog. She belongs to a wizard," Charmain said.

"This Wizard Norland who seems to have messed things up?" Calcifer asked.

"I don't think Great Uncle William messed things up," Charmain said. "He's a *dear*!"

"He seems to have looked in all the wrong places," Calcifer said. "You don't need to be nasty to make a mess. Look at Morgan." And he whisked away. He had this way, Charmain thought, of vanishing in one place and turning up in another, like a dragonfly flicking about over a pond.

The King came across to Charmain, jovially wiping his hands on a large, crisp napkin. "Better get back to work, my dear. We have to tidy up for the night."

"Yes, of course, Sire," Charmain said and followed him towards the door.

Before they got there, the angelic Twinkle somehow escaped from the angry Mrs Pendragon and pulled at the sleeve of the lady-in-waiting. "Pleathe," he asked charmingly, "do you have any toyth?"

The lady looked nonplussed. "I don't play with toys, dear," she said.

Morgan caught the word from her. "*Doy!*" he shouted, waving both arms, with a buttery muffin clutched in one fist. "Doy, doy, doy!"

A jack-in-the-box landed in front of Morgan, bursting its lid open, so that the jack popped out with a *boinng*. A large dolls' house crashed down beside it, followed by a shower of elderly teddy bears. An instant later, a shabby rocking horse established itself next to the tea trolley. Morgan shouted with delight.

"I think we'll leave my daughter to cope with her guests," the King said, ushering Charmain and Waif out of the parlour. He shut the door upon more and more toys appearing and the child Twinkle looking highly demure, while everyone else ran about in confusion. "Wizards are often very vigorous guests," the King remarked on the way back to the library, "although I had no idea they started so young. A bit trying for their mothers, I imagine."

Half an hour later, Charmain was on her way back to Great Uncle William's house with Waif pattering behind her looking as demure as the child Twinkle.

"Ooof!" Charmain said to her. "You know, Waif, I've never lived so much life in three days, *ever*!" She felt a bit wistful all the same. It made sense for the King to give her the bills and love letters, but she did wish they could have taken turns with the books.

She would have loved to spend some of the day at least going through a thoroughly elderly and musty leather-bound volume. It was what she had been hoping for. But never mind. As soon as she got back to

Great Uncle William's house, she could bury herself in *The Twelve-Branched Wand,* or perhaps *Memoirs of an Exorcist* would be better, since it seemed to be the kind of book you were happier to read by daylight. Or try a different book altogether maybe?

She was looking forward so much to a good read that she hardly noticed the walk, except to pick Waif up again when Waif began panting and toiling. With Waif in her arms, she kicked Great Uncle William's gate open and found herself confronting Rollo halfway up the path, scowling all over his small blue face.

"What is it *now*?" Charmain said to him, and seriously wondered whether to pick Rollo up too and throw him into the hydrangeas. Rollo was small enough to hurl beautifully, even when she had one arm wrapped round Waif.

"Them flowerheads you got all over that outside table," Rollo said. "You expect me to stick them back on, or something?"

"No, of course not," Charmain said. "They're drying in the sun. Then I'll have them in the house."

"Huh!" said Rollo. "Prettifying in there, are you? How do you think the wizard'll like that?"

"None of your business," Charmain said haughtily, and strode forward so that Rollo was forced to hop out of her way. He shouted something after her as she was opening the front door, but she did not bother to listen. She knew it was rude. She slammed the door shut on his yells.

Indoors, the smell of the living room was more than musty. It was like a stagnant pond. Charmain put Waif on the floor and sniffed suspiciously. So did Waif. Long brown fingers of something were oozing under the door to the kitchen. Waif tiptoed up to them warily. Charmain, equally warily, put out her toe and prodded the nearest brown trickle. It squished like a marsh.

"Oh, what has Peter done *now*?" Charmain exclaimed. She flung the door open.

Two inches of water rippled all over the kitchen floor. Charmain could see it seeping darkly up the six bags of laundry beside the sink.

"*Doh!*" she cried out, slammed the door shut, opened it again and turned left.

The corridor there was awash. Sunlight from the end window flared on the water in a way that suggested a strong current coming from the bathroom. Angrily, Charmain splashed her way there. All I wanted to do was sit down and read a book, she thought, and I come home to a flood!

As she reached the bathroom, with Waif paddling unhappily after her, its door opened and Peter shot out of it, damp down his front and looking thoroughly harassed. He had no shoes on and his trousers were rolled up to his knees.

"Oh good, you're back," he said, before Charmain could speak. "There's this hole in one of the pipes in here. I've tried six different spells to stop it, but all they do is make it move about. I was just going to turn the water off at that woolly tank through there – or try to anyway – but perhaps you could do something instead."

"Woolly tank?" Charmain said. "Oh, you mean that thing covered in blue fur. What makes you think that will do any good? Everywhere's *flooded*!"

"It's the only thing I haven't tried," Peter snarled at her. "The water *has* to come from there somehow. You can hear it trickling. I thought I might find a stopcock—"

"Oh, you're *useless*!" Charmain snarled back. "Let me have a look." She pushed Peter aside and flounced into the bathroom, raising a sheet of water as she went.

There was indeed a hole. One of the pipes between the washbasin and the bath had a lengthwise slit in it and water was spraying out of it in a merry fountain. Here and there along the pipe were grey magical-looking blobs which must have been Peter's six useless spells. And this is all *his* fault! she snarled to herself. *He* was the one who made the pipes red hot. Oh, *honestly*!

She rushed at the spraying slit and angrily planted both hands on it. "Stop this!" she commanded. Water sprayed out round her hands and into her face. "Stop it at *once*!"

All that happened was that the slit moved sideways from under her fingers for about six inches and sprayed water over her pigtail and her right shoulder.

Charmain scooped her hands along to cover it again. "Stop that! *Stop* it!"

The slit moved off sideways again.

"So that's how you want it, is it?" Charmain said to it, and scooped some more. The slit moved off. She followed it with her hands. In a moment or so she had it cornered above the bath and the water spraying harmlessly into the bath and running away down the plughole. She kept it there, by leaning on the pipe with one hand, while she thought what next to do. I wonder Peter didn't think of this, she thought in a sort of mutter, instead of running about casting useless spells. "Great Uncle William," she called out, "how do I stop the bathroom pipe leaking?"

There was no answer. This was obviously not something Great Uncle William thought Charmain would need to know.

"I don't think he knows much about plumbing," Peter said from the doorway. "There's nothing useful in the suitcase either. I had it all out to see."

"Oh, *did* you?" Charmain said nastily.

"Yes, some of the stuff in there is really *interesting*," Peter said. "I'll show you if you—"

"Be *quiet* and let me *think*!" Charmain snapped at him.

Peter seemed to realise that Charmain might not be in a very good mood. He stopped talking and waited while Charmain stood in the bath and leaned on the pipe, thinking. You had to come at this leak two ways, so that it couldn't slide off again. First you fixed it in one place and then you covered it up. But how? Quick, before my feet are quite soaked. "Peter," she said, "go and get me some dishcloths. At least *three*."

"Why?" said Peter. "You don't think—"

"*Now!*" said Charmain.

To her relief, Peter went crossly splashing off, muttering about bossy, bad-tempered *cats*. Charmain pretended not to hear. Meanwhile, she dared not let go of the slit and the slit kept spraying and she was getting wetter every second. Oh, *blast* Peter! She put her other hand on the farther end of the slit and began pushing and sliding her hands together as hard as she could. "Close up!" she ordered the pipe. "Stop leaking and close *up*!" Water spouted rudely into her face. She could feel the slit trying to dodge, but she refused to let it. She pushed and pushed. I can do magic! she thought at the pipe. I worked a spell. I can *make* you close up! "So close *up*!"

And it worked. By the time Peter came wading back with just two cloths, saying those were all he could find, Charmain was soaked through to her underclothes but the pipe was whole again. Charmain took the cloths and bound them around the pipe on either side of where the slit had been. Then she snatched up the long back brush from beside the bath – this being the only thing remotely like a wizard's staff that she could see – and batted at the cloths with it.

"Stay there. Don't dare move!" she told the cloths. She batted at the mended slit. "You stay shut," she told it, "or it'll be the worse for you!" After that she turned the back brush on Peter's blobby grey spells and batted at them too. "Go!" she told them. "Go away! You're *useless*!" And they all obediently vanished. Charmain, flushed with a sense of great power, batted at the hot tap beside her knees. "Run hot again," she told it, "and let's have no nonsense! *And* you," she added, reaching across to bat at the hot tap on the washbasin. "Both hot – but not too hot, or I'll give you grief. But you stay running cold," she instructed the cold taps, batting them. Finally, she came out of the bath with a great splash and batted at the water on the floor. "And you *go*! Go on, dry up, drain away. Go! Or else!"

Peter waded over to the washbasin, turned the hot tap on and held his hand under it. "It's warm!" he said. "You really did it! That's a relief. Thanks."

"Huh!" said Charmain, soaked and cold and grumpy. "Now I'm going to change into dry clothes and read a book."

Peter asked, rather pathetically, "Aren't you going to help mop up, then?"

Charmain did not see why she should. But her eye fell on poor Waif, struggling towards her with water lapping at her underside. It did not look as if the back brush had worked on the floors. "All right," she sighed. "But I have done a day's work already, you know."

"So have I," Peter said feelingly. "I was rushing about all day trying to stop that pipe leaking. Let's get the kitchen dry, at least."

As the fire was still leaping and crackling in the kitchen grate, it was not unlike a steam bath in there. Charmain waded through the tepid water and opened the window. Apart from the mysteriously multiplying laundry bags, which were sodden, everywhere but the floor was dry. This included the suitcase, open on the table.

Behind Charmain, Peter spoke strange words and Waif whimpered.

Charmain whirled round to find Peter with his arms stretched out. Little flames were flickering on them, from his fingers to his shoulders. "Dry, O waters on the floor!" he intoned. Flames began to flicker across his hair and down his damp front too. His face changed from smug to alarmed. "Oh dear!" he said. As he said this, the flames rippled all over him and he began to burn quite fiercely. By then he looked plain frightened. "It's hot! *Help!*"

Charmain rushed at him, seized one of his blazing arms and pushed him over into the water on the floor. This did no good at all. Charmain stared at the extraordinary sight of flames flickering away under the water and simmering bubbles appearing all round Peter, where the water was starting to boil, and hauled him up again double quick in a shower of hot water and steam. "Cancel it!" she shouted, snatching her hands off his hot sleeve. "What spell did you use?"

"I don't know how!" Peter wailed.

"What *spell*?" Charmain bawled at him.

"It was the spell to stop floods in *The Boke of Palimpsest*," Peter babbled, "and I've no idea how to cancel it."

"Oh, you are *stupid*!" Charmain cried out. She grabbed him by one flaming shoulder and shook him. "Cancel, spell!" she shouted. "*Ouch!* Spell, I order you to cancel at once!"

The spell obeyed her. Charmain stood shaking her scorched hand and watched the flames vanish in a sizzle, a cloud of steam and a wet, singeing smell. It left Peter looking brown and frizzled all over. His face and hands were bright pink and his hair was noticeably shorter. "Thanks!" he said, flopping over with relief.

Charmain pushed him upright. "Pooh! You smell of burned hair! How *can* you be so stupid! What other spells have you been doing?"

"Nothing," Peter said, raking burned bits out of his hair. Charmain was fairly sure he was lying, but if he was, Peter was not going to confess. "And it wasn't that stupid," he argued. "Look at the floor."

Charmain looked down to see that the water had mostly gone. The floor was once again simply tiles, wet, shiny and steaming, but not flooded any longer. "Then you've been very lucky," she said.

"I mostly am," Peter said. "My mother always says that too, whenever I do a spell that goes wrong. I think I'm going to have to change into different clothes."

"Me too," Charmain said.

They went through the inner door, where Peter tried to turn right and Charmain pushed him left, so that they went straight and arrived in the living room. The wet trickles on the carpet there were steaming and drying out rapidly, but the room still smelled horrible. Charmain snorted, turned Peter round and pushed him left through the door again. Here, the corridor was damp, but not full of water any longer.

"See?" Peter said as he went into his bedroom. "It did work."

"Huh!" Charmain said, going into her own room.

I wonder what *else* he's done. I don't trust him an inch.

Her best clothes were a wet mess. Charmain took them off sadly and hung them around the room to get dry. And nothing was going to cure the big scorch mark down the front of her best jacket. She would have to wear ordinary clothes tomorrow when she went to the Royal Mansion. And do I dare leave Peter alone here? she wondered. I bet he'll spend the time experimenting with spells. I know I would. She shrugged a little, as she realised she was no better than Peter really. She had been quite unable to resist the spells in *The Boke of Palimpsest* either.

She was feeling much more kindly towards Peter when she came back to the kitchen, dry again except for her hair and wearing her oldest clothes and her slippers.

"Find out how to ask for supper," Peter said, as Charmain put her wet shoes to dry in the hearth. "I'm starving." He was looking much more comfortable in the old blue suit that he had arrived in.

"There's food in the bag Mother brought yesterday," Charmain said, busy arranging the shoes in the best place.

"No, there isn't," Peter said. "I ate it all for lunch."

Charmain stopped feeling kindly towards Peter. "Greedy pig," she said, banging on the fireplace for food for Waif. Waif, in spite of all the crumpets she had eaten in the Royal Mansion, was delighted to see the latest dog dish. "And so are you a greedy pig," Charmain said, watching Waif gobble. "Where do you put it all? Great Uncle William, how do we get supper?"

The kindly voice was very faint now. "Just knock on the pantry door and say 'Supper', my dear."

Peter got to the pantry first. "Supper!" he bellowed, banging hard on the door.

There was a knobby, flopping sound from the table. Both of them whirled round to look. There, lying beside the open suitcase, were a small lamb chop, two onions and a turnip. Charmain and Peter stared at them.

"All raw!" Peter said, stunned.

"And not enough anyway," Charmain said. "Do you know how to cook it?"

"No," said Peter. "My mother does all the cooking in our house."

"Oh!" said Charmain. "*Honestly!*"

# CHAPTER NINE

### In which Great Uncle William's house
### proves to have many ways

Peter and Charmain naturally converged on the fireplace then. Waif scuttled out of the way as, one after another, they beat on the mantelpiece and cried out, "Breakfast!" But it seemed that this spell only worked properly in the morning.

"I wouldn't even have minded kippers," Charmain said, miserably surveying the two trays. They had rolls, honey and orange juice on them, and nothing else.

"I know how to boil eggs," Peter said. "Will Waif eat this lamb chop?"

"She'll eat almost anything," Charmain said. "She's as bad as – as we are. I don't think she'll eat a turnip though. I wouldn't."

They had a somewhat unsatisfactory supper. Peter's eggs were – well – solid. In order to take Charmain's mind off them, Peter asked her about her time in the Royal Mansion. Charmain told him, in order to take both their minds off the way hard boiled eggs did not mix with honey. Peter was highly intrigued by the way the King seemed to be looking for gold, and even more intrigued by the arrival of Morgan and Twinkle.

"And a fire demon?" he said. "Two infants with magical powers *and* a fire demon! I bet the Princess has her hands full. How long are they staying?"

"I don't know. Nobody said," Charmain said.

"Then I bet you two Afternoon Teas and a Morning Coffee that the Princess turns them out before the weekend," Peter said. "Have you finished eating? Then I want you to look through your great uncle's suitcase."

"But I want to read a *book*!" Charmain protested.

"No, you don't," Peter said. "You can do that any time. This suitcase is full of stuff you need to know. I'll show you." He pushed the breakfast trays aside and pulled the suitcase in front of her. Charmain sighed and put her glasses on.

The suitcase was full to the brim with paper. Lying

on top was a note in Great Uncle William's beautiful but shaky writing. "For Charmain," it said. "Key to the House." Under that was a large sheet of paper with a tangle of swirly lines drawn on it. The lines had labelled boxes drawn on them at intervals, and each line ended in an arrow at the edge of the page, with the word "Unexplored" written beside it.

"That's the short key you've got there," Peter said as Charmain picked this paper up. "The rest of the stuff in the suitcase is the proper map. It folds out. Look." He took hold of the next sheet of paper and pulled, and it came out with the next sheet joined to it, and then the next, folded back and forth to fit in the suitcase. It came out on to the table in a huge zigzag. Charmain stared at it resentfully. Each piece had carefully drawn rooms and corridors on it, and neatly written notes beside each thing. The notes said things like "Turn left twice here" and "Two steps right and one left here". The rooms had blocks of writing in them, some simple, like "Kitchen" and some eloquent, like the one that read "My store of wizardly supplies, kept constantly replenished by an intake spell I am rather proud of. Please note that the ingredients on the left hand wall are all highly dangerous and must be handled with great care". And some of the joined sheets seemed to be all criss-crossing corridors labelled "To unexplored North Section", "To Kobolds", "To Main

Cistern" or "To Ballroom: I doubt if we shall ever find a use for this".

"I was quite right to leave this suitcase shut," Charmain said. "It's the most confusing map I ever saw in my life! It *can't* all be this house!"

"It is. It's enormous," Peter said. "And if you look, you'll see that the way the map is folded is a clue to how you get to the different parts of it. See, here's the living room on the top page, but if you go to the next page, you don't get his study or the bedrooms because those are folded back, see. You get the kitchen instead because that's folded the same way…"

Charmain's head began to go round and she closed her ears to Peter's enthusiastic explanations. She looked at the swirling lines on the piece of paper in her hand instead. It almost seemed easier. At least, she could see "Kitchen" right in the middle of it, and "Bedrooms" and "Swimming Pool" and "Study". "Swimming Pool?" Not really, surely? An interesting swirl led off to the right, underneath these boxes, into a tangle containing a box labelled "Conference Room". An arrow pointed off from this box labelled "To Royal Mansion".

"Oh!" she exclaimed. "You can get to the King's house from here!"

"…out to a mountain meadow that says 'Stables', but I can't see how to get there from his workroom yet,"

Peter expounded, unfolding another zigzag. "And here's 'Food Store'. It says 'Stasis Spells operate'. I wonder how you take those off. But what interests me are the places like this one, where he's written 'Storage Space. Just Junk? Must investigate some day.' Do you think he created all this bent space himself? Or did he find it already there when he moved in?"

"He found it," Charmain said. "You can tell by these arrows that say 'Unexplored' that he doesn't know what's out there yet."

"You may be right," Peter said judiciously. "He really only uses the middle bits, doesn't he? We can do him a favour by exploring more of it."

"You can if you like," Charmain said. "I'm going to read my book." She folded up the paper with the swirly lines on it and stowed it in her pocket. This could save her a journey in the morning.

In the morning, Charmain's good clothes were still damp. She had to leave them draped depressingly around her room and get into her next-nicest, while she wondered if she could manage to leave Waif behind with Peter today. Perhaps not. Suppose Peter tried another spell and contrived to turn Waif inside out or something.

Waif of course came trotting eagerly after Charmain

into the kitchen. Charmain tapped the fireplace for dog
food and then, a little doubtfully, for her own breakfast.
It could be that she and Peter had thrown the spell out
by demanding breakfast yesterday evening.

But no. Today she got a full tray, with a choice of tea
or coffee, and toast, and a plate piled high with something
made with fish and rice, and a peach to follow. I think the
spell's apologising, she thought. She didn't like the fish
stuff much, so she gave most of it to Waif, who liked it the
way she always liked food and smelled quite fishy as she
trotted after Charmain when Charmain unfolded her
swirly paper, ready to go to the Royal Mansion.

Looking at the swirls confused Charmain. She found
she had been even more confused by the chart in the
suitcase. Bending the paper backwards and forwards to
try and reproduce what was in the suitcase did not help
at all. After several turns left and right, she found
herself walking into a place that was large and well
lighted by big windows overlooking the river. There
was a fine view of the town across the river, where,
most frustratingly, she could see the golden roof of the
Royal Mansion gleaming in the sunlight.

"But I'm trying to get *there*, not *here*!" she said,
looking around.

There were long wooden tables under the windows,
loaded with strange implements and more implements

stacked in the middle of the room. The other walls were full of shelves piled with jars, tins, and odd-shaped glassware. Charmain sniffed the smell of new wood here, which was overlaid by the same thunderstorm-and-spice smell she had noticed in Great Uncle William's study. The smell of magic having been done, she thought. This must be his workroom. To judge by the way Waif was trotting cheerily about, Waif knew this place well.

"Come on, Waif," Charmain said, pausing to look at a piece of paper on top of the strange implements in the middle of the room. It said, "Please do not touch." "Let's go back to the kitchen and start again."

It did not work out that way. A left turn from the workroom door brought them into a warm, warm place open to the sky, where a small blue pool rippled amid white stone surrounds. The place was fenced off by white stone trellises with roses growing up them, and there were white reclining chairs beside the roses, piled with large fluffy towels. Ready for when you'd finished swimming, Charmain supposed. But poor Waif was terrified of this place. She crouched against the gateway, whining and trembling.

Charmain picked her up. "Did someone try to drown you, Waif? Were you a puppy someone didn't want? It's all right. I'm not going near this water either. I've no idea how to swim." As she turned left through the gateway, it occurred to her that swimming was only one of a very large number of things she had no idea how to do. Peter had been right to object to her ignorance. "It's not that I'm lazy," she explained to Waif as they arrived in what seemed to be the stables, "or stupid. I've just not bothered to look round the edges of Mother's way of doing things, you see."

The stables were rather smelly. Charmain was relieved to see that the horses that must belong there were up in a meadow beyond a fence. Horses were another thing she had no idea about. At least Waif did not seem to be frightened here.

Charmain sighed, put Waif down, scrabbled up her glasses and looked at the confusing swirly chart again. "Stables" were here, up in the mountains somewhere. She needed two right turns from there to the kitchen again. She turned right twice, with Waif pattering behind, and found herself in near dark outside what seemed to be a large cave full of hurrying blue kobolds. Each one of them turned and glowered at Charmain. Charmain hurriedly turned right again. And this time she was in a store for cups, plates and teapots. Waif whined. Charmain stared at several hundred teapots, in rows on shelves, of every possible colour and size, and began to panic. It was getting late. Worse than that, when she put her glasses on again and consulted the plan, she found she was somewhere near the bottom lefthand part of the swirls, where the arrow pointing off to the edge had a note that said "A group of lubbockins live down this way. Care necessary."

"Oh," Charmain exclaimed. This is *ridiculous*! Come on, Waif." She opened the door they had just come through and turned right yet again.

This time they were in complete darkness. Charmain could feel Waif nosing anxiously up against her ankles. Both of them sniffed and Charmain said, "Ah!" This place had a damp stone smell that she remembered from the day she had arrived in the house. "Great Uncle William," she asked, "how do I get from here to the kitchen again?"

Much to her relief, the kindly voice answered. It sounded very faint and far away now. "If you are there, my dear, you are rather lost, so listen carefully. Make one turn clockwise…"

Charmain had no need to listen any more. Instead of making a complete turn, she turned carefully halfway and then peered forward. Sure enough, there was a dimly lighted stone corridor ahead, crossing the one she seemed to be standing in. She strode thankfully towards it, with Waif trotting behind her, and turned into that corridor. She knew she was now in the Royal Mansion. It was the same corridor where she had seen

Sim pushing a trolley on her first day in Great Uncle William's house. Not only did it smell right – with faint foody smells on top of the damp stone smell – but the walls had the typical Royal Mansion look, with lighter squares and oblongs where pictures had been taken away. The only trouble was that she had no idea whereabouts in the Mansion this was. Waif was no help. She simply plastered herself against Charmain's ankles and shivered.

Charmain picked Waif up and walked down the corridor, hoping to find somewhere she knew. She turned two corners without being any the wiser and then almost ran into the colourless gentleman who had passed the crumpets round yesterday. He jumped backwards, thoroughly startled.

"Dear me," he said, peering at Charmain in the gloom. "I had no idea you had arrived yet, Miss... er... Charming, is it? Are you lost? Can I assist?"

"Yes, please," Charmain said resourcefully. "I went to the... to the... er... um... you know, the one for ladies – and I must have turned the wrong way afterwards. Can you tell me the way back to the library?"

"I can do better than that," said the colourless gentleman. "I'll *show* you. Just follow me."

He turned round and led the way back where he had been coming from, along another dim corridor and across a large, cold lobby, where a flight of stone stairs led upwards. Waif's tail began to twitch slightly, as if she found this part familiar. But her tail stopped moving as they crossed in front of the stairs. Morgan's voice came booming down from the top of the flight.

"Don't *want* to! Don't *want*! *Don't* WANT!"

Twinkle's shriller voice joined in. "I can't wear *thethe*! I want my *thtwipey* oneth!"

Sophie Pendragon's voice echoed down too. "Be quiet, both of you! Or I'll do something dreadful, I warn you! I've no patience left!"

The colourless gentleman winced. He said to Charmain, "Small children bring so much life to a place, don't they?"

Charmain looked up at him, meaning to nod and grin. But something made her shudder instead. She was not sure why. She managed to give a little nod and that was all, before she followed the gentleman through an archway, where the booming of Morgan and the screaming of Twinkle died away into the distance.

Round another corner, the colourless gentleman opened a door that Charmain recognised as the door to the library. "Miss Charming seems to have arrived, Sire," he said, bowing.

"Oh, good," said the King, looking up from a pile of thin leather books. "Come in and sit down, my dear. I

found an absolute heap of papers for you last night. I'd
no idea we had so many."

Charmain felt as if she had never been away. Waif
settled down, rolled tummy upwards in the heat from
the brazier. Charmain settled down also, in front of a
toppling heap of different-sized papers, found pen and
paper, and started in. It was very companionable.

After a while, the King said, "This ancestor of mine,
who wrote these diaries, fancied himself as a poet. What
do you think of this one? To his lady love, of course.

*"You dance with the grace of a goat, my love,*
*And you sing soft like a cow on the mountains.*

"Would you call that romantic, my dear?"

Charmain laughed. "It's dreadful. I hope she threw
him over. Er... Your Majesty, who is the colour... er...
the gentleman who showed me in just now?"

"You mean my steward?" the King said. "Do you
know, he's been with us for years and years and years –
and I can never remember the poor fellow's name.
You'll have to ask the Princess, my dear. She
remembers things like that."

Oh, well, Charmain thought. I shall just have to
think of him as the colourless gentleman, then.

The day passed peacefully. It made, Charmain felt, a

pleasant change after such a hectic start. She sorted out
and made notes about bills from two hundred years ago,
bills from one hundred years ago and bills from a mere
forty years back. Oddly enough, the older bills were for
much larger sums of money than the newer ones. It
looked as if the Royal Mansion was spending less and less.
Charmain also sorted out letters from four hundred years
back, and more recent reports from ambassadors from
Strangia, Ingary and even Rajpuht. Some ambassadors
sent poems. Charmain read the worst ones out to the
King. Farther down the stack, she came upon receipts.
Papers saying things like "In payment for portrait of a
lady, reputed to be by a grand master, 200 guineas" began
to turn up more and more frequently, all from the last
sixty years. It looked to Charmain as if the Royal
Mansion had been selling its pictures for most of the
King's reign. She decided not to ask the King about it.

Lunch arrived, more of Jamal's delicious spicy things.
When Sim brought them, Waif jumped up, wagging her
tail, stopped, looked disappointed and trotted away out
of the library. Charmain had no idea if it was the cook's
dog or lunch that Waif wanted. Lunch, probably.

As Sim put the platter on the table, the King asked
jovially, "How are things going out there now, Sim?"

"A little noisily, Sire," Sim replied. "We have just
received our sixth rocking horse. Master Morgan seems

desirous of a live monkey, which, I am glad to report, Mrs Pendragon has refused to allow him to have. A certain uproar resulted. In addition, Master Twinkle seems convinced that someone is denying him a pair of stripey trousers. He has been very loud on the subject all morning, Sire. And the fire demon has adopted the fire in the front parlour as his roosting place of choice. Will you be taking tea with us in the front parlour today, Sire?"

"I think not," the King said. "I've nothing against the fire demon, but it gets a bit crowded in there with all those rocking horses. Be good enough to fetch us some crumpets here to the library, if you will, Sim."

"Certainly, Sire," Sim said, shakily backing from the room.

When the door was shut, the King said to Charmain, "It's not the rocking horses, really. And I quite like the noise. But it all makes me think how much I'd have enjoyed being a grandfather. Pity, that."

"Er..." said Charmain, "people in town always say that Princess Hilda was disappointed in love. Is that why she never married?"

The King seemed surprised. "Not that I know of," he said. "She had princes and dukes lining up to marry her for years when she was younger. But she's not the marrying kind. Never fancied the idea, so she tells me. Prefers her life here, helping me. It's a pity, though.

Here's my heir having to be Prince Ludovic, my fool of a cousin's son. You'll meet him soon, if we can only move a rocking horse or so – or maybe she'll use the Grand Parlour instead. But the real pity is that there are no more youngsters around the Mansion nowadays. I miss that."

The King did not seem too unhappy. He looked matter-of-fact rather than mournful, but Charmain was suddenly struck by what a sad place the Royal Mansion really was. Huge, empty and sad. "I understand, Your Majesty," she said.

The King grinned and bit into a Jamal tasty. "I know you do," he said. "You're a very intelligent young lady. You'll do your Great Uncle William great credit one day."

Charmain blinked a bit at this description. But before she could get too uncomfortable at being praised, she realised what the King had left out. I may be clever, she thought, quite sadly, but I'm not in the least kind or sympathetic. I think I may even be hard-hearted. Look at the way I treat Peter.

She brooded on this for the rest of the afternoon. The result was that, when it was time to stop for the day and Sim reappeared with Waif wandering along after him, Charmain stood up and said, "Thank you for being so good to me, Your Majesty."

The King seemed surprised and told her to think nothing of it. But I do, Charmain thought. He's been so kind that it should be a lesson to me. As she followed Sim's slow totter, with Waif, who seemed very sleepy and fat, toiling along behind both of them, Charmain made a resolution to be kind to Peter when she got back to Great Uncle William's house.

Sim had almost reached the front door, when Twinkle came rushing past from somewhere, energetically bowling a large hoop. He was followed at speed by Morgan, holding both arms out and bellowing, "Oop, *oop*, OOP!" Sim was sent reeling. Charmain tried to flatten herself against the wall as Twinkle shot past. There was an instant when she thought that Twinkle gave her a strange, searching look as he whipped by, but a yelp from Waif sent her speeding to the rescue and she thought no more about it. Waif had been knocked upside-down and was very upset about it. Charmain scooped her up and nearly ran into Sophie Pendragon, chasing after Morgan.

"Which way?" Sophie panted.

Charmain pointed. Sophie hauled her skirts high and raced off, muttering something about guts and garters as she ran.

Princess Hilda appeared in the distance and stopped to drag Sim to his feet. "I really do apologise, Miss Charming," she said as Charmain reached her. "That child is like an eel – well, they both are actually. I shall have to take steps, or poor Sophie will have no attention left for our problems. Are you steady now, Sim?"

"Perfectly, ma'am," said Sim. He bowed to Charmain and let her out through the front door into bright afternoon sunlight, as if nothing had happened.

If I ever marry, Charmain thought, striding across Royal Square with Waif in her arms, I shall never have children. They would make me cruel and hard-hearted after a week. Perhaps I shall be like Princess Hilda and never marry. That way, I might stand a chance of learning to be kind. Anyway, I shall practise on Peter, because he's truly hard work.

She was full of sternly kind resolve when she reached Great Uncle William's house. It helped, as she marched up the path between the ranks of blue hydrangeas, that there was no sign of Rollo. Being kind to Rollo was something Charmain was sure she could never do.

"Not humanly possible," she remarked to herself as she put Waif down on the living room carpet. The room struck her as being unusually clean and tidy. Everything was orderly, from the suitcase neatly put back beside one of the armchairs to the vase of variously coloured hydrangeas on the coffee table. Charmain frowned at this vase. It was surely the one that had disappeared when it was put on the trolley. Maybe Peter ordered Morning Coffee and it came back then, she thought – rather vaguely, because she suddenly remembered that she had left damp clothing all over her bedroom and bedclothes trailing over the floor. Bother! I have to tidy up.

She stopped short in the doorway of her bedroom. Someone had made her bed. Her clothes, dry now, were neatly folded on top of the chest of drawers. It was an outrage. Feeling anything but kind, Charmain stormed into the kitchen.

Peter was sitting at the kitchen table, looking so virtuous that Charmain knew he had been up to something. Behind him, on the fire, a large black pot was bubbling out strange, weak, savoury smells.

"What do you mean by tidying up my room?" Charmain demanded.

Peter looked injured, even though Charmain could tell he was full of secret, exciting thoughts. "I thought you'd be pleased," he said.

"Well, I'm *not*!" Charmain said. She was surprised to find herself almost in tears. "I was just beginning to learn that if I drop something on the floor it *stays* dropped unless I pick it up, and if I make a mess I have to clear it away because it doesn't go by itself, and then you go and clear it up *for* me! You're as bad as my mother!"

"I've got to do something while I'm alone here all day," Peter protested. "Or do you expect me to just sit here?"

"You can do anything you like," Charmain yelled. "Dance. Stand on your head. Make faces at Rollo. But don't spoil my learning process!"

"Feel free to learn," Peter retorted. "You've got a long way to go. I won't touch your room again. Are you interested in some of the things *I've* learned today? Or are you thoroughly self-centreed?"

Charmain gulped. "I was meaning to be kind to you this evening, but you make it very difficult."

"My mother says difficulties help you learn," Peter said. "You should be pleased. I'll tell you one thing I've learned today and that's how to get enough supper." He pointed with his thumb to the bubbling pot. That thumb had a piece of green string round it. The other thumb had red string and one of his fingers was decorated with blue string.

He's been trying to go in three directions at once, Charmain thought. Striving mightily to sound friendly, she said, "How do you get enough supper, then?"

"I kept banging on the pantry door," Peter said, "until enough things landed on the table. Then I put them in that pot to boil."

Charmain looked at the pot. "What things?"

"Liver and bacon," Peter said. "Cabbage. More turnips and a chunk of rabbit. Onions, two more chops and a leek. It was easy really."

Yuk! thought Charmain. In order not to say something really rude, she turned round to go to the living room.

Peter called after her, "Don't you want to know how I got that vase of flowers back?"

"You sat on the trolley," Charmain said coldly, and went away to read *The Twelve-Branched Wand*. But it was no good. She kept looking up and seeing that vase of hydrangeas and then looking over at the trolley and wondering if Peter had truly sat there and vanished away with an Afternoon Tea. Then wondering how he had got back. And every time she looked, she was more aware that her resolve to be kind to Peter had come to absolutely nothing. She stood it for nearly an hour and then went back to the kitchen. "I apologise," she said. "How did you get the flowers back?"

Peter was prodding at the stuff in the pot with a spoon. "I don't think this is ready yet," he said. "This spoon bounces off."

"Oh, come on," Charmain said. "I'm being polite."

"I'll tell you over supper," Peter said.

He kept his word, maddeningly. He hardly said a word for an hour, until the contents of the pot had been shared into two bowls. Dividing the food was not easy because Peter had not bothered to peel anything or cut it up before he put it in the pot. They had to hack the cabbage apart with two spoons. Nor had Peter remembered that a stew needs salt. Everything – white, soggy bacon, hunk of rabbit, whole turnip, and flabby onion – floated in weak watery juice. To put it mildly, the food was quite horrible. Doing her best to be kind, Charmain did not say it was.

The only good thing was that Waif liked it. That is to say, she lapped up the weak juice and then carefully ate the meaty bits out from among the cabbage. Charmain did much the same and tried not to shudder. She was glad to take her mind off it by listening to what Peter had to tell.

"Are you aware," he began, rather pompously, to Charmain's mind. But she could tell that he had everything worked out in his mind like a story and was going to tell it just as he had it worked out. "Are you aware that when things vanish from the trolley, they go back into the past?"

"Well, I suppose the past makes quite a good waste dump," Charmain said. "As long as you make sure it really *is* past and things don't turn up again all mouldy—"

"Do you want to hear or not?" Peter demanded.

Be kind, Charmain told herself. She ate another piece of nasty cabbage and nodded.

"And that parts of this house are in the past?" Peter continued. "I didn't sit on the trolley, you know. I just went exploring with a list of the ways I needed to turn, and I found out by accident really. I must have turned the wrong way once or twice."

Doesn't surprise me, Charmain thought.

"Anyway," said Peter, "I got to a place where there were hundreds of kobold ladies all washing teapots and stacking food on trays for breakfasts and teas and things. And I was a bit nervous of them, because of the way you'd annoyed them over the hydrangeas, but I tried to look pleasant as I went by and nodded and smiled and things. And I was really surprised when they all nodded and smiled back and said 'Good morning' in a perfectly friendly way. So I went on nodding and smiling and walking past, until I came to a room I hadn't seen before. As soon as I opened the door, the first thing I saw was that vase of flowers sitting on the front of a long, long table. The next thing I saw was Wizard Norland sitting behind the table—"

"Good gracious!" said Charmain.

"It surprised me too," Peter admitted. "I just stood there and stared, to tell the truth. He looked quite healthy – you know, strong and pink, and he had a lot more hair than I remembered – and he was busy working on the chart that was in the suitcase. He had it all spread out along the table and he'd only filled in about a quarter of it. I suppose that gave me a clue. Anyway, he looked up and said, quite politely, 'Would you mind closing the door?

There's quite a draught.' Then before I could say anything, he looked up again and said, 'Who on earth are *you*?'

"I said, 'I'm Peter Regis.'

"That made him frown. He said, 'Regis, Regis? Does that make you some relation of the Witch of Montalbino, perhaps?'

"'She's my mother,' I said.

"And he said, 'I didn't think she had any children.'

"'She only has me,' I said. 'My dad was killed in a big avalanche at Transmontain just after I was born.'

"He frowned some more and said, 'But that avalanche was only last month, young man. They're saying that a lubbock set it off and it certainly killed a lot of people – or are we talking about the avalanche forty years ago?' And he looked very stern and disbelieving at me.

"I wondered how I could make him believe what had happened. I said, 'I promise it's true. Some of your house must go back in time. It's where the Afternoon Teas disappear to. And – this should prove it – we put that vase of flowers on the trolley the other day and it came back here to you.' He looked at the vase, but he didn't say anything. I said, 'I came here to your house because my mother arranged for me to be your apprentice.'

"He said, 'Did she indeed? I must have been wanting to oblige her quite badly then. You don't seem to me to have any remarkable talent.'

"'I can do magic,' I said, 'but my mother can arrange anything when she wants to.'

"He said, 'True. She has a remarkably forceful personality. What did I say when you turned up?'

"'You didn't.' I said. 'You weren't there. A girl called Charmain Baker was looking after your house – or she was supposed to be, but she went off and worked for the King and met a fire demon—'

"He interrupted me then, looking shocked. 'A fire demon? Young man, those are very dangerous beings. Are you telling me that the Witch of the Waste will be in High Norland before long?'

"'No, no,' I said. 'One of the Royal Wizards in Ingary did for the Witch of the Waste nearly three years ago now. This one was something to do with the King, Charmain said. I suppose she's only just born from your point of view, but she said you were ill and the elves carried you off to cure you and her Aunt Sempronia arranged for Charmain to look after the house while you were gone.'

"He looked quite upset about this. He sat back in his chair and blinked a bit. 'I have a great-niece called Sempronia,' he said, sort of slowly and thinking about it. 'This *could* be so. Sempronia has married into a very respectable family, I believe—'

"'Oh, they are!' I said. 'You should just see

Charmain's mother. She's so respectable she doesn't let Charmain do anything.'"

Thank you very much, Peter! Charmain thought. Now he thinks I'm a complete waste of space!

"But he wasn't really interested," Peter went on. "He wanted to know what had made him ill and I couldn't tell him. Do *you* know?" he asked Charmain. Charmain shook her head. Peter shrugged and said, "Then he sighed, and said he supposed it didn't matter, because it seemed to have been unavoidable. But after that, he said, quite pathetically and all puzzled, 'But I don't know any elves!'

"I said, 'Charmain said it was the King who sent the elves.'

"'Oh,' he said, and he looked much happier. 'Of course it would be! The royal family has elf blood – several of them married elves and the elves do keep up the connection, I believe.' Then he looked at me and said, 'So this story begins to hang together.'

"I said, 'Well it should do. It's all true. But what I don't understand is what you did to make the kobolds so angry with you.'

"'Nothing, I assure you,' he said. 'Kobolds are my friends, they have been for years. They do a great many tasks for me. I would no more anger a kobold than I would anger my friend the King.'

"He seemed annoyed enough about this that I thought I'd better change the subject. I said, 'Then can I ask you about this house? Did you build it or find it?'

"'Oh, found it,' he said. 'Or at least I bought it when I was quite a young, struggling wizard, because it seemed small and cheap. Then I found it was a labyrinth of many ways. It was a delightful discovery, I can tell you. It seems once to have belonged to a Wizard Melicot, the same man who made the roof of the Royal Mansion appear to be gold. I have always hoped that, somewhere inside this house, there is hidden the actual gold that was in the Royal Treasury at the time. The King has been looking for that for years, you know.'

"And you can guess how that made me prick up my ears," Peter said. "But I never got to ask any more, because he said, looking at the vase on the table, 'So these are really flowers from the future, then? Do you mind telling me what sort they are?'

"I was quite astonished he didn't know. I told him they were hydrangeas from his own garden. 'The coloured ones the kobolds cut off,' I said. And he looked at them and murmured that they were quite magnificent, particularly the way they were so many different colours. 'I shall have to start growing them for myself,' he said. 'They have more colours than roses.'

"'You can get them to grow blue too,' I said. 'My

mother uses a spell with copper powder for ours.' And while he was murmuring about that, I asked him if I could take them back with me, so that I could prove to you that I'd met him.

"'Certainly, certainly,' he said. 'They are rather in the way here. And tell your young lady who knows the fire demon that I hope to have my chart of the house finished by the time she is grown up enough to need it.'

"So," Peter said, "I took the flowers and came away. Wasn't that extraordinary!"

"Very," said Charmain. "He wouldn't have grown hydrangeas if the kobolds hadn't cut them off and I hadn't picked them up and you hadn't got lost – It makes my head go round." She pushed aside her bowlful of cabbage and turnip. I shall be nice to him. I shall, I *shall*! "Peter, how would it be if I called in on my father on my way home tomorrow and asked him for a cookery book? He must have hundreds. He's the best cook in town."

Peter looked utterly relieved. "Good idea," he said. "My mother's never told me much about cooking. She always does it all."

And I shan't object to the way he's made Great Uncle William think of me, Charmain vowed. I shall be kind. But if he does that once again…

# CHAPTER TEN

### In which Twinkle takes
### to the roof

In the night, a worrying thought struck Charmain. If you could travel in time in Great Uncle William's house, what was to stop her arriving in the Royal Mansion ten years ago, to find that the King was not expecting her? Or ten years in the future, to find that Prince Ludovic was ruling now? It was enough to make her decide to walk to the Mansion in the usual way.

So, the next morning, Charmain set off along the road, with Waif pattering behind her, until they came by the cliff where the lubbock's meadow was, when Waif became so breathless and pathetic that Charmain picked her up. As usual, Charmain thought. I feel like a proper grown up working-girl, she added to herself as she strode towards town with Waif happily trying to lick her chin.

It had rained in the night again, but now it was one of those mornings of pale blue sky and huge white clouds. The mountains were silky blues and greens, and in the town, the sun glittered off wet cobbles and flared on the river. Charmain felt very contented. She was really looking forward to a day of sorting papers and chatting with the King.

As she crossed Royal Square, the sun glared so off the golden roof of the Royal Mansion that Charmain was forced to look down at the cobbles. Waif blinked and ducked and then jumped as a loud squealing sound came from the Mansion.

"Look at me! *Look at me!*"

Charmain looked, found her eyes full of tears from the dazzle, and looked again under a hand spared from Waif. The child Twinkle was sitting astride the golden roof, fully a hundred feet in the air, waving merrily to her. He almost overbalanced doing it. At the sight, Charmain forgot all the unkind thoughts she had had about children yesterday. She dumped Waif on the cobbles and ran for the Mansion door, where she clattered at the great knocker and rang the bell furiously.

"That little boy!" she gasped at Sim when he slowly and creakily opened the door. "Twinkle. He's sitting on the roof! Someone *has* to get him down!"

"Is that so?" said Sim. He tottered out on to the steps. Charmain had to wait while he tottered to a place where he could see the roof and craned shakily upwards. "Indeed he is, miss," he agreed. "Little demon. He'll fall. That roof is as slippery as ice."

Charmain was jigging with impatience by then. "Send someone to fetch him *in*! Quickly!"

"I don't know who," Sim said slowly. "Nobody much in this Mansion climbs too well. I *could* send Jamal, I suppose, but with only the one eye his balance is not too good."

Waif was prancing about, yapping to be carried up the steps. Charmain ignored her. "Then send me," she said. "Just tell me how to get there. Now. Before he slides off sideways."

"Good notion," Sim agreed. "You take the stairs at the end of the hall, miss, and keep on going up. Last flight's wooden and you'll find a small door—"

Charmain waited for no more. Leaving Waif to fend for herself, she raced off down the damp stone corridor until she came to the lobby with the stone stairs. There she began to climb for dear life, with her glasses bouncing on her chest and her footsteps ringing round the walls. Up she went, two long flights, her mind filled with horrible thoughts of a small body plummeting down and hitting the cobbles with... well... a *splash*, just about where she had left Waif. Panting hard, she hurried up a third, narrower flight. It seemed endless. Then she came to wooden stairs and clattered up those, almost out of breath. They seemed endless too. At last she came to a small wooden door. Praying she was still in time, Charmain flung open the door on to a blaze of sunlight and gold.

"I fort you were never coming," Twinkle said from the middle of the roof. He was wearing a pale blue velvet suit and his golden hair blazed as bright as the roof. He seemed perfectly calm, more like a strayed angel than a small boy in trouble on a roof.

"Are you very frightened?" Charmain panted anxiously. "Hold on very tight and don't move and I'll crawl out and get you."

"Pleathe do that," Twinkle said politely.

He doesn't know the danger he's in! Charmain thought. I shall have to keep very calm. Very cautiously, she climbed out through the wooden door and maneuvered until she was sitting astride the roof like Twinkle. It was highly uncomfortable. Charmain did not know which was worse: the fact that the tin tiles were hot, wet, sharp, and slippery, or the way the roof seemed to be cutting her in two. When she snatched a sideways look at Royal Square, far, far below, she had to remind herself, very seriously, that she had worked a spell only three days ago that had saved her from the lubbock and *proved* that she could fly. She might be able to grab Twinkle round his waist and float down with him.

Here she realised that Twinkle was moving backwards away from her as she worked her way towards him. "Stop that!" she said. "Don't you know how dangerous this is?"

"Of *courthe* I do," Twinkle retorted. "Heighth thcare me thilly. But thith ith the only plathe where I can talk to you without anyone overhearing. Jutht get yourthelf to the middle of the roof where I don't have to thout. And be quick. Printheth Hilda hath hired a nurthemaid for Morgan and me. The wretched girl will be along any minute now."

This sounded so grown up that Charmain blinked and stared at him. Twinkle smiled blindingly back, all big blue eyes and enchanting rosy lips. "Are you an infant genius, or something?" she asked him.

"Well, I am now," Twinkle said. "When I wath *really* thix yearth old, I wath about average, I think. With a thtrong gift for magic, of courthe. Move along, can't you."

"I'm trying." Charmain set herself to shunting along the roof, until she was only a foot or so away from the child. "So what are we supposed to be talking about?" she snapped into his face.

"Withard Norland firtht," Twinkle said. "They tell me you know him."

"Not really," Charmain said. "He's my great-aunt-by-marriage's great uncle. I'm keeping house for him while he's ill." She did not feel like mentioning Peter.

"And what ith hith houthe like?" Twinkle asked. He added chattily, "I live in a moving cathtle mythelf. Doeth Norland'th houthe move?"

"No," said Charmain. "But there's a door in the middle that takes you to about a hundred different rooms. They say Wizard Melicot made it."

"Ah. Melicot," Twinkle piped. He seemed very pleased. "Then I'll probably need to come and thee it, whatever Calthifer thayth. Ith that all right?"

"I suppose so," Charmain said. "Why?"

"Becauthe," Twinkle explained, "Thophie, Calthifer, and I have been hired to find out what became of the gold in the King'th treathury. At leatht, we *fink* that'th what they're wanting, but they're not being very clear. Half the time, they theem to be thaying that what they've lotht ith thomething called the Elfgift and nobody knowth what thith Elfgift *ith*. And the Printheth hath athked Thophie to find out what keepth happening to the money from the taxeth. And that theemth to be thomething different again. They've thold a lot of pictureth and other thingth and they're thtill ath poor ath church mithe – you mutht have notithed."

Charmain nodded. "I noticed. Couldn't they ask for more taxes?"

"Or thell thome of their library," Twinkle suggested. He shrugged. This made him sway about so precariously that Charmain shut her eyes. "Calthifer nearly got ordered to leave latht night when he thuggethted thelling thome bookth. And ath for taxeth, the King thayth High Norland people are well off and contented, and any extra tax money would probably jutht dithappear too. Tho that'th no good. What I want you to do—"

There was a shout down in the distance. Charmain opened her eyes and looked sideways. Quite a number of people had gathered in the square, all shading their eyes and pointing to the roof. "Hurry up," she said. "They'll be calling out the fire brigade any minute now."

"Do they have one?" Twinkle asked. "There'th thivilithed you are here." He smiled another of his blazing smiles. "What we need you to do—"

"Are you two quite happy out here?" a voice asked close behind Charmain. It was so near and so sudden that Charmain jumped and all but overbalanced.

"Watch it, Thophie!" Twinkle said urgently. "You nearly had her off then."

"That just goes to show what a harebrained scheme this was, even for you," Sophie said. By the sound, she was leaning out of the wooden door, but Charmain did not dare turn round to look.

"Have you done the magic I gave you?" Twinkle asked, leaning sideways to talk round Charmain.

"Yes, I have," Sophie said. "Everyone's running around the Mansion fussing, Calcifer's trying to stop that silly nursemaid having hysterics, and someone outside has just called the firemen in. I managed to slip into the library with your spell in the confusion. Satisfied?"

"Perfectly." Twinkle gave another angelic smile. "You thee how cunning my plan wath now." He leaned towards Charmain. "What I've done," he said to her, "ith to catht a thpell that maketh every book or piethe of paper that hath the thlighteht bearing on the King'th problemth light up with a light that only you can thee. When you thpot a lighted one, I want you to make a note of which it ith and what it thayth. Thecretly, of courthe. Thomething'th definitely wrong here and we don't want anyone to know what you're doing, in cathe it getth to the perthon cauthing the trouble. Can you do that for uth?"

"I suppose so," said Charmain. It sounded easy enough, although she did not like the idea of keeping secrets from the King. "When do you want my notes?"

"Tonight, please, before that princely heir gets here," Sophie said from behind Charmain. "There's no need to get *him* mixed up in this. And we're very grateful and it truly is important. It's the reason why we're here. Now for goodness' sake come inside, both of you, before they start putting up ladders."

"All right," Twinkle piped. "Here we go. I may arrive in two halveth, mind you."

"Serve you right," said Sophie. The roof started to buck and ripple under Charmain. She nearly screamed. But she clung on with both hands, reminding herself that she really could fly. Couldn't she? And the roof jiggled and rippled her backwards towards the way she had come out, while in front of her Twinkle jiggled onwards too. In moments, Charmain felt Sophie take hold of her under her armpits and lug her backwards, with a bit of a scramble, inside the Royal Mansion again. Sophie then leaned out and seized Twinkle and dumped him down beside Charmain.

Twinkle looked soulfully up at Charmain. "Back to infanthy again," he said, sighing. "You won't give me away, will you?"

"Oh, cut out the nonsense," Sophie said. "Charmain's all right." She said to Charmain, "His name's Howl really and he's enjoying himself quite disgustingly much, having his second childhood. Come along, my little man." She swept Twinkle up under one arm and carried him away down the stairs. There was a lot of kicking and screaming.

Charmain followed them, shaking her head.

On the main landing halfway down, everyone in the Mansion seemed to be gathered – including a number of people Charmain had not seen before – with Calcifer bobbing this way and that among them. Even the King was there, carrying Waif in an absent-minded way. Princess Hilda pushed aside a fat young woman, who was holding Morgan and sobbing, and shook Charmain's hand.

"My dear Miss Charming, thank you so very much. We were in such a panic. Sim, go and tell the firemen we don't need the ladders and we *certainly* don't need the hoses."

Charmain could hardly hear her. Waif had seen Charmain and she promptly leaped from the King's arms, yapping with hysterical relief that Charmain was *safe*. From somewhere in the background Jamal's dog answered with mournful howlings. The fat nursemaid went "Sniff... hooh!" Morgan bellowed, "Oof! Oof!" and everyone else jabbered. In the distance, Twinkle was yelling, "I am *not* naughty! I wath vewwy fwightened, I tell you!"

Charmain cut down some of the noise by scooping Waif up. Princess Hilda silenced most of the rest by clapping her hands and saying, "Back to work, everyone.

Nancy, take Morgan away before he deafens us all and make it very clear to him that he is not going out on the roof too. Sophie, dear, can you shut Twinkle up?"

Everyone moved away. Twinkle went "I am not a naughty—" and then stopped as if a hand had been clapped across his mouth. In next to no time, Charmain found herself walking down the rest of the stairs with the King, on the way to the library, with Waif ecstatically trying to lick her chin.

"It takes me right back," the King remarked. "I got out on the roof several times when I was a boy. Never failed to cause a silly panic. Firemen nearly hosed me off once by mistake. Boys will be boys, my dear. Are you ready to get down to work, or will you want to sit and recover a bit?"

"No, I'm fine," Charmain assured him.

She felt completely at home today as she settled into her seat in the library, surrounded by the smell of old books, with Waif toasting her tummy at the brazier and the King sitting opposite investigating a ragged pile of old diaries. So peaceful was it that Charmain all but forgot about Twinkle's spell. She became immersed in peeling apart a damp pile of old letters. They were all from a long-ago prince who was breeding horses and wanted his mother to coax more money out of the King. The prince was just feelingly describing the beauties of the new foal his best mare had given birth to, when Charmain looked up to see the fire demon flickering slowly this way and that around the library.

The King looked up too. "Good morning, Calcifer," he said courteously. "Is there something you need?"

"Just exploring," Calcifer answered in his small crackling voice. "I understand now why you might not want to sell these books."

"Indeed," said the King. "Tell me, do fire demons read much?"

"Not generally," Calcifer replied. "Sophie reads to me quite often. I like the kind of story with puzzles in, where you have to guess who did the murder. Have you any of those in here?"

"Probably not," said the King. "But my daughter is partial to murder mysteries too. Perhaps you should ask her."

"Thank you. I will," Calcifer said, and vanished.

The King shook his head and went back to his diaries. And, as if Calcifer had given Twinkle's spell a jog, Charmain instantly noticed that the diary the King was flipping through was glowing a faint, pale green. So was the next thing in her own pile, which was a rather squashed scroll, done up with tarnished golden tape.

Charmain took a large breath and asked, "Anything interesting in that diary, Sire?"

"Well," said the King, "it's rather nasty really. This

is the diary of one of my great-grandmother's ladies-in-waiting. Full of gossip. Just now, she's dreadfully shocked because the King's sister died giving birth to a son and the midwife seems to have killed the baby. Said it was purple and it frightened her. They're going to put the poor silly soul on trial for murder."

Charmain's mind flew to herself and Peter looking up "lubbock" in Great Uncle William's encyclopedia. She said, "I suppose she thought the baby was a lubbockin."

"Yes, very superstitious and ignorant," the King said. "No one believes in lubbockins these days." He went back to reading.

Charmain wondered whether to say that that long-ago midwife may have been quite right. Lubbocks existed. Why not lubbockins too? But she was sure the King would not believe her and she scribbled a note about it instead. Then she picked up the squashed scroll. But before she unrolled it, it occurred to her to look along the row of boxes where she had put the papers she had already read, in case any of them glowed too. Only one did, quite faintly. When Charmain pulled it out, she found it was the bill from Wizard Melicot for making the roof look like gold. This was puzzling, but Charmain made a note about that too, before she finally undid the tarnished gold tape and spread the scroll out.

It was a family tree of the kings of High Norland, rather scribbly and hasty, as if it was only a plan for a much more careful copy. Charmain had trouble reading it. It was full of crossings out and little arrows leading to scribbled additions and lopsided circles with notes inside them. "Sire," she said, "can you explain this to me?"

"Let's see." The King took the scroll and spread it out on the table. "Ah," he said. "We've got the fair copy of this hanging in the throne room. I haven't properly looked at it for years, but I know it's much plainer than this family tree – just names of rulers and who they married and so on. This one seems to have notes on it, written by several different people by the looks of it. See. Here's my ancestor, Adolphus I. The note beside him is in really old writing. It says... hm... 'Raised walls to the towne by virtue of the Elfgift.' Not much sign of those walls nowadays, is there? But they say that Embankment Street down beside the river is part of the old walls—"

"Excuse me, Sire," Charmain interrupted, "but what is the Elfgift?"

"No idea, my dear," the King said. "I wish I knew. It was said to bring prosperity and protection to the kingdom, whatever it was, but it seems to have vanished long ago. Hmm. This is *fascinating*." The King ran his large finger across to one note after another. "Here, beside my ancestor's wife, it says, 'Was Elf-woman, so called.' They always told me that Queen Matilda was only half elf, but here is her son, Hans Nicholas, labelled as 'Elf childe' so maybe that's why he never got to be King. Nobody really trusts elves. Great mistake, in my opinion. They crowned Hans Nicholas's son instead, a very boring person called Adolphus II, who never did anything much. He's the one King on this scroll who doesn't have a note beside him. Tells you something. But *his* son – here he is – Hans Peter Adolphus, he has a note that says, 'Reaffirmed the safetie of the realm in partnership with the Elfgift', whatever that means. My dear, this is so interesting. Would you do me the favour of making a good readable copy of all these people's names and the notes beside them? You can miss out cousins and things if they don't have notes. Would you mind very much?"

"Not at all, Sire," Charmain said. She had been wondering how she could write all this down secretly for Sophie and Twinkle, and this was how.

She spent the rest of that day making two copies of the scroll. One was a muddly first draft, where she was constantly having to ask the King about this note or that one, and the second copy was in her best writing for the King himself. She became as interested as the King was. Why did Hans Peter III's nephew take to "banditry in the hills"? What made Queen Gertrude "a witche to be feared"? And why was her daughter Princess Isolla labelled "blueman lover"?

The King could not answer those questions, but he said he had a good idea why Prince Nicholas Adolphus was labelled "drunkarde". Had Charmain looked at where it said the prince's father, Peter Hans IV, was called "a dark tyrant and a wizarde besides"? "Some of my ancestors were not nice people," he said. "I bet this one bullied poor Nicholas horribly. They tell me it can be like that when elf blood goes sour, but I think it's just people, really."

Quite late in the day, when Charmain was down near the bottom of the scroll, where nearly every ruler seemed to be called Adolphus, or Adolphus Nicholas, or Ludovic Adolphus, she was fascinated to come upon a Princess Moina who "married a great Lorde of Strangia, but died giving birth to a loathesome lubbockin". Charmain was sure Moina was the one in the lady-in-waiting's diary. It looked as if *someone* had believed the midwife's story. She decided not to mention this to the King.

Three lines farther down she came upon the King himself, "much lost among his books", and Princess Hilda, "refused marriage with a kinge, 3 lordes and a wizard". They were rather squeezed to one side to make room for the descendants of the King's uncle, Nicholas Peter, who seemed to have had a great many children. The children's children filled the whole bottom row. *How on earth do they remember who is which?* Charmain wondered. Half the girls were called Matilda and the other half Isolla, while the boys were mostly Hans or Hans Adolphus. You could only tell them apart by the tiny scribbled notes, calling one Hans "a great lout, drowned" and another "murdered by accident" and yet another "died abroad". The girls were worse. One Matilda was "a tedious proude girl", another "to be feared like Q. Gertrude" and a third "of no good nature". The Isollas were all either "poisoned" or "of evil ways". The King's heir, Ludovic Nicholas, stood out from what Charmain began to think was a truly dreadful family, by having no note beside him at all, like the dull Adolphus of long ago.

She wrote it all out, names, notes and all. By the end of the afternoon, her right forefinger was quite numb and blue with ink.

"*Thank* you, my dear," the King said as Charmain handed him her good copy. He started reading through it so eagerly that Charmain was easily able to gather up her scribbly copy and her other notes and cram them into her pockets, without the King seeing. As she stood up, the King looked up to say, "I hope you will forgive me, my dear. I shall not be needing you for the next two days. The Princess insists that I come out of the library and play host to young Prince Ludovic this weekend. She is not at her best with male visitors, you know. But I shall see you again on Monday, I hope."

"Yes, of course," Charmain said. She collected Waif, who came pottering towards her from the kitchen, and set off towards the front door, wondering what to do with her copy of the scroll. She was not sure she trusted Twinkle. Could you trust someone who looked like a little boy and obviously wasn't quite? And then there's what Peter said Great Uncle William said about fire demons. Can you trust someone that dangerous? she thought unhappily as she went.

She found herself face to face with Sophie. "How did it go? Did you find anything?" Sophie asked, smiling at her.

It was such a friendly smile that Charmain decided she could trust Sophie anyway. She hoped. "I got some things," she said, pulling papers out of her pockets.

Sophie took them even more eagerly and gratefully than the King had taken his good copy. "Marvelous!" she said. "These should at least give us a clue. We're really in the dark at the moment. Howl – I mean, Twinkle – says divining spells just don't seem to work here. And that's odd, because I don't think either the King or the Princess do magic, do you? Enough to block a divining spell, I mean."

"No," Charmain said. "But a lot of their ancestors did. And there's more to the King than meets your eye."

"You're right," said Sophie. "Are you able to stay and go through these notes with us?"

"Ask me things on Monday," Charmain told her. "I have to go and see my father before his bakery closes."

# CHAPTER ELEVEN

### In which Charmain
### kneels on a cake

The shop was closed when Charmain reached it, but she could see, dimly through the glass, someone moving about inside, cleaning up. Charmain rapped on the door and, when that did no good, put her face to the glass and shouted, "*Let me in!*"

The person inside at length shuffled over and opened the door enough to put his face round it. He proved to be an apprentice about Peter's age whom Charmain had never met. "We're closed," he said. His eyes went to Waif in Charmain's arms. The open door had let out a gust of recent doughnut smells and Waif had her nose into it, sniffing rapturously. "And we don't allow dogs," he said.

"I need to see my father," Charmain said.

"You can't see anyone," the apprentice said. "The bake house is still busy."

"My father is Mr Baker," Charmain told him, "and I know he'll see me. Let me in."

"How do I know that's the truth?" the apprentice said suspiciously. "It's as much as my job's worth—"

Charmain knew this was the sort of time when she needed to be polite and tactful, but she ran out of patience, just as she had with the kobolds. "Oh, you silly boy!" she interrupted him. "If my father knew you weren't letting me in, he'd sack you on the spot! Go and fetch him if you don't believe me!"

"Hoity-toity!" said the apprentice. But he backed away from the door, saying, "Come in, then, but you leave the dog outside, understand?"

"No, I don't," Charmain said. "She might be stolen. She's a highly valuable magical dog, I'll have you know, and even the King lets her in. If he can, so can you."

The apprentice looked scornful. "Tell that to the lubbock on the hills," he said.

Things might have become very difficult then, if Belle, one of the ladies who served in the shop, had not come in through the bake house door just then. She was tying on her headscarf and saying, "I'm leaving now, Timmy. Mind you wash down all the—" when she saw Charmain. "Oh, hallo, Charmain! Want to see your dad, do you?"

"Hallo, Belle. Yes, I do," Charmain said. "But he won't let me bring Waif in."

Belle looked at Waif. Her face melted into a smile. "What a sweet little creature! But you know what your dad thinks of dogs coming in here. Better leave her in the shop for Timmy to look after. You'll take care of her, won't you, Timmy?"

The apprentice made a grudging noise and glowered at Charmain.

"But I warn you, Charmain," Belle continued in her usual chatty way, "they're very busy through there. There's an order on for a special cake. So you won't stay long, will you? Put your little dog down here and she'll be quite safe. And, Timmy, I want those shelves cleaned down properly this time, or I'll have words to say to you tomorrow. Ta-ra, night-night!"

Belle swept out of the shop and Charmain swept past her into it. Charmain did have thoughts of sweeping onwards into the bake house with Waif, but she knew Waif's record with food was not good. So she deposited Waif beside the counter, gave Timmy a cold nod – And he'll hate me for the rest of his life, she thought – and stalked on alone past the empty glass cases and the cool marble shelves and the clusters of white tables and chairs, where the citizens of High Norland were accustomed to sit for coffee and rich cakes. Waif gave a desperate whine as Charmain pushed open the bake house door, but Charmain hardened her heart and pushed the door shut behind herself.

It was busy as a hive in there and tropically hot, and full of scents that would certainly have driven Waif mad with greed. There was the smell of new dough and dough cooking, the sweet scent of buns and tarts and waffles, overlaid with savoury smells from pasties and quiches, which were all overlaid in turn by strong odours of cream and flavoured icing from the large, many-layered cake that several people were decorating on the table nearest the door. Rosewater! Charmain thought, inhaling those scents. Lemon, strawberry, almonds from south Ingary, cherries and peaches!

Mr Baker was striding from worker to worker, instructing, encouraging and inspecting as he went. "Jake, you have to put your back into kneading that dough," Charmain heard him saying as she came in. And a moment later, "A light hand with that pastry, Nancy. Don't *hammer* it or it'll be like a rock." A moment after that, he was off down to the baking ovens at the other end, telling the young man there which oven to use. And wherever he went, he got instant attention and obedience.

Her father, Charmain knew, was a king in his bake house – more of a king than the real King in the Royal Mansion, she thought. His white hat sat on his head like a crown. It suited him too, Charmain thought. He was thin-faced and ginger haired like she was herself, though much more freckly.

She ran him down by the stoves, where he was tasting a savoury meat filling and telling the girl making it that there was too much spice in it.

"It tastes *good*, though!" the girl protested.

"Maybe," said Mr Baker, "but there's a world of difference between a good taste and a perfect one, Lorna. You cut along and help them with the cake or they'll be at it all night, and I'll have a go rescuing this filling." He took the saucepan off the flames as Lorna hurried off, looking mightily relieved. He turned round with it and saw Charmain. "Hallo, sweetheart! I wasn't expecting *you*!" A slight doubt came over him. "Did your mother send you?"

"No," Charmain said. "I came by myself. I'm looking after Great Uncle William's house. Remember?"

"Oh, so you are," her father said. "What can I do for you?"

"Er…" Charmain said. This was hard to say now that she had been reminded what an expert her father was.

He said, "Just a moment," and turned to search

through rows of powdered herbs and spices on a shelf beside the stoves. He selected a jar, uncapped it and shook just a sprinkle of something into the saucepan. He stirred the mixture, tasted it and nodded. "That'll do now," he said, putting the saucepan down to cool. Then he looked questioningly at Charmain.

"I don't know how to cook, Dad," she blurted out, "and the food for the evening comes raw in Great Uncle William's house. You don't happen to have any instructions written down, do you? For apprentices or something?"

Mr Baker pulled at his freckly chin with his clean, clean hand, thinking. "I always told your mother you'd need to know some of those things," he said. "Respectable or not. Let's see. Most of what I've got will be a bit advanced for you. Patisserie and gourmet sauces and such. I expect my apprentices to come to me knowing the basics, these days. But I think I still may have some of the elementary, *simple* notes from back when I started. Let's go and see, shall we?"

He led the way across the bake house, among the thronging, busy cooks, to the far wall. There were a few rickety shelves there, piled higgledy-piggledy with notebooks, pieces of paper with jam stains on them and fat files covered with floury fingerprints. "Wait a moment," Mr Baker said, pausing by the leftovers table beside these shelves. "I'd better give you some food to go on with, while you're reading up on it, hadn't I?"

Charmain knew this table well. Waif would have loved it. On it were any pieces of baking that had not turned out quite perfect: broken tarts, lopsided buns and cracked pasties, together with all the things from the shop that had not been sold that day. The bake house workers were allowed to carry these home if they wanted. Mr Baker picked up one of the sacking bags the workers used and began swiftly filling it. A whole cream cake went in at the bottom, followed by a layer of pasties, then buns, doughnuts and finally a large cheese flan. He left the bulging bag on the table while he searched about on the shelves.

"Here we are," he said, pulling forth a floppy brown notebook, dark with old grease. "I *thought* I still had it! This was from when I started as a lad in the restaurant on Market Place. I was as ignorant as you are then, so it should be just what you need. Do you want the spells that go with the recipes?"

"*Spells!*" said Charmain. "But, Dad—!"

Mr Baker looked as guilty as Charmain had ever seen him. His freckles for a moment were drowned in redness. "I know, I know, Charmain. Your mother would have seventy fits. She will insist that magic is low, vulgar stuff. But I was born a magic user and I can't help myself, not when I'm cooking. We use magic all the time, here in the bake house. Be a good, kind girl and don't let your mother know. Please?" He pulled a thin yellow notebook off the shelves and flapped it wistfully. "These, in here, are all plain, simple spells that work. Do you want this?"

"Yes, *please*!" Charmain said. "And of course I won't say a word to Mother. I know what she's like as well as you do."

"Good girl!" said Mr Baker. He swiftly slid both notebooks down into the bag beside the cheese flan and passed Charmain the bag. They grinned at one another like conspirators. "Happy eating," Mr Baker said. "Good luck."

"You too," Charmain said. "And thank you, Dad!" She stretched up and kissed him on his floury, freckled cheek, just below the cook's hat, and then made her way out of the bake house.

"You lucky thing!" Lorna called out to her while Charmain was pushing open the door. "I had my eye on that cream cake he gave you."

"There were two of them," Charmain called over her shoulder, as she went through into the shop. There, to her surprise, she found Timmy sitting on the glass-and-marble counter with Waif in his arms. He explained, rather defensively, "She was really upset when you left her. Started howling her head off."

Perhaps we won't be lifelong enemies after all! Charmain thought, as Waif leaped out of Timmy's arms, shrieking with delight. She danced about Charmain's ankles and generally made such a noise that Timmy evidently did not hear Charmain thank him. Charmain made sure to give a great smile and to nod at him as she went out into the street, with Waif frisking and squeaking round her feet.

The shop and bake house were on the other side of the town from the river and the embankment. Charmain could have cut across to there, but it was shorter – with Waif having to walk, because Charmain was carrying the bulging bag – to go along High Street instead. High Street, although it was one of the main streets, was far from seeming that way. It was twisting and narrow, with no sidewalks, but the shops on either side were some of the best. Charmain walked slowly along, looking into shops to give Waif time to keep up, dodging late shoppers and people just strolling before supper, and thinking. Her thoughts were divided between satisfaction – Peter has no excuse now for making any more horrible food – and amazement. Dad is a *magic user*! He always has been. Up until then, Charmain had felt a lot of hidden guilt at the way she had experimented with *The Boke of Palimpsest*, but she found that had gone now. I think I may have inherited

Dad's magic! Oh, *great*! Then I know I *can* do spells. But why does Dad always do what Mother says? He insists on me being respectable as much as Mother does. Honestly, *parents*! Charmain found she was feeling very jolly altogether about this.

At this point there was a tremendous clatter of horse hooves coming up behind her, mixed with rumbling and deep shouts of "Clear the way! Clear the way!"

Charmain glanced round and found riders in some kind of uniform filling the street, coming so fast that they were almost on top of her already. People on foot were flattening themselves against shops and walls on either side of the street. Charmain whirled round, reaching for Waif. She tripped over someone's doorstep and half-knelt on the bag of food, but she got Waif and managed not to drop the bag. Holding Waif and the bag in both arms, she backed against the nearest wall, while horses' legs and men's feet in stirrups pounded past in front of her nose. Those were followed by a whole string more of galloping horses, shining black ones in long leather traces and a whip cracking across their backs. After them a great colourful coach thundered by, glinting with gold and glass and painted shields, with two men in feathered hats swaying on the back of it. This was followed by yet more uniforms on horses, galloping deafeningly.

Then they were gone, away down the street and round the next bend. Waif whimpered. Charmain sagged against the wall. "What on earth was *that*?" she said to the person flattened against the wall beside her.

"That," said the woman, "was Crown Prince Ludovic. On his way to visit the King, I suppose." She was a fair and slightly fierce-looking lady, who reminded Charmain just a little of Sophie Pendragon. She was clutching a small boy, who might have reminded Charmain of Morgan, except that he was not making any noise at all. He looked to be shocked white, rather the way Charmain felt herself.

"He ought to know better than to go that fast in a narrow street like this!" Charmain said angrily. "Someone could have been hurt!" She looked into her bag and discovered that the flan had broken in half and folded up, which made her angrier than ever. "Why couldn't he have gone down the embankment, where it's wide?" she said. "Doesn't he care?"

"Not a lot," said the woman.

"Then I shudder to think what he'll be like when he's King!" Charmain said. "He's going to be *dreadful*!"

The woman gave her a strange, meaningful stare. "I didn't hear you say that," she said.

"Why?" asked Charmain.

"Ludovic doesn't like criticism," the woman said. "He

has lubbockins to enforce his feelings. *Lubbockins*, you hear, girl! Let's hope I was the only one who heard what you said." She heaved the little boy higher in her arms and walked away.

Charmain thought about this as she trudged through the town with Waif under one arm and the bag pulling at the other. She found herself hoping hard that her King, Adolphus X, would go on living for a very long time. Or I might have to start a revolution, she thought. And, my goodness, it feels a long way to Great Uncle William's house today!

She got there in the end, however, and put Waif down thankfully on the garden path. Indoors, Peter was in the kitchen, sitting on one of the ten bags of laundry, staring moodily at a big red slab of meat on the table. Beside it were three onions and two carrots.

"I don't know how to cook these," he said.

"You don't have to," Charmain said, dumping her bag on the table. "I went to see my father this evening. And here," she added, fishing out the two notebooks, "are recipes and the spells that go with them." Both notebooks were rather the worse for flan. Charmain wiped them on her skirt and handed them over.

Peter brightened up wonderfully and jumped off the laundry bag. "That's really useful!" he said. "And a bag of food is better."

Charmain unpacked bent flan, broken pasties and squashed buns. The cream cake at the bottom had a knee-shaped dent in it and it had oozed into some of the pasties. This made her angry with Prince Ludovic all over again. She told Peter all about it while she tried to reassemble the pasties.

"Yes, my mother says he's got the makings of a real tyrant," Peter said, a little absently because he was flipping through the notebooks. "She says that's why she left this country. Do I do these spells while I cook the food, or before, or after, do you know?"

"Dad didn't say. You'll have to work it out," Charmain said and went away to Great Uncle William's study to find a soothing book to read. *The Twelve-Branched Wand* was interesting, but it made her feel as though her mind had broken into a hundred little pieces. Each branch of the Wand had twelve more branches growing out of it, and twelve more from each of those. Much more and I'd turn into a tree, Charmain thought as she searched the shelves. She chose a book called *The Magician's Journey*, which she hoped would be an adventure story. And it was, in a way, but she very soon realised that it was also a step-by-step account of how a magician learned his skills.

This set her thinking again of how Dad had turned out to be a magic user. And I *know* I've inherited it, she thought. I learned to fly and I mended the pipes in the bathroom, all in no time. But I ought to learn how to do it smoothly and quietly, instead of shouting and bullying things. She was still sitting, pondering this, when Peter yelled to her to come and eat.

"I used the spells," he said. He was very proud of himself. He had warmed up the pasties and made a truly tasty mixture of the onions and carrots. "And," he added, "I was quite tired after a day of exploring."

"Looking for gold?" Charmain said.

"It's the natural thing to do," Peter said. "We know it's somewhere in this house. But what I found instead was the place where the kobolds live. It's like a huge cave and they were all in there making things. Cuckoo clocks mostly, but some of them were making teapots, and some more were making something like a sofa near the entrance. I didn't speak to them – I didn't know if they were in the past or nowadays, so I just smiled and watched. I didn't want them angry again. What did you do today?"

"Oh, goodness!" Charmain said. "It was quite a day. It started with Twinkle out on the roof. I was so scared!" And she told him all the rest.

Peter frowned. "This Twinkle," he said, "and this Sophie – are you quite sure they're not up to something sinister? Wizard Norland said fire demons were dangerous beings, you know."

"I did wonder," Charmain admitted. "But I think

they're all right. It looks as if Princess Hilda has called them in to help. I wish I knew how to find what the King is looking for. He got so excited when I found that family tree. Did you know that Prince Ludovic has eight second cousins, mostly called Hans and Isolla, and nearly all of them have met with sticky ends?"

"Because they were all bad lots," Peter said. "My mother says that Hans the cruel was poisoned by Isolla the murderess, and she was killed by Hans the drunkard when he was drunk. Then that Hans fell downstairs and broke his neck. His sister Isolla was hanged over in Strangia for trying to kill the lord she married there... How many am I up to?"

"Five," said Charmain, quite fascinated. "Three to go."

"Those are two Matildas and another Hans," Peter said. "Hans Nicholas, that one was, and I don't know how he died, except that he was somewhere abroad when he did. One of the Matildas was burned when her manor house caught fire, and they say the other one is such a dangerous witch that Prince Ludovic has her shut up in an attic in Castel Joie. Nobody dares go near her, not even Prince Ludovic. She kills people just by looking at them. Is it all right that I gave Waif that lump of meat?"

"Probably," said Charmain. "If she didn't choke. How do you know all about these cousins? I'd never heard of them before today."

"That's because I come from Montalbino," Peter said. "Everyone at my school knows all about the Nine Bad Cousins of High Norland. But I suppose that in this country neither the King nor Prince Ludovic want it to get about that their relatives were so vile. They say Prince Ludovic is as bad as the rest too."

"And we're such a *nice* country, really!" Charmain protested. She felt quite hurt that her own High Norland should have given birth to nine such awful people. It seemed hard on the King, as well.

# CHAPTER TWELVE

### Concerns laundry and
### lubbock eggs

Charmain woke early the following day, because Waif stuck her small cold nose into Charmain's ear, obviously thinking they needed to go to the Royal Mansion as usual.

"No, I *don't* need to go!" Charmain said crossly. "The King has to look after Prince Ludovic today. Go away, Waif, or I may turn into an Isolla and poison you! Or a Matilda and do evil magic at you. Just go!"

Waif pattered sadly away, but Charmain was awake by then. Before long she got up, soothing her crossness by promising herself that she would spend a fine, lazy day reading *The Magician's Journey*.

Peter was up too and he had other ideas. "We're going to do some of this laundry today," he said. "Have you noticed that there are ten bags of it in here now and ten more in Wizard Norland's bedroom? I think there may be ten in the pantry as well."

Charmain glowered at the laundry bags. She could not deny that they filled the kitchen up rather.

"Let's not bother," she said. "It must be those kobolds doing it."

"No, it isn't," Peter said. "My mother says that laundry breeds if you don't wash it."

"We have a washerwoman," Charmain said. "I don't know how to wash things."

"I'll show you how," Peter said. "Stop hiding behind your ignorance."

Angrily wondering how it was that Peter always managed to set her to work, Charmain shortly found herself pumping hard at the pump in the yard, filling buckets with water for Peter to carry to the wash house and empty into the great copper boiler. After about the tenth bucketful, Peter came back, saying, "We need to light the fire under the copper now, but I can't find any fuel. Where do you think he keeps it?"

Charmain wiped sweaty hair back from her face with an

exhausted hand. "It must work like the kitchen fire," she said. "I'll go and see." She led the way to the shed, thinking, And if this doesn't work, we can stop trying. Good. "We need just one thing that will burn," she told Peter.

He looked blankly round. Inside the shed there was nothing but a stack of wooden tubs and a box of soapflakes. Charmain eyed the place at the bottom of the boiler. It was black with old fires. She eyed the tubs. Too big. She eyed the soapflakes and decided not to risk another storm of bubbles. She went outside and plucked a twig from the unhealthy tree. Shoving this into the blackened fireplace, she slapped the side of the boiler and said, "Fire!" And had to leap quickly backwards as flames thundered into being underneath. "There," she said to Peter.

"Good," he said. "Back to the pump. We need the copper full now."

"*Why?*" said Charmain.

"Because there's thirty sacks of washing, of course," Peter said. "We'll need to run hot water into some of these tubs to soak the silks and do the woollens in. And then we'll need water for rinsing. Buckets and buckets more."

"I don't *believe* this!" Charmain muttered to Waif, who was pottering about watching. She sighed and went back to pumping.

Meanwhile, Peter fetched out a kitchen chair and put

it in the shed. Then, to Charmain's indignation, he set out the tubs in a row and began pouring bucketfuls of her hard-worked-for cold water into them. "I thought those were for the copper!" she protested.

Peter climbed on the chair and began hurling handfuls of soapflakes into the top of the boiler. It was now steaming and making simmering noises. "Stop arguing and keep pumping," he said. "It's nearly hot enough for the whites now. Four more buckets should do it, and then you can start putting shirts and things in."

He climbed off the chair and went away into the house. When he came back, he was lugging two of the laundry bags, which he left propped against the shed while he went back for more. Charmain pumped and panted and glowered and climbed on the chair to pour her four full buckets into the soapy clouds of steam rising from the copper. Then, glad to be doing something else, she untied the strings that held the first laundry bag closed. There were socks inside, and a red wizardly robe, two pairs of trousers, and shirts and underclothes below that, all smelling of mildew from Peter's bathroom flood. Oddly enough, when Charmain untied the second bag, there were the same, identical things inside it.

"Wizard's washing was bound to be peculiar," Charmain said. She took armfuls of the washing, climbed on the chair, and heaved the clothes into the copper.

"No, no, no! *Stop!*" Peter shouted, just as Charmain had emptied the second bagful in. He came rushing across the grass, towing eight more bags all tied together.

"But you *said* to do it!" Charmain protested.

"Not before we've sorted it out, you fool!" Peter said. "You only boil the *white* things!"

"I didn't know," Charmain said sullenly.

She spent the rest of the morning sorting laundry into heaps on the grass, while Peter hurled shirts in to boil and ran off soapy water into tubs to soak robes and socks and twenty pairs of wizardly trousers in.

At length he said, "I think the shirts have boiled enough," and pulled forward a swilling tub of cold water. "You put the fire out while I run the hot water off."

Charmain had not the least idea how you put a magical fire out. Experimentally, she slapped the side of the copper. It burned her hand. She said, "*Ow!* Fire, go *out!*" in a sort of scream. And the fire obediently flickered down and disappeared. She sucked her fingers and watched Peter open the tap at the bottom of the copper and send steaming pink suds gushing away down the drain. Charmain peered through the steam as the tap ran.

"I didn't know the soap was pink," she said.

"It wasn't," Peter said. "Oh, my heavens! Look what you've done *now!*" He leaped up on the chair and began heaving out steaming shirts with the forked stick meant for the purpose. Every one of them, as it splashed into the cold water, turned out to be bright cherry pink. After the shirts, he forked out fifteen tiny shrunken socks, all of which would have been too small for Morgan, and a baby-sized pair of wizardly trousers. Finally, he fished up a very small red robe and held it out accusingly, dripping and steaming, for Charmain to see. "That's what you did," he said. "You *never* put red wool in with white shirts. The dye runs. *And* it's turned out almost too small for a kobold. You *are* an utter fool!"

"How was I to know?" Charmain demanded passionately. "I've lived a sheltered life! Mother never lets me go near our wash house."

"Because it's not respectable. I know," Peter said disgustedly. "I suppose you think I should be sorry for you! Well, I'm not. I'm not going to trust you anywhere near the mangle. The lord knows what you'd do with that! I'm going to try a bleaching spell while I do the mangling. *You* go and get the clothesline and that tub of clothes pegs from the pantry and hang everything up to dry. Can I trust you not to hang yourself or something while you do that?"

"I'm not a fool," Charmain said haughtily.

An hour or so later, when Peter and Charmain, both weary and damp with steam, were soberly chewing yesterday's leftover pasties in the kitchen, Charmain could not help thinking that her efforts with the clothesline were rather more successful than Peter's with the mangle and the bleaching spell. The clothesline zigzagged ten times back and forth across the yard. But it stayed up. The shirts now flapping from the pegs on it were not white. Some were streaked with red. Some had curious pink curlicues all over them and some others were a delicate blue. Most of the robes had white stripes on them somewhere. The socks and the trousers were all creamy white. Charmain thought it very tactful of her that she did not point out to Peter that the elf, who was ducking and dodging among the zigzags of washing, was staring at it in grave amazement.

"There's an *elf* out there!" Peter exclaimed with his mouth full.

Charmain swallowed the rest of her pasty and opened the back door to see what the elf wanted. The elf bent his tall fair head under the doorway and stalked into the middle of the kitchen, where he put the glass box he was carrying down on the table. Inside the box were three roundish white things about the size of tennis balls. Peter and Charmain stared at them and then at the elf, who simply stood there without speaking.

"What are these?" Peter said at length.

The elf bowed, very slightly. "These," he said, "are the

three lubbock eggs that we have removed from the wizard William Norland. It was a very difficult operation, but we have performed it successfully."

"*Lubbock eggs!*" Peter and Charmain exclaimed, almost together. Charmain felt her face draining white and very much wished she had not eaten that pasty. All Peter's freckles showed up brown in his white face. Waif, who had been begging for lunch under the table, set up a frantic whining.

"Why... why have you brought the eggs here?" Charmain managed to say.

The elf said calmly, "Because we have found it impossible to destroy them. They defeat all our efforts, magical and physical. We have finally concluded that only a fire demon is capable of destroying them. Wizard Norland informs us that Miss Charming will by now have contact with a fire demon."

"Wizard Norland's *alive*? He's talking to you?" Peter said eagerly.

"Indeed," said the elf. "He is recovering well and should be ready to return here in three or four days at the most."

"Oh, I'm so glad!" Charmain said. "So it was lubbock eggs making him ill?"

"That is so," the elf agreed. "It seems that the wizard encountered a lubbock some months ago while walking in a mountain meadow. The fact that he is a wizard has caused the eggs to absorb his magic and become nearly impossible to destroy. You are warned not to touch the eggs or attempt to open this box that they are in. They are extremely dangerous. You are advised to obtain the services of the fire demon as soon as possible."

While Peter and Charmain gulped and stared at those three white eggs in their box, the elf gave another small bow and stalked away through the inner door. Peter pulled himself together and ran after him, shouting to know more. But he arrived in the living room to see the front door slamming shut. When he, followed by Charmain, followed by Waif, rushed out into the front garden, there was no sign of the elf at all. Charmain caught sight of Rollo peering slyly round the stalks of a hydrangea, but the elf was gone completely.

She picked up Waif and planted her in Peter's arms. "Peter," she said, "keep Waif *here*. I'll go and get Calcifer at once." And she set off at a run down the garden path.

"Be quick!" Peter shouted after her. "Be *very* quick!"

Charmain did not need Peter to tell her that. She ran, followed by Waif's despairing and squeaky howls, and ran, and went on running, until she had rounded the great cliff and could see the town ahead. There she had to drop to a hasty walk and clutch at the stitch in her side, but she kept on as fast as she could. The thought of those round white eggs sitting on the kitchen table was enough to make her break into a trot as soon as her breath came back. Suppose the eggs hatched before she had found Calcifer. Suppose Peter did something stupid, like trying to put a spell on them. Suppose— She tried to take her mind off all the other awful possibilities by panting to herself, "I am *so* stupid! I could have asked that elf what the Elfgift was! But I clean forgot. I *should* have remembered. I'm *stupid*!" But her heart was not really in it. All she could see in her mind was Peter mumbling spells over the glass box. It would be just like him to try.

It came on to pour with rain as she entered the town. Charmain was pleased. That should take Peter's mind off the lubbock eggs. He would have to rush outside and bring the washing in before it got soaked again. Just so long as he hadn't done something stupid before that!

She arrived at the Royal Mansion soaked through and almost out of breath entirely, where she clattered at the knocker and rang the bell even more frantically than she had when Twinkle was on the roof. It seemed an age before Sim opened the door.

"Oh, Sim," she gasped. "I need to see Calcifer at once! Can you tell me where he is?"

"Certainly, miss," Sim replied, not in the least put

out by Charmain's soaking hair and dripping clothes. "Sir Calcifer is presently in the Grand Lounge. Allow me to show you the way."

He shut the door and shuffled off, and Charmain dripped her way after him, down the long damp hallway, past the stone staircase, to a grand doorway somewhere near the back of the Mansion, where Charmain had never been before.

"In here, miss," he said, throwing the grand but shabby door open.

Charmain went in, to a roar of voices and a crowd of finely dressed people, who all seemed to be shouting at one another while they walked about eating cake off elegant little plates. The cake was the first thing she recognised. It stood grandly on a special table in the middle of the room. Although only half of it was there by now, it was definitely the same cake that her father's cooks had been working on yesterday evening. It was like seeing an old friend among all these finely dressed strangers. The nearest man, who was dressed in midnight blue velvet and dark blue brocade, turned and stared haughtily at Charmain and then exchanged disgusted looks with the lady beside him. This lady was wearing – not exactly a ball dress, not at *teatime*! Charmain thought – silks and satins so sumptuous that she would have made Aunt Sempronia look shabby, had Aunt Sempronia been there. Aunt Sempronia was not there, but the Lord Mayor was, and so was his lady, and so were all the most important people in town.

"Sim," asked the man in midnight blue, "just who *is* this wet little commoner?"

"Lady Charming," Sim replied, "is the new assistant to His Majesty, Your Highness." He turned to Charmain. "Allow me to present you to His Highness, Crown Prince Ludovic, my lady." He stepped backwards and shut himself outside the room.

Charmain felt that the floor would be doing her a favour if it opened under her soaking wet feet and dropped her into the cellars. She had clean forgotten the visit of Crown Prince Ludovic. Princess Hilda had obviously invited all the Best People of High Norland to meet the prince. And she, ordinary Charmain Baker, had gate-crashed the tea party.

"Pleased to meet you, Your Highness," she tried to say. It came out as frightened whisper. Prince Ludovic probably did not hear. He laughed and said, "Is Lady Charming some kind of nickname the King calls you, little girl?" He pointed with his cake fork at the lady in not-quite-evening-dress. "I call my assistant Lady Moneybags. She costs me a fortune, you see."

Charmain opened her mouth to explain what her name really was, but the lady in not-quite-evening-dress got in first. "You'd no call to say that!" she said angrily. "You spiteful thing, you!"

Prince Ludovic laughed and turned away to talk to the colourless gentleman, who was approaching in a colourless grey silk outfit. Charmain would have tiptoed away at once to find Calcifer, except that, as the Prince turned, the light from the big chandelier overhead caught him in side face. The eye she could see glowed deep purple.

Charmain stood like a cold statue of horror. Prince Ludovic was a lubbockin. For a moment she could not move, knowing she was showing her horror, knowing that people would see how horrified she was and wonder why. The colourless gentleman was already looking at her, with curiosity in his mild mauve eyes. Oh, heavens! *He* was a lubbockin too. That was what had worried her before, when she met him near the kitchens.

Fortunately, the Lord Mayor moved away from beside the cake table just then, to bow deeply to the King, and gave Charmain a glimpse of a rocking horse – no, there were *many* rocking horses, Charmain saw. It quite distracted her from her horror. For some reason, rocking horses were lined up all round the walls of the grand room. Twinkle was sitting on the one nearest to the large marble fireplace, staring at her earnestly. Charmain could tell he knew she had had a shock of some kind and wanted her to tell him what had caused it.

She began edging her way across to the fireplace. This gave her a sight of Morgan, sitting by the marble fender playing with a box of bricks. Sophie was standing over him. In spite of Sophie's peacock blue dress and her air of being part of the tea party, Charmain had a moment when she saw Sophie as a very large lioness with its teeth bared, standing guard on its small lion cub.

"Oh, hallo, Charming," Princess Hilda said, more or less in Charmain's ear. "Would you like some cake, since you're here?"

Charmain shot a regretful look at the cake and inhaled its luscious smell instead. "No thank you, ma'am," she said. "I only came with a message for… er… Mrs Pendragon, you see." Where was Calcifer?

"Well, there she is, just over there," Princess Hilda said, pointing. "I must say the children are behaving beautifully at the moment. Long may it last!"

She swished away to offer another finely dressed person some cake. For all its swishing, her dress was nothing like as fine as the others in the room. It was faded almost white in places and reminded Charmain rather of the laundry after Peter had worked his bleaching spell. Oh, *please* don't let Peter try any spells on those lubbock eggs! Charmain prayed as she walked over to Sophie.

"Hallo," Sophie said, smiling rather tensely. Beyond her, Twinkle was rocking on the rocking horse, going *creak-creak-creeak*, quite irritatingly. The fat nursemaid was standing beside him going, "Master Twinkle, pray *do* get down from there. You're making such a noise, Master Twinkle. Master Twinkle, I don't want to have to tell you twice!" Over and over. This was probably even more irritating.

Sophie knelt down and passed Morgan a red brick. Morgan held the brick out towards Charmain. "Boo bick," he told her.

Charmain knelt down too. "No, it isn't blue," she said. "Try again."

Sophie murmured out of the side of her mouth, "Glad to see you. I don't care for this Prince at all, do you? Nor for that overdressed floozie with him."

"Urple?" Morgan guessed, holding the brick out again.

"I don't blame you," Charmain whispered to Sophie. "No, it's not purple, it's red. But the Prince is purple, or his eyes are. He's a lubbockin."

"A *what*?" Sophie said, puzzled.

"Dead?" asked Morgan, looking at his brick disbelievingly. *Creak-creeak*, went the rocking horse.

"Yes. Red," said Charmain. "I can't explain here. Tell me where Calcifer is – I'll explain to him and he can tell you. I need Calcifer urgently."

"Here I am," Calcifer said. "What *do* you need me for?"

Charmain looked round. Calcifer was roosting among the flaming logs in the fireplace, mingling his blue flames with the orange ones from the logs and looking so peaceful that Charmain had quite failed to notice him until he spoke. "Oh, thank goodness!" she said. "Can you come with me *at once* to Wizard Norland's house? We've got an emergency there that only a fire demon can deal with. Please!"

# Chapter Thirteen

### In which Calcifer
### is very active

Calcifer's orange eyes turned to Sophie. "Do you need me to keep guard here still?" he asked her. "Or can you manage with just the two of you?"

Sophie gazed worriedly out at the well-dressed, chattering crowd. "I don't *think* anyone's going to try anything just now," she said. "But come back quickly. I have a horrible foreboding feeling. I don't trust that mauve-eyed fellow an inch. Or that nasty Prince either."

"All right. Quick it is," Calcifer crackled. "Stand up, young Charming. I'm going to sit on your hands."

Charmain got to her feet, expecting to be burned – or at least singed – any moment. Morgan objected to her going by waving a yellow brick at her and raising a booming shout of "Geen, geen, *geen!*"

"Shush!" Sophie and Twinkle said together, and the fat nursemaid added, "Master Morgan, we don't shout, not here in front of the King."

"It's yellow," Charmain said, waiting for all the staring faces to turn away. She was beginning to see that none of the fine guests knew that Calcifer was part of the fire and that Calcifer wanted to keep it that way.

As soon as everyone lost interest and turned back to their chatter, Calcifer hopped up out of the fire and landed just slightly above Charmain's nervous fingers in the exact likeness of a plate of cake. He did not hurt a bit. In fact, Charmain could scarcely feel him.

"Clever," she said.

"Pretend to hold me," Calcifer replied, "and walk out of the room with me."

Charmain curled her fingers round the false plate and walked towards the door. Prince Ludovic, to her relief, had moved away, but the King was coming towards her instead. He nodded and smiled at Charmain.

"Got yourself some cake, I see," he said. "Good, isn't it? Wish I knew why we have all these rocking horses. Don't happen to know, do you?"

Charmain shook her head and the King turned away, still smiling. "Why do we?" Charmain asked. "Have all these rocking horses?"

"Protection," said the plate of cake. "Open the door and let's get out of here."

Charmain took one hand from the false plate, opened the door and slipped out into the damp, echoing hallway. "But who's being protected from what?" she asked, closing the door as quietly as possible.

"Morgan," said the plate of cake. "Sophie got an anonymous note this morning. It said, 'Stop your investigation and leave High Norland, or your child suffers.' But we can't leave, because Sophie's promised the Princess she'll stay until we find out where all the money's gone. Tomorrow we're going to pretend to go—"

Calcifer was interrupted by shrill barking. Waif came dashing round the corner and hurled herself delightedly on to Charmain's ankles. Calcifer jumped and floated free in his own shape, as a fiery blue teardrop hovering by Charmain's shoulder. Charmain scooped Waif up. "How did you—?" she began, trying to keep her face out of the way of Waif's eager tongue. Then she realised that Waif was not in the least wet. "Oh, Calcifer, she must have come the quick way through the house! Can you find me the Conference Room? I can get us back from there."

"Easy." Calcifer darted off like a blue comet, so fast that Charmain had trouble keeping up. He whirled round several corners and into the corridor where the kitchen smells were. In next to no time, Charmain was standing with her back to the door of the Conference Room with Waif in her arms and Calcifer floating by her shoulder, while she tried to remember just what you did from here. Calcifer said, "It's like *this*," and zigzagged away in front of her. Charmain followed as best she could and found herself in the corridor where the bedrooms were. Sunlight was blazing in the window beyond Great Uncle William's study. Peter came dashing towards them, looking pale and urgent.

"Oh, good dog, Waif!" he said. "I sent her to fetch you. Just come and take a look at *this*!"

He turned and galloped back to the other end of the corridor, where he pointed rather shakily at the view out of the window.

Out in the mountain meadow, the rain was just passing away in big, melting, dark grey clouds that were obviously still raining below on the town. A rainbow arched across the mountains, lurid in front of the clouds and pale and misty across the meadow. The meadow grass blazed and twinkled so with sunlit wetness, that Charmain was dazzled for a moment and could not see what Peter was pointing at.

"That's the lubbock," Peter said, rather hoarsely. "Right?"

The lubbock was there, towering huge and purple in the middle of the meadow. It was bending slightly to listen to a kobold, who was hopping up and down, pointing at the rainbow and evidently shouting at the lubbock.

"That's the lubbock, all right," Charmain said, shivering. "And that's Rollo."

As she said it, the lubbock laughed and rolled its bundles of insect eyes towards the rainbow. It stepped carefully backwards until the misty rainbow stripes seemed to be right beside its insect feet. There it bent and dragged a small earthenware pot out of the turf. Rollo capered about.

"That must be the crock of gold at the end of the rainbow!" Peter said wonderingly.

They watched the lubbock pass the pot to Rollo, who took it in both arms. It was evidently heavy. Rollo stopped capering and staggered about with his head thrown back in greedy joy. He turned to stagger away. He did not see the lubbock slyly extend its long purple proboscis behind him. He did not seem to notice when the proboscis stabbed into his back. He just sank away into the meadow grass, still clutching the pot and laughing. The lubbock laughed too, standing in the middle of the meadow and waving its insect arms.

"It's just laid its eggs in Rollo," Charmain

whispered, "and he didn't even notice!" She felt ill. The same thing had so nearly happened to her. Peter looked quite green and Waif was shivering. "You know," she said, "I think the lubbock may have promised Rollo a crock of gold for making trouble between the kobolds and Great Uncle William."

"I'm sure it did," Peter said. "Before you got here, I could hear Rollo yelling that he needed to be paid."

He opened the window to listen, Charmain thought. The silly fool.

"I have to declare war," Calcifer said. He had gone rather wispy and pale. He added in a small hiss that trembled slightly, "I have to fight that lubbock or I won't deserve the life that Sophie gave me. One moment." He stopped speaking and hung in the air, long and stiff, with his orange eyes closed.

"Are you the fire demon?" Peter asked. "I've never seen one bef—"

"Quiet," said Calcifer. "I'm concentrating. This has to be right."

There was a slight rumbling from somewhere. Then, overhead and across the window from behind, came what Charmain at first took for a thundercloud. It threw a large black, turretted shadow along the meadow, which very quickly reached the rejoicing lubbock. The lubbock looked round as the shadow fell across it and froze for an instant. Then it started to run. By this time the turreted shadow had been followed by the castle that was making it, a tall black castle built of huge blocks of dark stone with turrets on all four corners. They could see the big stones it was made of shaking and grinding together as it moved. It came after the lubbock faster than the lubbock could run.

The lubbock dodged. The castle swerved after it. The lubbock spread its small fuzzy wings for more speed and went bounding in furious strides to the tall rocks at the end of the meadow. As soon as it reached the rocks, it turned round and came rushing the other way, towards the window. It must have hoped that the castle would crash into the rocks. But the castle reversed itself with no trouble at all and came after it faster than ever. Big puffs of black smoke went belching from the castle's turrets and floating away across the fading rainbow. The lubbock swivelled one of its multiple eyes as it ran, then put its insect head down and pelted, feelers flapping, wings beating, in a big curve that took it along the very edge of the cliff. Although its wings were now purple blurs, it seemed not to be able to fly with them at all. Charmain understood why it had not tried to follow her down from the cliff: it would not have been able to fly back up. Instead of jumping off the cliff to escape, the lubbock simply kept on running, tempting the castle to follow and fall off the edge.

The castle did follow. It came steaming and puffing and grinding at speed along the cliff, and seemed perfectly balanced in spite of the way half of it was hanging over the edge. The lubbock gave out a despairing hoot, changed direction again and rushed out into the centre of the meadow. There it played its last trick and went small. It shrank into a tiny purple insect and plunged in among the grass and flowers.

The castle was on to that spot in instants. It shuddered to a stop over the place where the lubbock had vanished and floated there. Flames began to come out of its flat underside, yellow flames first, then orange, then angry red, and finally a white hotness that was too bright to look at. Flames and thick smoke licked up its sides and joined the dark smokes streaming from its turrets. The meadow filled with hot black fog. For what seemed hours, but was probably only minutes, the castle was a dim, hovering shape over smoky brightness, like the sun seen through clouds. They could hear the roar of burning even behind the magical window.

"Right," Calcifer said. "I think that's done it." He turned to Charmain and she noticed that his eyes were now a strange shining silver. "Will you open the window, please? I have to go and make sure."

As Charmain turned the catch and swung the window open, the castle rose up and moved sideways. All the smokes and fogs collected into one large dark puff, which rolled across the edge of the cliff and out into the valley, where it shredded away to nothing. When Calcifer floated forward into the meadow, the castle was standing demurely, with only a wisp of smoke coming from each turret, beside a big square patch of black earth. A perfectly horrible smell rolled in through the window.

"Ugh!" said Charmain. "What is that?"

"Roast lubbock, I hope," Peter said.

They watched Calcifer float to the burned square. There he became a blue streak of action, whirling this way and that across the blackness until he had covered every tiny scrap of it.

He came floating back with his eyes a normal orange again. "That's it," he said cheerfully. "Gone."

And so are a lot of flowers, Charmain thought, but it did not seem polite to say so. The important thing was that the lubbock was gone, truly gone. "The flowers will grow again next year," Calcifer said to her. "What did you come and fetch me for? This lubbock?"

"No. The lubbock *eggs*," Peter and Charmain said together. They explained about the elf and what the elf had said.

"Show me," said Calcifer.

They went to the kitchen, all except Waif, who whined and refused to go in there. There Charmain had a fine sunlit view of the yard out of the window, full of dripping pink, white and red laundry still on the clotheslines. Peter had obviously not bothered to fetch it in. She wondered what he *had* been doing. The glass box was still on the table, still with the eggs in it, but it had sunk into the table somehow, so that only half of it was showing.

"What made it do that?" Charmain asked. "The magic in the eggs?"

Peter looked a little self-conscious. "Not exactly," he said. "That happened when I put my safety spell on it. I was going back to the study to look up another spell when I saw Rollo talking to the lubbock."

Isn't that *typical*! Charmain thought. This fool always thinks he knows best!

"The elf spells would have been quite enough," Calcifer said, floating above the embedded glass box.

"But he said it was *dangerous*!" Peter protested.

"You've made it more dangerous," Calcifer said. "Don't either of you come any nearer. No one can touch the box now. Does one of you know of a good stout layer of rock where I can go to destroy these eggs?"

Peter tried not to look chastened. Charmain remembered her fall from the cliff and how she had nearly landed on big rocks before she started to fly. She did her best to describe to Calcifer where those crags were.

"Under the cliff. I see," Calcifer said. "One of you open the back door, please, and then stand back." Peter hurried to open the door. Charmain could see he was quite ashamed of what he had done to the glass box. But it won't stop him doing something just as silly another time, she thought. I wish he'd *learn*!

Calcifer hovered over the glass box for a moment and then whirled to the open door. Halfway through the doorway, he seemed to stick, jerking and trembling, until he gave a mighty heave, doubling himself up like a large blue tadpole and then slamming himself straight again, and shot forward across the colourful washing. The glass box came loose with a scrape and a sound like someone throwing wooden planks about, and shot after him. It floated over the yard, eggs and all, following Calcifer's small blue teardrop shape. Peter and Charmain went to the door and watched the glass box glinting its way up and across the green hillside towards the lubbock's meadow, until it was out of sight.

"Oh!" Charmain said. "I forgot to tell him that Prince Ludovic is a lubbockin!"

"Is he? Really?" Peter said as he shut the door. "That must explain why my mother left this country, then."

Charmain had never had much interest in Peter's mother. She turned impatiently away and saw that the table was now flat again. That was a relief. She had been wondering what you did with a table that had a square trench in the middle of it. "What safety spell did you use?" she said.

"I'll show you," Peter said. "I want to have another sight of that castle anyway. Do you think we dare open the window and climb out near to it?"

"No," said Charmain.

"But the lubbock's definitely dead," Peter said. "There can't be any harm in it."

Charmain had a very strong feeling that Peter was asking for trouble. "How do you know there was only one lubbock?" she said.

"The encyclopedia *said*," Peter argued. "Lubbocks are solitary."

Arguing fiercely about it, they wrangled their way through the inner door and turned left into the corridor. There Peter made a defiant dash for the window. Charmain dashed after him and held him back by his jacket. Waif dashed after them, squeaking with distress, and contrived to tangle herself with Peter's feet so that he fell forward with both hands on the window. Charmain looked nervously out at the meadow, gleaming peacefully in orange sunset light, where the castle was still squatting beside the burned black patch. It was one of the queerest buildings she had ever seen.

There was a flash of light so bright that it blinded them.

Instants later there came the clap of an explosion as loud as the light was bright. The floor beneath them jiggled and the window blurred in its frame. Everything shook. Through tears of dazzle mixed with blots of blindness, Charmain thought she saw the castle vibrating all over. With ears fuzzy and deaf, she thought she heard rocks crash and grind and tumble.

Clever Waif! she thought. If Peter had been outside, he might be dead by now.

"What do you think that was?" Peter asked when they could almost hear again.

"Calcifer destroying the lubbock eggs, of course," said Charmain. "The rocks he went to are straight under the meadow."

They both blinked and blinked, trying to clear away blobs of blue and grey and yellow dazzle that would keep floating inside their eyes. They both peered and peered. It was hard to believe it, but nearly half the meadow was now missing. A curved piece, like a huge bite, had gone from the sloping green space. Below that, there must have been quite a landslide.

"Hmm," said Peter. "You don't think he destroyed himself as well, do you?"

Charmain said, "I hope *not*!"

They waited and watched. Sounds came back to their

ears, almost as usual apart from a little fizzing. The blots gradually faded from their eyes. After a while, they both noticed that the castle was drifting, in a sad, lost way, across the meadow towards the rocks at the other end. They waited and watched until it drifted up over the rocks and out of sight along the mountainside. There was still no sign of Calcifer.

"He probably came back to the kitchen," Peter suggested.

They went back there. They opened the back door and peered out among the laundry, but there was no sign anywhere of a floating blue teardrop shape. They went through the living room and opened the front door. But the only blue out there was the hydrangeas.

"*Do* fire demons die?" Peter said.

"I've no idea," Charmain said. As always, in times of trouble, she knew what she wanted to do. "I'm going to read a book," she said. She sat on the nearest sofa, pulled her glasses up, and picked *The Magician's Journey* up off the floor. Peter gave an angry sigh and went away.

But it was no good. Charmain could not concentrate. She kept thinking of Sophie, and of Morgan too. It was quite plain to her that Calcifer was, in some strange way, part of Sophie's family. "It would be even worse than losing you," she said to Waif, who had come to sit on her shoes. She wondered if she should go to the Royal Mansion and tell Sophie what had happened. But it was dark now. Sophie was probably having to have formal supper, sitting opposite the lubbockin Prince, with candles and things. Charmain did not think she dared interrupt another occasion in the Mansion. Besides, Sophie was worried sick about that threat to Morgan. Charmain did not want to worry her more. And perhaps Calcifer would turn up in the morning. He was made of fire after all. On the other hand, that explosion was enough to blow anything to bits. Charmain thought of bits of blue flame scattered about inside a landslide...

Peter came back into the living room. "I know what we ought to do," he said.

"Yes?" Charmain said eagerly.

"We ought to go and tell the kobolds about Rollo," Peter said.

Charmain stared. Took her glasses off and stared more clearly. "What have the kobolds got to do with Calcifer?"

"Nothing," Peter said, rather puzzled. "But we can prove that the lubbock paid Rollo to make trouble." Charmain wondered whether to spring up and hit him round the head with *The Magician's Journey*. *Bother* the kobolds!

"We ought to go now," Peter began persuasively, "before—"

"In the morning," Charmain said, firmly and definitely.

"In the morning, *after* we've been up to those rocks to see what happened to Calcifer."

"But—," said Peter.

"Because," Charmain said, quickly thinking of reasons, "Rollo's going to be off somewhere hiding his crock of gold. He ought to be there when you accuse him."

To her surprise, Peter thought about this and agreed with her. "And we ought to tidy Wizard Norland's bedroom," he said, "in case they bring him back tomorrow."

"You go and do that," Charmain said – before I throw my book at you, she thought, and probably the vase of flowers after that!

# CHAPTER FOURTEEN

## Which is full of
## kobolds again

Charmain was still thinking of Calcifer when she got up next morning. As she came out of the bathroom, she saw that Peter was busily engaged in changing the sheets on Great Uncle William's bed and stuffing the old sheets into a laundry bag. Charmain sighed. More work.

"Still," she said to Waif as she put down the usual bowl of dog food, "it keeps him busy and happy while I look for Calcifer. Now, are you coming up to those rocks with me?"

Waif, as always, was only too pleased to go wherever

Charmain went. After breakfast, she trotted eagerly after Charmain through the living room to the front door. But they never went to the rocks. As Charmain put out her hand to the doorknob, Waif charged out from behind her and burst the door open. And there was Rollo on the doorstep in the act of reaching his small blue hand out for his daily crock of milk. Uttering tiny snarls, Waif sprang upon him, got her jaws round Rollo's neck and pinned him to the ground.

"*Peter!*" Charmain roared, standing in a pool of spilled milk. "Come quickly! We need a bag!" She put one foot on Rollo to keep him in place. "*Bag! Bag!*" she screamed. Rollo kicked madly and bounced about under her shoe, while Waif let go of him in order to bark. Rollo added to the din by yelling, "Help! Murder! *Assault*!" in a strong grating howl.

Peter, to do him justice, arrived at a run. He took one look at the scene in the doorway and snatched up one of Mrs Baker's embroidered food bags, which he managed to get over Rollo's flailing legs before Charmain could draw breath to explain. Next second, Peter had the bag entirely over Rollo and was holding it up, bulging, twisting, and dripping milk, while he tried to reach one of his own pockets.

"Nice work!" he said. "Get some string out of that pocket, will you? We don't want him getting away."

And when Charmain had fumbled out a length of purple string from the pocket, he added, "Have you had breakfast? Good. Tie the top of the bag really tight. Then take it and hold it *fast* while I get ready. Then we can go straight there."

"Hluph, hlruther!" uttered the bag as Peter passed it over.

"Shut up," Charmain said to it and hung on to the bag with both hands just above the purple string. The bag twisted this way and that, while Charmain watched Peter drag loops of coloured string from pockets all over his coat. He put red string round his left thumb and green round his right, then purple, yellow and pink round the first three fingers of his right hand, followed by black, white and blue around the first three fingers of his left hand. Waif stood on the doorstep, frayed ears cocked, staring up at the process with interest. "Are we going to find the end of the rainbow or something?" Charmain asked.

"No, but this is how I've memorised the way to the kobolds," Peter explained. "Right. Shut the front door and let's go."

"*Harrabluph!*" shouted the bag.

"And the same to you!" Peter said, leading the way to the inner door. Waif trotted after and Charmain followed with the writhing bag.

They turned right through the door. Charmain was

too preoccupied to say she thought that was the way to the Conference Room. She was remembering how easily all the kobolds had vanished and reappeared, and how Rollo himself had sunk into the earth of the mountain meadow. It seemed to her that it was only a matter of time before Rollo sank out of the bottom of the embroidered bag. She kept one hand underneath it, but she was sure that was not enough. With milk dripping between her fingers, she tried to keep Rollo in with a spell. The trouble was, she had no idea how you did this. The only thing she could think of was to use the way she had dealt with Peter's leaking pipe spells. *Stay inside! Stay INSIDE!* she thought at Rollo, massaging the bottom of the bag. Each massaging produced another muffled yell from the bag, which made her surer than ever that Rollo was getting away. So she simply followed Peter as he turned this way or that and never noticed how you got to the kobolds at all. She only noticed when they were there.

They were standing outside a large well-lighted cave full of little blue people rushing about. It was hard to see what most of them were doing because the view was partly blocked by a very strange object in the entrance. This object looked a little like one of the horse-drawn sleds that people used in High Norland when the winter snows came down and made it impossible to use a cart or a carriage, except that this thing had no way to hitch a horse to it. It had a huge curvy handle at the back instead. It had curls and curvy bits all over it. Dozens of kobolds were working at it, climbing this way and that over it as they worked. Some were lining the inside with padding and sheepskin, some were hammering and carving, and the rest were painting the outside with curly blue flowers on a gold background. It was going to be very magnificent when it was finished, whatever it was.

Peter said to Charmain, "Can I trust you to be polite this time? Can you remember to be tactful at least?"

"I can try," Charmain said. "It depends."

"Then let me do the talking," Peter told her. He tapped the nearest busy kobold on the back. "Excuse me. Can you tell me where I can find Timminz, please?"

"Halfway down the cave," the kobold piped, pointing with her paintbrush. "Working on the cuckoo clock. What do you want him for?"

"We've something very important to tell him," Peter said.

This attracted the attention of most of the kobolds working on the object. Some of them turned and looked apprehensively at Waif. Waif at once looked sprightly, demure and lovable. The rest stared at Charmain and the writhing embroidered bag. "Who have you got there?" one of them asked Charmain.

"Rollo," said Charmain.

Most of them nodded, without seeming at all surprised. When Peter asked, "Is it all right to go and speak to Timminz?" they all nodded again and told him, "Go ahead." Charmain got the feeling that nobody liked Rollo very much. Rollo seemed to know this because he stopped writhing and made no kind of noise while Peter edged his way past the strange object. Charmain came after him, holding the bag sideways so as not to get paint on it.

"What are you making?" she asked the nearest kobolds as she went.

"Commission from the elves," one of them answered. Another added, "Going to cost a lot." And a third said, "Elves always pay well."

Charmain came out into the cave feeling none the wiser. The place was huge, and there were tiny kobold children tearing about among the busy adults. Most of the children screamed and ran away when they saw Waif. Their parents mostly moved prudently round to the back of whatever they were working on and went on painting, polishing or carving. Peter led the way past rocking horses, dolls' houses, baby-chairs, grandfather clocks, wooden settles and wind-up wooden dolls, until they came to the cuckoo clock. It was unmistakable. It was enormous. Its giant wooden casing stretched all the way up to the magically lighted roof; its huge clock face was propped up separately, filling most of the wall beside the casing; and the cuckoo for it, which a score of kobolds were diligently covering with feathers, was rather larger than Charmain and Peter together. Charmain wondered whoever might want a cuckoo clock that big.

Timminz was climbing about in the massive clockwork with a tiny spanner. "There he is," Peter said, recognising him by his nose. Peter went up to the giant works and cleared his throat. "Excuse me. Hrrmp. Excuse us."

Timminz swung himself round a mighty coil of metal and glowered at them. "Oh, it's you." He eyed the bag. "Kidnapping people now, are you?"

Rollo must have heard Timminz's voice and felt he was among friends. "*Hrluphuph! Hlewafaphauph!*" the bag bellowed.

"That's Rollo," Timminz said accusingly.

"That's right," Peter said. "We've brought him here to confess to you. The lubbock on the mountain paid him to make trouble between you and Wizard Norland."

"Hipughphy *hlephy*-phiph!" the bag shouted.

But Timminz had gone silvery blue with horror. "The *lubbock?*" he said.

"That's right," said Peter. "We saw him yesterday, asking the lubbock for his reward. And the lubbock gave him the crock of gold from the end of the rainbow."

"Hiphiphuph!" denied the bag loudly. "Hlephlyiph!"

"Both of us saw it," Peter said.

"Let him out," Timminz said. "Let him speak."

Peter nodded at Charmain. She took her hand away from the bottom of the bag and stopped doing what she hoped was her spell. Rollo instantly fell through on to the floor, where he sat spitting out milky ends of embroidery wool and old crumbs and glaring at Peter.

I really did some magic! I kept him in there! Charmain thought.

"You see what they're like?" Rollo said angrily. "Bag a person up and fill his mouth with stale fuzz so that he can't answer back while they tells lies about him!"

"You can answer now," Timminz said. "*Did* you get a crock of gold from the lubbock for setting us at odds with the wizard?"

"How could I have done?" Rollo asked virtuously. "No kobold would be seen dead talking to a lubbock. You all know that!"

Quite a crowd of kobolds had gathered around by now – at a safe distance from Waif – and Rollo waved dramatic arms at them.

"Bear witness!" he said. "I'm victim of a pack of lies!"

"Go and search his grotto, some of you," Timminz ordered.

Several kobolds set off at once. Rollo jumped to his feet. "I'll go with you!" he cried out. "I'll prove there's nothing there!"

Rollo had gone three steps when Waif seized him by the back of his blue jacket and bumped him to the floor again. She stayed there, teeth in Rollo's jacket, frayed tail wagging, with one ear cocked towards Charmain as if to say, "Didn't I do well?"

"You did wonderfully well," Charmain told her. "Good dog."

Rollo shouted, "Call it off! It's hurting my back!"

"No. You can stay there until they come back from searching your grotto," Charmain said. Rollo folded his arms and sat looking righteous and sulky. Charmain turned to Timminz. "Is it all right to ask you who wants such a big clock? While we wait," she explained, seeing Peter shaking his head at her.

Timminz looked up at the vast pieces of clock. "Crown Prince Ludovic," he said, with a gloomy sort of pride. "He wanted a whopper for Castel Joie." Gloom swallowed up his pride. "He hasn't paid us a penny yet. He never does pay. When you think how rich he is—"

He was interrupted by the kobolds coming back at a run. "Here it is!" they shouted. "Is this it? It was under his bed!"

The kobold in front was carrying the crock in both arms. It looked like an ordinary clay pottery crock, the kind someone might use to make a stew in an oven, except that it had a sort of glow around it, in faint rainbow colours.

"That's the one," Peter said.

"Then what do you think he did with the gold?" the kobold asked.

"What do you *mean*, what did I do with the gold?" Rollo demanded. "That there pot was stuffed full—" He stopped, realising he was giving himself away.

"It isn't now. Take a look if you don't believe me," the other kobold retorted. He dumped the crock down between Rollo's outstretched legs. "This is just how we found it."

Rollo bent to look inside the pot. He uttered a cry of grief. He plunged his hand into it and brought out a handful of dry, yellow leaves. Then he brought out another handful and another, until he had both hands inside the empty crock and was sitting surrounded in dead leaves.

"It's *gone*!" he howled. "It's turned into dead leaves! That lubbock *cheated* me!"

"So you admit the lubbock paid you to make trouble?" Timminz said.

Rollo scowled up sideways at Timminz. "I don't admit to anything, except that I've been robbed."

Peter coughed. "Ahem. I'm afraid the lubbock cheated him worse than that. It laid its eggs in him as soon as his back was turned."

There were gasps from all round. Big-nosed kobold faces stared at Rollo, pale blue with horror, noses and all, and then turned to Peter.

"It's true. We both saw it," Peter said.

Charmain nodded when they turned to her. "True," she said.

"It's a lie!" Rollo howled. "You're pulling my leg!"

"No we are *not*!" Charmain said. "The lubbock stuck out its egg-laying prong and got you in the back just before you went down into the earth. Didn't you say just now that your back hurt you?"

Rollo's eyes popped at Charmain. He believed her. His mouth opened. Waif scrambled hastily away as he began to scream. He threw the pot aside, he drummed his heels in a storm of dry leaves and yelled until his face was navy blue. "I'm a *goner*!" he blubbered. "I'm walking dead! There's *things* breeding inside of me! *Help!* Oh, please *help* me, somebody!"

Nobody helped him. All the kobolds backed away, still staring in horror. Peter looked disgusted. One lady kobold said, "What a *disgraceful* display!" and this seemed so unfair to Charmain that she could not help feeling truly sorry for Rollo.

"The elves can help him," she said to Timminz.

"What did you say?" Timminz snapped his fingers. There was sudden silence. Although Rollo continued to drum his heels and to open and shut his mouth, nobody could hear the noise. "*What* did you say?" Timminz said to Charmain.

"The elves," Charmain said. "They know how to get lubbock eggs out of a person."

"Yes, they do," Peter agreed. "Wizard Norland had had lubbock eggs laid in him. That was why they took him away to cure him. An elf came yesterday with the eggs they'd taken out of him."

"Elves charge high," remarked a kobold by Charmain's right knee, sounding very impressed.

"I think the King paid," Charmain said.

"Hush!" Timminz's brow was wrinkling right down into his nose. He sighed. "I suppose," he said, "we can give the elves their sled chair for nothing, in exchange for them curing Rollo. Curses! That's two commissions we won't get paid for now! Put Rollo to bed, some of you, and I'll talk to the elves. And I warn all of you again not to go near that meadow."

"Oh, that's all right now," Peter said cheerfully. "The lubbock's dead. The fire demon killed it."

"*What?*" shrieked all the other kobolds. "*Dead?*" they clamoured. "*Really?* You mean the fire demon

274

that's visiting the King? Did he actually *kill* it?"

"Yes, really," Peter shouted through the noise. "He killed the lubbock and then he destroyed the eggs the elf brought."

"And we think he destroyed himself too," Charmain added. She was fairly sure none of the kobolds heard her. They were all too busy dancing, cheering and throwing their small blue hats into the air.

When the noise had died down a little and four sturdy kobolds had carried Rollo away, still soundlessly kicking and screaming, Timminz said seriously to Peter, "That lubbock kept all of us in fear, it being the parent of the Crown Prince and all. What can we give the fire demon to show our gratitude, do you think?"

"Put Wizard Norland's kitchen taps back," Peter said promptly.

"That," said Timminz, "goes without saying. It was Rollo's doing they were taken away. I meant, what can mere kobolds do for a fire demon that it can't do for itself?"

"I know," Charmain said. Everyone was respectfully quiet as she went on. "Calcifer and his… er… family were trying to find out where all the King's money keeps disappearing to. Can you help them do that?"

There were murmurs from all round Charmain's knees of, "Easy, that is!" and "That's no problem!" and quite a ripple of laughter, as if Charmain had asked a stupid question. Timminz was so relieved that his brow unwrinkled entirely, making his nose – and his whole face – twice as long. "That is easy to do," he said, "and costs nothing." He glanced across to the other side of the cave, where at least sixty cuckoo clocks hung, all wagging their pendulums in sixty different rhythms. "If you come with me now, I think we should be just in time to see the money going. Are you sure the fire demon would be pleased by this?"

"Absolutely," Charmain said.

"Then follow me, please," Timminz said. He led the way towards the back of the cave.

Wherever they were going to turned out to be quite a long walk. Charmain became as confused as she had been on the way to the kobolds' cave. They were in half-dark the whole distance, and the route seemed to be all bends and sharp turns and hairpin corners. Every so often Timminz would say, "Three short steps and turn right" or "Count eight human-size steps and turn left, then sharp right, then left again," and this went on for so long that Waif became tired out and whined to be picked up. Charmain carried her for what seemed more than half the way.

"I must explain that the kobolds here belong to a different clan," Timminz said, when at last there seemed to be a little daylight ahead. "I like to think that

my clan would have managed better than they do."
Then, before Charmain could ask what he meant, he
went into a flurry of sharp rights and slow lefts, with a
couple of zigzags thrown in, and she found they were
at the end of an underground passage in cool, green
daylight. Marble steps all greened over with mildew led
up into some bushes. The bushes must once have been
planted on either side of the steps, but they had grown
to fill the space entirely.

Waif began to growl, sounding like a dog twice her size.

"Hush!" Timminz whispered. "No noise at *all* from
here onward."

Waif stopped growling at once, but Charmain could
feel her small, hot body throbbing with hidden growls.
Charmain turned to Peter to make sure he had the
sense to keep quiet too.

Peter was not there. There was only herself, Waif
and Timminz.

Charmain, wholly exasperated, knew just what had
happened. Somewhere along the confusing way, when
Timminz had said, "Turn left," Peter had turned right.
Or the other way round. Charmain had no idea at what
point this had happened, but she knew it had.

Never mind, she thought. He has enough coloured
string round his fingers to find his way to Ingary and
back. He'll probably arrive at Great Uncle William's

house long before I do. So she forgot about Peter and concentrated on tiptoeing up the slippery, mildewed steps, and then on peering out from among the bushes without rustling so much as one leaf.

There was blazing sunlight beyond, blazing on very green, very beautifully kept grass, with a blindingly white garden path beyond that. The path led up between trees that had been carved into knobs and points and cones and disks, like a lesson in geometry, to a small storybook palace – one that had many small pointed towers with little blue roofs. Charmain recognised it as Castel Joie, where Crown Prince Ludovic lived. She was slightly ashamed to realise that it was the building she always thought of when any book she was reading mentioned a palace.

I must be very unimaginative, she thought. Then, No. Whenever her father made shortbreads to sell in boxes for May Day, a picture of Castel Joie always appeared on the top of the box. Castel Joie was, after all, the pride of High Norland. No wonder it was so far to walk! she thought. We must be halfway down the Norland Valley here! And it still *is* my idea of a perfect palace, so there!

Footsteps crunched on the hot, white path and Prince Ludovic himself appeared, magnificent in white and azure silk, sauntering towards the palace. Just before he was level with the bush where Charmain was, he stopped and turned. "Come along, can't you!" he said angrily. "Get a move on!"

"We're trying, Highness!" piped a small panting voice.

A line of kobolds trudged into view, each bowed down under a knobby leather sack. They were all more greyish green than blue and looked most unhappy. Some of the unhappiness may have been due to the sunlight – for kobolds preferred to live in the dark – but Charmain thought their colour looked more like bad health. Their legs wobbled. One or two were coughing badly. The last one in the row was so unwell that he stumbled and fell down, dropping his sack, which spilled a scatter of gold coins across the blazing white path.

At this, the colourless gentleman strode into view. He advanced on the fallen kobold and started kicking him. He did not kick particularly hard, nor did he look particularly cruel: it was more as if he was trying to get a machine going again. The kobold scrambled about under the kicks, desperately picking up gold coins until he had them all back in the sack, and managed to stagger to his feet again. The colourless gentleman left off kicking him and came to stroll beside Prince Ludovic.

"It's not as if it was even a heavy load," he said to the Prince. "It's probably the last. They've no more money left, unless the King sells his books."

Prince Ludovic laughed. "He'd rather die than do that – which suits me, of course. We'll have to think of some other way to get money, then. Castel Joie is so dashed expensive to run." He looked back at the trudging, wobbling kobolds. "Move along there, will you! I have to get back to the Royal Mansion for tea."

The colourless gentleman nodded and strode back to the kobolds, ready to start kicking again, and the Prince waited for him, saying, "Mind you, if I never see another crumpet in my life, it will be too soon for me!"

The kobolds saw the colourless gentleman coming and did their best to hurry. All the same, it seemed an age to Charmain until the procession was out of sight and she could no longer hear their footsteps crunching. She kept her arms tight round the throbbing Waif, who seemed to want to jump down and chase the procession, and looked down through the leaves at Timminz.

"Why haven't you told anyone about this before? Why didn't you at least tell Wizard Norland?"

"Nobody asked," Timminz said, looking injured.

No, of *course* nobody asked! Charmain thought. This was why Rollo was paid to make the kobolds angry with Great Uncle William! He'd have got round to asking them in the end, if he hadn't been ill. She thought it was just as well that the lubbock was dead. If it was Prince Ludovic's parent, as Timminz had said, then it had probably meant to kill the Crown Prince and rule the country instead of him. It had more or less told her so, after all. But that still leaves Prince Ludovic to deal with, she thought. I really *have* to tell the King about him.

"It seems a bit hard on those kobolds," she said to Timminz.

"It is," Timminz agreed. "But they have not asked for help yet."

And of course it never occurred to you to help them without being asked, did it? Charmain thought. Honestly! I give up! "Can you show me the way home?" she asked.

Timminz hesitated. "Do you think the fire demon will be glad to know the money goes to Castel Joie?" he asked.

"Yes," Charmain said. "Or his family will."

# CHAPTER FIFTEEN

### Wherein the child Twinkle
### is kidnapped

Timminz, rather grudgingly, took Charmain the long, confusing way back to the kobolds' cave. There, he said cheerfully, "You'll know the way from here," and disappeared inside the cave, leaving Charmain alone with Waif.

Charmain did not know the way from there. She stood beside the object that Timminz had called a sled chair for several minutes, wondering what to do and watching kobolds painting and carving and upholstering the object and never sparing Charmain a glance. At length, it occurred to her to put Waif down on the ground.

"Show me the way to Great Uncle William's house, Waif," she said. "Be clever."

Waif trotted off with a will. But Charmain soon began seriously to doubt that Waif was being clever. Waif trotted and Charmain walked, and they turned left, and then right, and right again, for what seemed hours. Charmain was so busy thinking about what she had discovered that, several times, she missed the moment when Waif turned left or right and had to wait, standing in the near-dark, shouting, "Waif! *Waif!*" until Waif came back and found her. Quite probably, Charmain doubled the distance like this. Waif began toiling and panting, with her tongue hanging out longer and longer, but Charmain did not dare pick her up in case they never got home at all. She talked to Waif instead, to encourage them both.

"Waif, I *must* tell Sophie what has happened. She must be worrying about Calcifer by now. And I must tell the King about the money too. But if I go to the Royal Mansion as soon as I get home, horrible Prince Ludovic will be there, pretending to like crumpets. *Why* doesn't he like them? Crumpets are *nice*. Because he's a lubbockin, I suppose. I don't dare tell the King in front of him. We'll have to wait to go until tomorrow, I think. When do you think Prince Ludovic means to leave? Tonight? The King did tell me to come back in two days, so Ludovic *should* be gone by then. If I get there early, I can speak to Sophie first— Oh, dear! I've just remembered. Calcifer said they were going to pretend to leave, so we may not find Sophie there. Oh, Waif, I wish I knew what to do!"

The more Charmain talked about it, the less she knew what to do. In the end, she was too tired to talk and just stumbled after the pale shape of the limping, panting Waif, pattering along in front of her. Until at long last, Waif barged a door open and they were in Great Uncle William's living room, where Waif gave a moan and fell over on her side, breathing in hundreds of quick little gasping breaths. Charmain stared out of the windows at the hydrangeas all pink and purple in sunset light. We've been all day, she thought. No wonder Waif's so tired! No wonder my feet hurt! At least Peter should be home by now, and I do hope he's got supper ready.

"*Peter!*" she shouted.

When there was no answer, Charmain picked Waif up and went into the kitchen. Waif feebly licked Charmain's hand in gratitude for not having to walk a step farther. Here the sunset light was falling on the zigzags of pink and white washing, still hanging gently flapping in the yard outside. There was no sign of Peter.

"Peter?" Charmain called.

There was no answer. Charmain sighed. Evidently

Peter had got thoroughly lost, even worse than she had, and there was no knowing when he would turn up now.

"Too many pieces of coloured string!" Charmain muttered to Waif as she tapped the fireplace for dog food. "Stupid boy!"

She felt far too tired to do any cooking. When Waif had eaten two dishes of food and drunk the water Charmain fetched from the bathroom, Charmain staggered into the living room and had Afternoon Tea. After some thought, she had Afternoon Tea a second time. Then she had Morning Coffee. Then she wondered whether to go to the kitchen and have breakfast, but found she was too tired and picked up a book instead.

A long time later, Waif woke her up by climbing on the sofa beside her.

"Oh, bother this!" Charmain said. She went to bed without even trying to wash and fell asleep with her glasses still on her nose.

When she woke next morning, she could hear that Peter was back. There were bathroom noises and footsteps and the sound of doors opening and shutting. He sounds awfully brisk, Charmain thought. I wish I did. But she knew she really had to get to the Royal Mansion today, so she groaned and got up. She dug out her last set of clean clothes and took such great care washing and doing her hair that Waif arrived anxiously from somewhere to fetch her.

"Yes. Breakfast. All right. I know," Charmain said. "The trouble is," she admitted, as she picked Waif up, "I'm *scared* of that colourless gentleman. I think he's even worse than the Prince." She shoved the door open with one foot, turned, and turned left into the kitchen, where she stopped and stared.

A strange woman was sitting at the kitchen table calmly eating breakfast. She was the kind of woman who you know at once is completely efficient. She had efficiency all over her narrow sun-weathered face and competence all over her strong narrow hands. Those hands were busy efficiently cutting up a mighty pile of pancakes in syrup and slicing the stack of crispy bacon beside it.

Charmain stared, both at the pancakes and the woman's gypsy-like clothes. She wore bright, faded flounces all over and a colourful scarf across her faded fairish hair. The woman turned and stared back.

"Who are you?" they both said at once, the woman with her mouth full.

"I'm Charmain Baker," Charmain said. "I'm here to look after Great Uncle William's house while he's away being cured by the elves."

The woman swallowed her mouthful. "Good," she said. "I'm glad to see he left *someone* in charge. I didn't like to think of the dog being left all alone with Peter.

She's been fed, by the way. Peter is not a dog person. Is Peter still asleep?"

"Er...," said Charmain. "I'm not sure. He didn't come in last night."

The woman sighed. "He *always* vanishes as soon as I turn my back," she said. "I know he must have got here safely." She waved a fork loaded with pancake and bacon at the window. "That washing out there has Peter all over it."

Charmain felt her face go hot and red. "Some of it was my fault," she admitted. "I boiled a robe. Why do you think it was Peter?"

"Because," said the woman, "he has never been able to get a spell right in his life. I should know. I'm his mother."

Charmain was rather shaken to realise she was talking to the Witch of Montalbino. She was impressed. Of course Peter's mother is hyper-efficient, she thought. But what is she doing *here*? "I thought you'd gone to Ingary," she said.

"I had," said the Witch. "I'd got as far as Strangia, when Queen Beatrice told me that Wizard Howl had gone to High Norland. So back I came across the mountains and dropped in on the elves, where they told me that Wizard Norland was with them. I was extremely alarmed then, because I realised that Peter was probably all alone here. I'd sent him here to be safe, you see. I came here at once."

"I think Peter was safe," Charmain said. "Or he was until he got lost yesterday."

"He'll be safe now that I'm here," the Witch said. "I can feel he's somewhere quite near." She sighed. "I suppose I'll have to go and look for him. He doesn't know his right hand from his left, you see."

"I know," Charmain said. "He uses coloured string. He's quite efficient, really." But she thought as she spoke that to someone as super-efficient as the Witch of Montalbino, Peter was bound to seem as hopeless as Peter thought Charmain herself was. Parents! she thought. She put Waif on the floor and asked politely, "Excuse me for asking, but how did you get the breakfast spell to send you those pancakes?"

"By giving the right order, of course," said the Witch. "Want some?" Charmain nodded. The Witch flicked efficient fingers towards the fireplace. "Breakfast," she commanded, "with pancakes, bacon, juice and coffee." The loaded tray appeared at once, with a most satisfactory heap of pancakes trickling in syrup in the centre of it. "See?" said the Witch.

"Thank you," Charmain said, gratefully taking hold of the tray.

Waif's nose tilted up at the smell and she ran round in little circles, squeaking. It was clear that, to Waif, being fed by the Witch did not count as proper breakfast.

Charmain put the tray on the table and gave Waif the crunchiest piece of bacon.

"That's an enchanting dog you've got there," the Witch remarked, going back to her own breakfast.

"She is rather sweet," Charmain admitted as she sat down and began to enjoy the pancakes.

"No, I didn't mean that," the Witch said impatiently. "I never gush. I meant that is what she *is* – an enchanting dog." She ate more pancake and added with her mouth full, "Enchanting dogs are quite rare and very magical. This one is doing you a great honour by adopting you as her human. I'm guessing that she even changed her sex to match yours. I hope you appreciate her as you should."

"Yes," said Charmain. "I do." And I'd almost rather have breakfast with Princess Hilda, she thought. Why does she have to be so severe? She went on with her breakfast, remembering that Great Uncle William had seemed to think that Waif was a male dog. Waif had *seemed* to be a male dog at first. Then Peter had picked her up and said she was female. "I'm sure you're right," Charmain added politely. "Why is Peter not safe here on his own? He's my age, and I am."

"I imagine," the Witch said dryly, "that your magic works rather better than Peter's." She finished her pancakes and went on to toast. "If Peter can possibly bungle a spell, he will," she asserted, buttering the toast.

"Don't tell me," she said taking a large, crunchy bite, "because I won't believe you, that your magic doesn't do exactly what you mean it to, however you do it."

Charmain thought of the flying spell and the plumbing spell and then of Rollo in the bag and said, "Yes," through a mouthful of pancake. "I suppose—"

"Whereas," the Witch interrupted, "Peter is just the opposite. His method is always perfect, but the spell always misfires. One of my reasons for sending him to Wizard Norland was that I hoped the wizard could improve Peter's magic. William Norland owns *The Boke of Palimpsest*, you see."

Charmain felt her face hotting up again. "Er...," she said, passing Waif half a pancake, "what does *The Boke of Palimpsest* do, then?"

"That dog will be too fat to walk if you go on feeding her like that," said the Witch. "*The Boke of Palimpsest* gives a person the freedom to use all the magics of earth, air, fire and water. It only gives fire if the person is trustworthy. And of course the person has to have magical ability in the first place." Her severe face showed just a trace of anxiety. "I think Peter *has* the ability."

Charmain thought, Fire. I put the fire out on Peter. Am I trustworthy, then? "He must have the ability," she told the Witch. "You can't make a spell go wrong if you can't do magic in the first place. What other reasons made you send Peter here?"

"Enemies," said the Witch, sombrely sipping her coffee. "I have enemies. They killed Peter's father, you know."

"You mean lubbocks?" Charmain asked. She put everything back on her tray and took a last swig of coffee, preparing to get up and go.

"There is," said the Witch, "only the one lubbock so far as I know. It seems to have killed all its rivals. But yes, it was the lubbock that started the avalanche. I saw it."

"Then you can stop worrying," Charmain said, standing up. "The lubbock's dead. Calcifer destroyed it the day before yesterday."

The Witch was astonished. "Tell me!" she said eagerly.

Although she was itching to be off to the Royal Mansion, Charmain found she had to sit down, pour herself another cup of coffee and tell the Witch the whole story, not only about the lubbock and the lubbock eggs, but also about Rollo and the lubbock. And this is unfair use of witchcraft, she thought as she found herself telling the Witch how Calcifer seemed to be missing.

"Then what are you sitting about here for?" the Witch said. "Run along to the Royal Mansion and tell Sophie at once! The poor woman must be out of her mind with worry by now! Hurry it up, girl!"

And not even, Thank you for telling me, Charmain

thought sourly. I'd rather have my mother than Peter's any day. And I'd *definitely* rather have breakfast with Princess Hilda!

She got up and said a polite goodbye. Then, with Waif racing at her heels, she rushed through the living room and down the garden into the road. Lucky I didn't tell her about the Conference Room way, she thought, pounding along with her glasses bouncing on her chest. Or she'd make me go that way and I'd never get a chance to look for Calcifer.

Just before the road bent, she came to the place where Calcifer had exploded the lubbock eggs. A huge lump of the cliff had fallen off there, sending a hill of boulders almost as far as the road. Several people who looked like shepherds were climbing about on the pile, searching for buried sheep and scratching their heads as if they were wondering what had caused the damage. Charmain hesitated. If Calcifer was to be found, those people would have found him by now. She dropped to a walk and stared at the heap of broken stone carefully as she passed. There did not seem to be a trace of blue among the rocks, or a sign of a flame anywhere.

She made up her mind to have a thorough search later and broke into a run again, hardly noticing that the sky was a clear blue and that there was gauzy blue haze over the mountains. It was going to be one of

High Norland's rare scorching days. The only way this affected Charmain was that Waif soon began to look seriously overheated, panting, rolling from side to side as she ran and hanging her pink tongue out so far that it almost brushed the road.

"Oh, you! I suppose it was that pancake," Charmain said, snatching her up and pounding onwards. "I wish the Witch had not said that about you," she confessed as she ran. "It makes me worried about liking you so much."

By the time she reached the town, Charmain was as hot as Waif, so hot that she almost wished she had a tongue to hang out like Waif's did. She had to drop to a brisk walk, and even though she took the shortest way, it still seemed to take forever to reach Royal Square. At last she swung round the corner into the square and found her way blocked by a staring crowd. Half the citizens of High Norland seemed to be gathered there to stare at the new building standing a few feet away from the Royal Mansion. It was almost as tall as the Mansion, long and dark and coaly-looking, and it had a turret on each corner. It was the castle Charmain had last seen floating vaguely and sadly away across the mountains. She stared at it in as much amazement as everyone else in the square.

"How did it get here?" people were asking one another, as Charmain tried to push her way towards it. "However did it *fit*?"

Charmain looked at the four roads that led into Royal Square and wondered the same thing. None of the roads was more than half as wide as the castle was. But there it sat, solid and tall, as if it had built itself in the square overnight. Charmain elbowed her way towards it with growing curiosity.

As she came close under its walls, blue fire leaped from one of the turrets and plunged towards her. Charmain ducked. Waif wriggled. Someone screamed. Everyone in the crowd backed away in a hurry and left Charmain standing there on her own facing a blue teardrop of flame hovering just level with her face. Waif's frayed tail pounded on Charmain's arm, wagging a greeting.

"If you're going into the Mansion," Calcifer crackled at them, "tell them to hurry it up. I can't keep the castle here all morning."

Charmain was almost too delighted to speak. "I thought you were dead!" she managed to say. "What *happened*?"

Calcifer bobbled in the air and seemed a trifle ashamed. "I must have knocked myself silly," he confessed. "I was under a heap of rocks somehow. It took me all yesterday to worm my way out. When I did get out I had to find the castle. It had gone drifting off for miles. I've only just got it here, really. Tell Sophie. She was supposed to be pretending to leave today. And tell her I'm almost out of logs to burn. That should fetch her."

"I will," Charmain promised. "Are you sure you're all right?"

"Just hungry," Calcifer said. "Logs. Remember."

"Logs," Charmain agreed and went up the steps to the Mansion door, feeling suddenly that life was very much better and happier and freer than it had seemed before.

Sim opened the great door to her surprisingly quickly. He looked out at the castle and the staring crowd and shook his head. "Ah, Miss Charming," he said. "This is surely becoming a rather difficult morning. I'm not sure that His Majesty is quite ready to begin work in the library yet. But do please to come inside."

"Thanks," Charmain said, putting Waif down on the floor. "I don't mind waiting. I have to speak to Sophie first anyway."

"Sophie… er… Mrs Pendragon, that is to say," Sim said as he heaved the door shut, "seems to be some of the difficulty this morning. The Princess is highly put out and— But come this way and you will see what I mean."

He shuffled away down the damp corridor, beckoning Charmain to follow. Before they even got to the corner, to the place where the stone stairs came down, Charmain could hear the voice of Jamal the cook, saying, "And how is a person to know what to cook when guests are always leaving and not leaving and then leaving again, I ask you!" This was followed by fruity growls from Jamal's dog and quite a chorus of other voices.

Sophie was standing in the space below the stairs, holding Morgan in her arms, with Twinkle clinging anxiously and angelically to her skirt, while the fat nursemaid stood by looking useless as usual. Princess Hilda stood by the stairs, more intensely royal and polite than Charmain had ever seen her. And the King was there too, red in the face and obviously in a right royal rage. One look at all their faces and Charmain knew that there was no point in mentioning logs here yet. Prince Ludovic was leaning on the end of the banisters, looking amused and superior. His lady was beside him, looking disdainful, in what was very nearly a ball dress, and to Charmain's dismay, the colourless gentleman was there too, respectfully beside the Prince.

*You wouldn't think he'd just been robbing the King of all his money, the beast!* Charmain thought.

"I call this an utter abuse of my daughter's hospitality!" the King was saying. "You had no right to make promises you don't intend to keep. If you were one of our subjects, we would forbid you to leave."

Sophie said, trying to sound dignified, "I *do* mean to keep my promise, Sire, but you can't expect me to stay when my child has been threatened. If you'll let me take him away to safety first, then I'll be free to do whatever Princess Hilda wants."

Charmain saw Sophie's problem. With Prince Ludovic and the colourless gentleman standing there, she dared not say that she was only pretending to leave. And she did have to keep Morgan safe somehow.

The King said angrily, "Don't give us any more false promises, young woman!"

By Charmain's feet, Waif suddenly began growling. Behind the King, Prince Ludovic laughed and clicked his fingers. What followed took everyone by surprise. The nursemaid and the Prince's young lady both burst out of their dresses. The nursemaid became a burly purple person with glistening muscles and bare, clawed feet. The Prince's lady's ball dress peeled away to show a thick mauve body in a black leotard that had holes cut in the back to make room for a pair of useless-looking small purple wings. Both lubbockins advanced on Sophie with big purple hands outstretched.

Sophie yelled something and whirled Morgan away from the clutching hands. Morgan yelled too, in surprise and terror. Everything else was drowned out by the high yapping of Waif and immense fruity growls from Jamal's dog as it charged after the Prince's lady. Before the dog could get near either lubbockin, the Prince's lady, little wings whirring, had dived on

Twinkle and snatched him up. Twinkle screamed and flailed blue velvet legs. The nursemaid lubbockin put herself in front of Sophie to stop her trying to rescue Twinkle.

"You see," Prince Ludovic said, "you *are* leaving or your child suffers."

# CHAPTER SIXTEEN

### Which is full of escapes
### and discoveries

"This," said Princess Hilda, "is an outra—"
She had got this far when Twinkle somehow
got away. He twisted out of the lubbockin's purple
arms and went racing away up the stairs, shrieking,
"Help! Help! Don't let them touch me!"

Both lubbockins pushed Princess Hilda aside and
charged upstairs after Twinkle. Princess Hilda reeled into
the banisters and clung there, red in the face and suddenly
far from stately. Charmain found herself racing upstairs
after the lubbockins, shouting, "Leave him *alone*! How

299

*dare* you!" Afterwards, she thought it was the sight of Princess Hilda looking like an ordinary person that did it.

Down below, Sophie hovered a second and then shoved Morgan into the arms of the King. "Keep him safe!" she gasped at the King. Then she hauled her skirts up and raced upstairs after Charmain, shouting, "You just stop that! Do you hear!"

Jamal loyally laboured up after them, yelling, "Stop – thief! Stop – thief!" and panting hugely. Behind him clambered his dog, as loyal as its master, uttering huge rasping growls, while Waif ran backwards and forwards at the bottom of the stairs making a soprano thunderstorm of barking.

Prince Ludovic hung over the banisters opposite Princess Hilda and laughed at the lot of them.

The two lubbockins caught Twinkle near the top of the flight, in a blur of uselessly fanning wings and shiny mauve muscles. Twinkle surged and kicked mightily. For a moment, his blue velvet legs seemed to be big, strong man-sized legs. One big leg landed hard in the nursemaid lubbockin's stomach. The other came down on the stairs and braced him while Twinkle's right fist landed on the second lubbockin's nose with a meaty man-sized smack. Leaving both lubbockins in a heap on the landing, Twinkle sped nimbly on upwards. Charmain saw him look earnestly backwards and down as he whirled on to the next flight of stairs, making sure that she and Sophie and Jamal were still following.

They followed, because the two lubbockins picked themselves up with incredible speed and pelted upwards after Twinkle. Charmain and Sophie pelted upstairs too, and Jamal and the dog toiled on behind.

Halfway up that next flight, the lubbockins caught Twinkle again. Again there were hefty smacking sounds and Twinkle got loose once more, and once more sped upwards, into the third flight of stairs. He made it most of the way to the top of those, before the lubbockins reached him and threw themselves on top of him. All three went down into a walloping, writhing heap of legs, arms and fluttering purple wings.

By this time, Charmain and Sophie were flagging and nearly out of breath. Charmain distinctly saw Twinkle's angelic face emerge from the tangle of bodies and watch them carefully. When Charmain had toiled across the landing and started on that flight, followed by Sophie, who was clutching a stitch in her side, the bundle of bodies suddenly exploded apart. The purple bodies rolled aside and Twinkle, loose again, went fleeting up the final flight of wooden stairs. By the time the lubbockins had picked themselves up and started after him, Charmain and Sophie were not far behind. Jamal and his dog were a long way in the rear.

Up the wooden stairs they clattered, all the front five. Twinkle was climbing quite slowly now. Charmain was fairly sure this was artistic. But the lubbockins gave shouts of triumph and put on speed.

"Oh no! Not again!" Sophie groaned, as Twinkle banged open the door at the top and shot out on to the roof. The lubbockins shot out after him. When Charmain and Sophie toiled their way up there and stared out through the open door while they tried to get their breath back, they saw the two lubbockins sitting astride the golden roof. They were about halfway along and looking very much as if they wished they were anywhere else. There was no sign of Twinkle. "*Now* what is he up to?" Sophie said.

Almost as she said it, Twinkle appeared in the doorway, flushed and laughing angelic laughter, with his golden curls in a windblown halo. "Come and thee what I've found!" he said gleefully. "Jutht follow me."

Sophie clutched her side and pointed out at the roof. "What about those two?" she panted. "Do we just hope they fall off?"

Twinkle grinned enchantingly. "Wait and thee!" He cocked his golden head, listening. Down below, the growling and scrabbling of the cook's dog was getting louder. It had overtaken its master and was now snarling and clattering its way up the wooden stairs, panting horribly. Twinkle nodded and turned towards the roof. He made a small gesture and muttered a word. The two lubbockins perched out there suddenly shrank, with an unpleasant squelching sound, and became two purplish small flopping things, wagging about on the ridge of the golden roof.

"What—?" said Charmain.

Twinkle's grin grew, if possible, even more angelic. "Thquid," he said blissfully. "The cook'th dog will thell itth thoul for thquid."

Sophie said, "Eh? Oh, squids. I get you."

The cook's dog arrived as she spoke, with its legs going like pistons and drool hanging from its gnarly jaws. It shot out of the door and along the roof like a brown streak. Halfway along, its jaws went *snap-crunch*, and then *snap-crunch* again, and the squids were gone. Only then did the dog seem to notice where it was. It froze, with two legs on one side of the roof and two legs stiffly on the other, and whined piteously.

"Oh, poor thing!" Charmain said.

"The cook will rethcue it," Twinkle said. "You two follow me clothely. You have to turn left through thith door before your foot toucheth the roof." He stepped through the door leftward and vanished.

Oh, I think I understand! Charmain thought. This was like the doors in Great Uncle William's house, except that it was unnervingly high up. She let Sophie step through first so that she could catch hold of Sophie's skirt if Sophie went wrong. But Sophie was more used to magic than Charmain. She stepped left and vanished with no trouble at all. Charmain had a distinctly wobbly moment before she dared to follow. She shut her eyes and stepped. But her eyes shot open of their own accord as she went and she had a sideways, sliding view of the golden roof giddily blazing past her. Before she could decide to scream "Ylf!" to invoke the flying spell, she was elsewhere, in a warm triangular space with rafters in the roof.

Sophie said a bad word. In the dim light, she had stubbed her toe on one of the many dusty bricks piled around the place.

"Naughty-naughty," Twinkle said.

"Oh, shut up!" Sophie said, standing on one leg to hold her toe. "Why don't you grow up?"

"Not yet. I told you," Twinkle said. "We thtill have Pwinthe Ludovic to detheive. Ah, look! Thith happened when I wath here jutht now too."

A golden light was spreading over the largest pile of bricks. The bricks picked up the light and glowed golden as well, under the dust. Charmain realised that they were not bricks at all but ingots of solid gold. To make this quite clear, a golden banner appeared, floating in front of the ingots. Old-fashioned letters on it said:

𝔓raiſe tɧe 𝔚iſzarỏ 𝔐eɫicot wɧo
ɧiỏỏe tɧe 𝔎inge ɧiſ goɫỏ.

"Huh!" Sophie snorted, letting go of her toe. "Melicot must have lisped just like you. Proper soulmates, you and he would have been! Same size in swelled heads. He couldn't resist having his name up in lights, could he?"

"I don't *need* my name up in ligth," Twinkle said with great dignity.

"Doh!" said Sophie.

"Where are we?" Charmain asked quickly, because it rather looked as if Sophie was going to pick up a golden brick and brain Twinkle with it. "Is this the Royal Treasury?"

"No, under the golden roof," Twinkle told her. "Cunning, ithn't it? Everyone knowth the roof ithn't really gold, tho nobody thinkth of looking for the gold here." He tipped up one golden brick, thumped it on the floor to knock the dust off and dumped it into Charmain's hands. It was so heavy that she nearly dropped it. "You carry the evidenthe," he said. "I think the King ith going to be very glad to thee thith."

Sophie, who seemed to have recovered her temper a

little, said, "That lisp! It's driving me crazy! I think I hate it even more than I hate those golden curls!"

"But think how *utheful*," Twinkle said. "Nathty Ludovic tried to kidnap me and forgot all about Morgan." He turned his big blue eyes soulfully up at Charmain. "I had a mitherable childhood. Nobody loved me. I think I have a right to try again, looking pwettier, don't you?"

"Don't listen to him," Sophie said. "It's all a pose. Howl, how do we get out of here? I left Morgan with the King, and Ludovic's down there too. If we don't get back downstairs quickly, Ludovic's going to be thinking of grabbing Morgan any moment now."

"And Calcifer asked me to tell you to be quick," Charmain put in. "The castle's waiting in Royal Square. I really came to tell you—"

Before she could finish her sentence, Twinkle had done something that made the dusty loft rotate around them, so that they were once more standing beside the open door to the roof. Beyond the door, Jamal was lying on his face along the roof ridge, shaking all over, with one hand stretched out, clutching his dog's left hind leg. The dog was growling horrendously. It hated having its leg held and it hated the roof, but it was too frightened of falling to move.

Sophie said, "Howl, he's only got one eye and he's not balanced at all."

"I know," Twinkle said. "I know, I know!"

He waved a hand and Jamal came sliding backwards towards the door, towing the snarling dog. "I may be dead!" Jamal gasped, as the two landed in a heap by Twinkle's feet. "Why are we not dead?"

"Goodneth knowth," Twinkle said. "Excuthe uth. We need to thee a King about a thlab of gold."

He went pattering away down the stairs. Sophie raced after him and Charmain followed, lumbering rather because of the weight of the gold brick. Down they rushed, and down, and down again, until they swung round the corner at the top of the final flight. They arrived there just at the moment when Prince Ludovic shouldered Princess Hilda aside, barged past Sim and pulled Morgan out of the King's arms.

"Bad man!" Morgan boomed. He seized Prince Ludovic's beautifully curled hair and dragged. The hair came off, leaving the Prince's head smooth, bald and purple.

"I told you so!" Sophie screamed, and seemed to take wing. She and Twinkle raced down the stairs side by side.

The Prince looked up at them and down at Waif, who was trying to bite his ankle, and tried to drag his wig out of Morgan's hands. Morgan was beating Ludovic's face with it, still screaming "BAD MAN!" The colourless gentleman called out, "This way,

Highness!" and the two lubbockins raced for the nearest door.

"*Not in the library!*" the King and the Princess shouted with one voice.

They meant it so much and were so commanding that the colourless gentleman actually stopped, turned and led the Prince off in another direction. This gave Twinkle just time to catch up with Prince Ludovic and hang on to the Prince's trailing silken sleeve. Morgan gave a yell of delight and threw the wig down on Twinkle's face, more or less blinding him. Twinkle was towed helplessly along to the next nearest door, with the colourless gentleman sprinting ahead and Waif chasing, barking up a shrill tempest, and Sophie behind Waif, shouting, "*Put him* DOWN *or I'll* KILL *you!*" Behind her, the King and the Princess gave chase too.

"I say, this is a bit much!" the King called out. The Princess simply ordered them to "Stop!"

The Prince and the colourless gentleman tried to fling themselves and the children through the door and slam it in the faces of Sophie and the King. But the moment it slammed, Waif somehow burst the door open again and the rest of them came chasing through.

Charmain was last, with Sim. By this time her arms were aching. "Can you hold this?" she said to Sim. "It's evidence."

She passed Sim the gold brick while he was saying, "Certainly, miss." His hands and arms went right down with the weight of it. Charmain left him juggling with it and scuttled into what turned out to be the big room with the rocking horses lining the walls. Prince Ludovic was standing in the middle of it, looking very strange with his bald purple head.

He was now holding Morgan with one arm across Morgan's neck and Waif was jumping and dancing round his feet, trying to reach Morgan. The wig was lying on the carpet like a dead animal.

"You'll do what I say," the Prince was saying, "or this child suffers." Charmain's eye was caught by a sudden plunging blue flash from the fireplace. She looked and saw it was Calcifer, who must have come down the chimney in search of logs. He settled in among the unlighted wood there with a sigh of pleasure. When he saw Charmain looking at him, he winked one orange eye at her.

"Suffers, I say!" Prince Ludovic said dramatically.

Sophie looked at Morgan wriggling about in the Prince's arms and then down at Twinkle, who was just standing there, staring at his fingers as if he had never seen them before. She glanced across at Calcifer and seemed to be trying not to laugh. Her voice came out wobbly as she said, "Your Highness, I warn you, you are making a big mistake."

"You certainly are," the King agreed, panting and red in the face from the chase. "We in High Norland do not as a rule go in for treason trials, but we shall take pleasure in trying *you*."

"How can you?" the Prince demanded. "I'm not one of your subjects. I'm a lubbockin."

"Then you cannot, by law, be King after my father," Princess Hilda stated. Unlike the King, she was quite cool again and very royal.

"Oh, can't I?" said the Prince. "My parent, the lubbock, says I am to be King. It intends to rule the country though me. It got rid of the wizard so that nothing can stand in our way. You must crown me King at once or this child suffers. I'm keeping him as a hostage. Apart from that, what wrong have I done?"

"You've taken all their money!" Charmain called out. "I saw you – *both* you lubbockins – making the kobolds carry all the tax money to Castel Joie! And you're to let that little boy go before he strangles!" Morgan's face was bright red by then and he was struggling frantically. I don't think lubbockins have any real feelings, she thought. And I don't understand why Sophie thinks it's so funny!

"My goodness!" said the King. "So *that's* where it all went, Hilda! There's one puzzle solved at any rate. *Thank you*, my dear."

Prince Ludovic said disgustedly, "Why are you so

pleased? Didn't you *listen* to me?" He turned to the colourless gentleman. "He'll be offering us all crumpets next! Get on and work your spell. Get me out of here."

The colourless gentleman nodded and spread his faintly purple hands out in front of him. But that was the moment when Sim shuffled in with the gold brick in his arms. He shuffled swiftly across to the colourless gentleman and dropped the gold brick on the gentleman's toe.

After that, a lot of things happened very quickly.

As the gentleman, now purple with agony, hopped about yelling, Morgan seemed to arrive at his last gasp. His arms waved in a strange, convulsive pattern. And Prince Ludovic found himself trying to carry a tall, full-grown man in an elegant blue satin suit. He dropped the man, who promptly turned round and hit the Prince in the face.

"How *dare* you do that!" the Prince screamed. "I'm not used to it!"

"Bad luck," said Wizard Howl, and hit him again. This time Prince Ludovic caught his foot in the wig and sat down with a thump. "Only language a lubbockin understands," the wizard remarked over his shoulder to the King. "Had enough, Ludy old boy?"

At the same time, Morgan, who seemed to be wearing Twinkle's blue velvet suit, very crumpled and much too big for him, rushed at the wizard, booming, "Dad – *Dad* – DAD!"

Oh, I see! Charmain thought. They changed places somehow. That's pretty good magic. I'd like to learn how you do that. She wondered, while she watched the wizard carefully keeping Morgan away from the Prince, why Howl had wanted to be prettier than he was. He was most people's idea of a very handsome man, although, she thought, his hair was perhaps a little unreal. It fell over his blue satin shoulders in improbably beautiful flaxen curls.

But, also at the same time, Sim stood back – while the colourless gentleman hopped about in front of him – and seemed to be trying to make a formal announcement of some kind. But Morgan was raising such a clamour and Waif was barking so hard that all anyone could hear was "Your Majesty" and "Royal Highness."

While Sim was speaking, Wizard Howl looked across at the fireplace and nodded. There was something that happened then, between the wizard and Calcifer, that was not exactly a flash of light and not exactly a flash of invisible light either. While Charmain was still trying to describe it to herself, Prince Ludovic humped into himself and vanished downwards. So did the colourless gentleman. In their places were two rabbits.

Wizard Howl looked at them and then at Calcifer. "Why rabbits?" he asked, swinging Morgan up into his arms. Morgan at once stopped yelling and there was a moment of silence.

"All that hopping about," Calcifer said. "It put me in mind of rabbits."

The colourless gentleman was still hopping about, but he was now hopping as a large white rabbit with bulging purple eyes. Prince Ludovic, who was a pale fawn colour with even bigger purple eyes, seemed too astonished to move. He twitched his ears and wobbled his nose...

This was when Waif attacked.

Meanwhile, the visitors Sim had been trying to announce were already in the room. Waif killed the fawn-coloured rabbit almost under the runners of the kobolds' painted sled chair, which was being pushed by the Witch of Montalbino. Great Uncle William, rather pale and thin but evidently much better, was propped on a pile of blue cushions inside the chair. He, and the Witch, and Timminz, who was standing on the cushions, all leaned over the chair's carved blue side to watch Waif give a tiny snarl and toss the fawn coloured rabbit sideways by its neck and then, with another miniature snarl, hurl it across her back to land with a *flump*, dead, on the carpet.

"Good gracious!" said Wizard Norland, the King, Sophie and Charmain. "I'd have thought Waif was too small to *do* that!"

Princess Hilda waited for the rabbit to land and sailed across to the sled chair. She ignored, grandly, the frantic

313

rushing and scrambling as Waif chased the white rabbit round and round the room. "My dear Princess Matilda," the Princess said, holding both hands out to Peter's mother. "What a long time it is since we've seen you here. I do hope you mean to make us a long visit."

"That depends," the Witch said dryly.

"My daughter's second cousin," the King explained to Charmain and Sophie. "Prefers to be called the Witch of Somewhere usually. Always gets irritated if anyone calls her Princess Matilda. My daughter makes a point of it, of course. Hilda doesn't hold with inverted snobbery."

By this time, Wizard Howl had hoisted Morgan up on to his shoulders so that they could both watch as Waif cornered the white rabbit behind the fifth rocking horse along. There was some more tiny snarling. Presently the white rabbit's corpse came flying out across the rockers, dead and limp.

"Hooray!" Morgan boomed, beating his fists on his father's flaxen head.

Howl rather hastily hoisted Morgan down and handed him on to Sophie. "Have you told them about the gold yet?" he asked her.

"Not yet. The evidence got dropped on someone's foot," Sophie said, taking firm charge of Morgan.

"Tell them now," Howl said. "There's something

else that's strange here." He bent down and caught Waif as she trotted back to Charmain. Waif squirmed and whined and craned and did everything she could to make it clear that it was Charmain she wanted to go to. "Shortly, shortly," Howl said, turning Waif around in a puzzled way. Eventually he carried her over to the sled chair, where the King was jovially shaking Wizard Norland's hand while Sophie showed the gold ingot to them. The Witch and Timminz and Princess Hilda all crowded round Sophie, staring and demanding to know where Sophie had found the gold.

Charmain stood in the middle of the room feeling quite left out. I know I'm being quite unreasonable, she thought. I'm just the same as I always was. But I want Waif back. I want to take her with me when they send me back home to Mother. It was obvious to her that Peter's mother was going to look after Great Uncle William now, and where did that leave Charmain?

There was a terrific crash.

The walls shook, causing Calcifer to shoot out of the fireplace and hover over Charmain's head. Then, in very slow motion, a large hole opened in the wall beside the fireplace. The wallpaper peeled away first, followed by the plaster underneath it. Then the dark stones behind the plaster crumbled away and vanished, until nothing was left but a dark space. Finally, not in slow motion at all, Peter shot backwards through the hole and landed lying in front of Charmain.

"Hole!" boomed Morgan, pointing.

"I think you're right," Calcifer agreed.

Peter did not seem in the least put out. He looked up at Calcifer and said, "So you're not dead then. I knew she was making a stupid fuss. She's never sensible about things."

"Oh, thank you, Peter!" Charmain said. "And when have you ever been sensible? Where have you *been*?"

"Yes, indeed," said the Witch of Montalbino. "I'd like to know that too." She pushed the sled chair right up to Peter, so that Great Uncle William and Timminz were gazing down on Peter, along with everyone else, except for Princess Hilda. Princess Hilda was looking ruefully at the hole in the wall.

Peter did not seem worried at all. He sat up. "Hallo, Mum," he said cheerfully. "Why aren't you in Ingary?"

"Because Wizard Howl is here," said his mother. "And you?"

"I've been in Wizard Norland's workshop," Peter said. "I went there as soon as I gave Charmain the slip." He waved his hands with the rainbow of strings tied round his fingers to show how he got there. But he gave Wizard Norland a slightly anxious look. "I've been very careful in there, sir. Really."

"Have you indeed?" said Great Uncle William,

looking at the hole in the wall. It seemed to be slowly healing up. The dark stones were closing gently in towards the middle of it and the plaster was growing across after the stones. "And what were you doing there for a whole day and a night, may I ask?"

"Divining spells," Peter explained. "They take ages. It was lucky you had all those food spells in there, sir, or I'd have been really hungry by now. And I used your camp bed. I hope you don't mind." By the look on Great Uncle William's face, it was clear that he *did* mind. Peter added hurriedly, "But the spells worked, sir. The Royal Treasure must be here, where we all are, because I told the spell to take me to wherever it was."

"And so it is," said his mother. "Wizard Howl has already found it."

"Oh," said Peter. He looked very cast down. But then he brightened up. "I did a spell that worked, then!"

Everyone looked at the slowly healing hole. The wallpaper was now moving softly in across the plaster, but it was obvious that the wall would never be quite the same again. It had a soggy, wrinkled look. "I'm sure this is a great comfort to you, young man," Princess Hilda said bitterly. Peter looked at her blankly, obviously wondering who she was.

His mother sighed. "Peter, this is Her Highness Princess Hilda of High Norland. Perhaps you would be good enough to get up and bow to her and to her father the King. They are, after all, near relations of ours."

"How come?" Peter asked. But he scrambled to his feet and bowed in a very mannerly way.

"My son, Peter," said the Witch, "who is now most probably heir to your throne, Sire."

"Pleased to meet you, my boy," the King said. "This has all become very confusing. Won't somebody give me an explanation?"

"I will give you one, Sire," the Witch said.

"Perhaps we should all sit down," the Princess suggested. "Sim, be good enough to remove these two... er... dead rabbits, please."

"Very good, ma'am," Sim said. He shuffled rapidly about the room, gathering up the two corpses. He was clearly so anxious not to miss whatever the Witch was going to say, that Charmain was sure he simply dumped the rabbits outside the door. By the time he hurried back into the room, everyone had settled on to the grand but faded sofas, except for Great Uncle William, who lay back on his cushions looking thin and weary, and Timminz, who sat himself on a cushion beside Great Uncle William's ear. Calcifer went back to roost in the grate. Sophie took Morgan on her knee, where Morgan put his thumb in his mouth and went to sleep. And Wizard Howl at last handed Waif back to

Charmain. He did it with such a dazzlingly apologetic smile that Charmain felt quite flustered.

I like him much better as a grown up man, she thought. No wonder Sophie was so annoyed with Twinkle! Waif meanwhile squeaked and bounced and put her paws on Charmain's dangling glasses in order to lick her chin. Charmain rubbed Waif's ears and stroked the frayed hair on the top of Waif's head while she listened to what Peter's mother had to say.

"As you may know," the Witch said, "I married my cousin Hans Nicholas, who was at that time third in succession to the throne of High Norland. I was fifth, but as a woman I didn't really count, and besides, the only thing I wanted in the world was to be a professional witch. Hans was not interested in being King either. His passion was for climbing mountains and discovering caves and new passes among the glaciers. We were quite content to leave our cousin Ludovic to be heir to the throne. Neither of us *liked* him, and Hans always said Ludovic was the most selfish and unfeeling person he knew, but we both thought that if we went away and showed we had no interest in the throne, he wouldn't bother us.

"So we moved to Montalbino, where I took up office as Witch and Hans became a mountain guide; and we were very happy until just after Peter was born, when it became dreadfully plain that our other cousins were dying like flies. And not only dying, but also said to be wicked and dying because of their wickedness. When my cousin Isolla Matilda, who was the kindest and gentlest of girls, was killed while apparently attempting to murder someone, Hans became positive that Ludovic was doing it. 'Systematically killing off all the other heirs to the throne,' he said. 'And giving us all a bad name while he does it.'

"I became simply terrified for Hans and for Peter. By that time Hans was next heir after Ludovic and Peter came after that. So I got out my broomstick, put Peter into a sling on my back and flew all the way down to Ingary to consult Mrs Pentstemmon, who had trained me as a witch. I believe," the Witch said, turning to Howl, "that she trained you too, Wizard Howl."

Howl gave her one of his scintillating smiles. "That was much later. I was her very last pupil."

"Then you know that she was the best," said the Witch of Montalbino. "You agree?" Howl nodded. "You could trust everything she told you," the Witch went on. "She was always right." Sophie nodded too at this, a little ruefully. "But when I consulted her," said the Witch, "she was not sure that there was anything I could do except take Peter and go very far away. Inhico, she thought. I said, 'But what about Hans?' and she agreed I was right to be worried. 'Give me half a day,' she said, 'to find an answer for you,' and she went and shut herself into her workroom. Less than half a day later, she came out almost in a panic. I'd never seen her so upset before. 'My dear,' she said, 'your cousin Ludovic is a vile creature called a lubbockin, offspring of a lubbock that roams the hills between High Norland and Montalbino, and he is doing just what your Hans suspected he was doing, no doubt with the help of that lubbock. You must hurry home to Montalbino at once! Let us pray you get there in time. And on no account tell anyone who this little lad of yours is – don't tell him or anyone else, or the lubbock will try to kill him too!'"

"Oh, is that why you never told me all this before?" Peter said. "You should have done. I can look after myself."

"That," said his mother, "is exactly what poor Hans thought too. I should have made him come to Ingary with us. Don't interrupt, Peter. You nearly made me forget the last thing Mrs Pentstemmon said to me, which was, 'There is an answer, my dear. In your native land, there is, or was, something called the Elfgift belonging to the royal family, which has the power to keep the King safe and the whole country with him. Go and ask the King of High Norland to lend this Elfgift to Peter. It will keep him safe.' So I thanked her and put Peter on my back again and flew as fast as I could to Montalbino. I meant to ask Hans to come with me to High Norland to ask for the Elfgift, but when I got home they told me Hans was up in the Gretterhorns with the mountain rescue team. I had the most horrible premonition then. I flew straight on up into the mountains, with Peter still on my back. He was crying with hunger by then, but I didn't dare stop. And I just got there in time to see the lubbock start the avalanche that killed Hans."

The Witch stopped here, as if she could not bear to go on. Everyone waited respectfully while she swallowed and dabbed at her eyes with a multicoloured handkerchief. Then she shook her shoulders efficiently and said, "I put protections round Peter at once, of course, the strongest possible. They've never once been off him. I let him grow up as secretly as possible and I didn't mind at all when Ludovic began telling people that I was a mad prisoner in Castel Joie. That meant no one knew about Peter, you see. And the day after the avalanche, I left Peter with a neighbour and went to High Norland. You probably remember me coming, don't you?" she asked the King.

"Yes, I do," said the King. "But you said nothing about Peter, or Hans, and I had no idea it was all so sad and urgent. And of course I hadn't got the Elfgift. I didn't even know what it looked like. All you did was to start me off, together with my good friend Wizard Norland here, looking for the Elfgift. We've been hunting for it for thirteen years now. And we haven't got very far, have we, William?"

"We've got nowhere at all," Great Uncle William agreed from the sled chair. He chuckled. "But people *will* keep thinking that I'm the expert on the Elfgift. Some folks even say that I'm the Elfgift and *I* guard the King. I do try to guard him, of course, but not like an Elfgift would."

"That's one of the reasons I sent Peter to you," said the Witch. "It was always possible that the rumours were true. And I knew you could keep Peter safe anyway. I've been looking for that Elfgift myself for years, because I thought it could probably get rid of Ludovic. Beatrice of Strangia told me that Wizard Howl of Ingary was better at divination than any wizard in the world, so I went to Ingary to ask him to find it for me."

Wizard Howl threw his flaxen head back and began to laugh. "And you have to admit that I did find it!" he said. "Most unexpectedly. There it sits, on Miss Charming's lap!"

"What – *Waif*?" said Charmain. Waif wagged her tail and looked demure.

Howl nodded. "That's right. Your little enchanting dog." He turned to the King. "Don't those records of yours talk about a dog anywhere?"

"Frequently," said the King. "But I had no idea – My great-grandfather held a State Funeral for his dog when it died, and I simply wondered what all the fuss was about!"

Princess Hilda coughed gently. "Of course, most of our oil paintings have been sold now," she said, "but I do remember that a lot of our earlier kings were painted with a dog at their sides. They were generally a little... er... nobler looking than Waif, however."

"I imagine they come all sizes and shapes," Great Uncle William put in. "It looks to me as if the Elfgift is something certain dogs inherit, and the later kings forgot to breed them properly. Now, for instance, when Waif has her puppies a bit later this year—"

"*What?*" said Charmain. "*Puppies!*" Waif wagged her tail again and looked even more demure. Charmain pushed Waif's chin up and stared accusingly into her eyes. "The cook's dog?" she asked. Waif blinked bashfully. "Oh, Waif!" Charmain wailed. "Goodness knows what they'll look like!"

"We must wait and hope," said Great Uncle William. "One of those pups will have inherited the Elfgift. But there is one other important aspect to this, my dear. Waif has adopted you, and this makes you High Norland's Elfgift Guardian. Also, since the Witch of Montalbino here tells me that *The Boke of Palimpsest* has adopted you too... It *has*, hasn't it?"

"I... er... um. It did make me do spells out of it," Charmain admitted.

"Then that settles it," Great Uncle William said, nestling contentedly back on his cushions. "You come and live with me as my apprentice from now on. You need to learn how to help Waif protect the country properly."

"Yes... oh... but..." Charmain babbled, "Mother won't allow me... She says magic's not respectable. My dad won't mind, probably," she added. "But my mother—"

"I'll fix her," said Great Uncle William. "If necessary, I'll set your aunt Sempronia on her."

"Better still," said the King, "I'll make it a Royal Decree. Your mother will be impressed by that. You see, we need you, my dear."

"Yes, but I want to help you with the *books*!" Charmain cried out.

Princess Hilda gave another of her gentle coughs. "I shall be rather busy," she said, "redecorating and renovating this Mansion." The gold ingot was lying on the carpet by her feet. She gave it a tender prod with one sensible shoe. "Now we are solvent again," she said happily. "I suggest that you stand in for me in the library with my father twice a week, if Wizard Norland will spare you."

"Oh, *thank* you!" Charmain said.

"And," added the Princess, "as for Peter—"

"There's no need to concern yourself with Peter," the Witch interrupted. "I shall be staying with Peter and Charmain to look after the house at least until Wizard Norland is back on his feet. Maybe I shall live there permanently."

Charmain, Peter and Great Uncle William exchanged looks of horror. *I see why she got to be so efficient, being left all alone with Peter to protect,* Charmain thought. *But if she stays in that house, I'll go back to live with Mother!*

"Nonsense, Matilda," said Princess Hilda. "Peter is very much our concern, now that it is clear that he is our Crown Prince. Peter will live *here* and commute to Wizard Norland for lessons in magic. You must go back to Montalbino, Matilda. They need you there."

"And us kobolds will look after the house, the way we always used to," Timminz piped.

*Oh, good,* Charmain thought. *I don't think I'm really house trained yet – and Peter certainly isn't!*

"Bless you, Timminz. Bless you, Hilda," Great Uncle William murmured. "The thought of all that efficiency in my house—"

"I shall be fine, Mum," Peter said. "You don't have to protect me any more."

"If you're sure," the Witch said. "It seems to me—"

"Now," said Princess Hilda, at least as efficiently as

the Witch, "it only remains for us to say goodbye to our kind, helpful, if somewhat eccentric guests, and wave them off in their castle. Come along, all of you."

"Woops!" said Calcifer and shot away up the chimney.

Sophie stood up, dislodging Morgan's thumb from his mouth. Morgan woke, looked round, saw that his father was there, and looked round some more. His face crumpled up. "Dinkle," he said. "Where *Dinkle*?" He started to cry.

"Now look what you've started!" Sophie said to Howl.

"I can always turn into Twinkle again," Howl suggested.

"Don't you *dare*!" Sophie said, and marched away into the damp hallway after Sim.

Five minutes later, they were all gathered on the front steps of the Mansion to watch Sophie and Howl hauling the struggling, crying Morgan through the door of the castle. As the door shut on Morgan's yells of "Dinkle, Dinkle, Dinkle!" Charmain bent and murmured to Waif in her arms, "You *did* protect the country, didn't you? And I never even noticed!"

By this time, half the people in High Norland were gathered in Royal Square to stare at the castle. They all watched with disbelief as the castle rose slightly into the air and glided towards the road that led southward.

It was hardly more than an alley really. "It'll never fit!" people said. But the castle somehow squeezed itself narrow enough to drift away along it and out of sight.

The citizens of High Norland gave it a cheer as it went.

# Diana Wynne Jones

# Howl's Moving Castle

*"How about making a bargain with me?"
said the demon. "I'll break your spell if you
agree to break this contract I'm under."*

In the land of Ingary, where seven-league boots
and cloaks of invisibility exist, pretty Sophie
Hatter is cursed into the shape of an old woman.
Determined to make the best of things, she
travels to the one place where she might find
help – the moving castle on the nearby hills.

But the castle belongs to the dreaded Wizard
Howl whose appetite, they say, is satisfied
only by the hearts of young girls...

HarperCollins *Children's Books*

# Diana Wynne Jones

# Castle in the Air

*"I never said my wishes were supposed to do anyone
any good," said the genie. "In fact, I swore that they
weould always do as much harm as possible."*

By day Abdullah is a humble carpet merchant, but
in his dreams he is a prince. Then his dreams start
to come true when he meets the lovely Flower-in-
the-Night. Fate has destined them for each other,
but a bad-tempered genie, a hideous djinn and
various villanous bandits have their own ideas.

When Flower is carried off, Abdullah is
determined to rescue her – but how can he
succeed with only a bad-tempered genie and an
unreliable magic carpet to help him?

HarperCollins *Children's Books*

# Diana Wynne Jones

## THE Game

"*I swear not to say a word about what we do in this game to anyone outside...*"

When Hayley is packed off to Ireland to live with her aunts, she is bewildered by how different it is from Grandma's. It's noisy and chaotic, and full of assorted cousins! But here she is introduced to "the game" that takes her into the forbidden mythosphere – a place Hayley has glimpsed briefly before, and which holds the answers to her family's secrets.

HarperCollins *Children's Books*

*"There's one absolute rule," said Chrestomanci.
"No witchcraft of any kind is to be practised by
children without supervision. Is that understood?"*

No witchcraft? Gwendolen Chant – a gifted
witch in the making – has other ideas and
is determined to get the better of the great
enchanter. Her brother Cat, who has no
magical gift, is powerless to stop her.

Winner of the Guardian Award.

HarperCollins *Children's Books*

*"You lying Petrocchi swine! Kidnapper!"*
*"Swine yourself! Spell-bungler! Traitor!"*

The Dukedom of Caprona is a place where music
is enchantment and spells are as slippery as
spaghetti. The magical business is run by two
families – the Montanas and the Petrocchis – and
they are deadly rivals. So when all the spells start
going wrong, they naturally blame each other.

Chrestomanci suspects an evil enchanter; others
say it is a White Devil. Or maybe a different kind
of magic is needed to save Caprona…

HarperCollins *Children's Books*

# WITCH WEEK

## Diana Wynne Jones

*SOMEONE IN THIS CLASS IS A WITCH*

When the note, written in ordinary ballpoint, turns
up in the homework books Mr Crossley is
marking, he is very upset. For this is Larwood
House, a school for witch-orphans, where
witchcraft is utterly forbidden. And yet magic
keeps breaking out all over the place – like measles!

The last thing they need is a visit from the
Divisional Inquisitor. If only Chrestomanci
could come and sort out all the trouble.

HarperCollins *Children's Books*

# THE PINHOE EGG

*The egg was large and round and mauvish.*
*It sat in a nest of old moth-eaten blankets.*
*The moment Cat touched it he knew it was*
*very strange and valuable indeed.*

Spells always have consequences and it's
Chrestomanci's job to make sure everything is
safely under control. Even so, in the village
around Chrestomanci Castle, all sorts of secret
magical misuse is going on. And when Cat Chant
finds the Pinhoe egg, chaos is just the beginning!

HarperCollins *Children's Books*

# Diana Wynne Jones

# FIRE AND HEMLOCK

Polly has always loved the fire and hemlock photograph
which hangs above her bed, but now it sparks memories
that don't seem to exist any more. Memories of Thomas
Lynn, who became her greatest friend… Memories of
the stories they made up together – adventures in which
Tom is a great hero and Polly is his assistant… Memories
that these adventures had a nasty habit of coming true…

Why has Tom been erased from Polly's mind, and from
the rest of the world as well? And why is Polly so sure
that she must have done something dreadful?
Determined to uncover the truth, she casts her mind
back ten years to when it all started. At the funeral…

HarperCollins *Children's Books*